The door burst open, and three men lunged into the room

Bolan fired at point-blank range, nailing the last man in. His two companions whirled, one stitching the wall behind the warrior with a burst from a silenced Uzi.

The Executioner dived to the floor, the 9 mm bullets gouging plaster from the walls. He squeezed off a round, catching the sluggish gunner on the cheekbone.

The third man backed up, raising one hand over his head. But the .45 in his other hand was still wavering. Bolan watched the man for a heartbeat, then, as the pistol swung in his direction, the warrior fired a 3-round burst, catching the hit man in the chest.

Bolan got to his feet slowly, swinging the Beretta toward the gaping doorway. Catfooting to the opening, he looked out into the hallway and saw that it was empty. He holstered his weapon and was halfway across the room when four *federales* filled the doorway.

"That was fast."

"*Señor*, you are under arrest. Please come with us."

"Under arrest for what?"

The lieutenant in charge smiled. "You *narcotraficantes* are such kidders." He snapped his fingers and nodded to an underling. "Take his weapons."

MACK BOLAN®

The Executioner

#60 Sold for Slaughter
#61 Tiger War
#62 Day of Mourning
#63 The New War Book
#64 Dead Man Running
#65 Cambodia Clash
#66 Orbiting Omega
#67 Beirut Payback
#68 Prairie Fire
#69 Skysweeper
#70 Ice Cold Kill
#71 Blood Dues
#72 Hellbinder
#73 Appointment in Kabul
#74 Savannah Swingsaw
#75 The Bone Yard
#76 Teheran Wipeout
#77 Hollywood Hell
#78 Death Games
#79 Council of Kings
#80 Running Hot
#81 Shock Waves
#82 Hammerhead Reef
#83 Missouri Deathwatch
#84 Fastburn
#85 Sunscream
#86 Hell's Gate
#87 Hellfire Crusade
#88 Baltimore Trackdown
#89 Defenders and Believers
#90 Blood Heat Zero
#91 The Trial
#92 Moscow Massacre
#93 The Fire Eaters
#94 Save the Children
#95 Blood and Thunder
#96 Death Has a Name

#97 Meltdown
#98 Black Dice
#99 Code of Dishonor
#100 Blood Testament
#101 Eternal Triangle
#102 Split Image
#103 Assault on Rome
#104 Devil's Horn
#105 Countdown to Chaos
#106 Run to Ground
#107 American Nightmare
#108 Time to Kill
#109 Hong Kong Hit List
#110 Trojan Horse
#111 The Fiery Cross
#112 Blood of the Lion
#113 Vietnam Fallout
#114 Cold Judgment
#115 Circle of Steel
#116 The Killing Urge
#117 Vendetta in Venice
#118 Warrior's Revenge
#119 Line of Fire
#120 Border Sweep

Stony Man Doctrine
Terminal Velocity
Resurrection Day
Dirty War
Flight 741
Dead Easy
Sudden Death
Rogue Force
Tropic Heat
Fire in the Sky
Anvil of Hell
Flash Point
Flesh and Blood

DON PENDLETON's EXECUTIONER

MACK BOLAN.

Border
Sweep

A GOLD EAGLE BOOK FROM
W RLDWIDE.

TORONTO • NEW YORK • LONDON • PARIS
AMSTERDAM • STOCKHOLM • HAMBURG
ATHENS • MILAN • TOKYO • SYDNEY

First edition December 1988

ISBN 0-373-61120-X

Special thanks and acknowledgment to
Charlie McDade for his contribution to this work.

Justice is the constant and perpetual wish to render everyone his due.

—Justinian c. 482-565

The worst kind of man tries to cash in on the hopes and dreams of his fellow men—individuals striving to build a better life for themselves and their families. That man will one day stand judgment for his actions. And the price he will pay will be costly.

—Mack Bolan

To the men and women
of the Border Patrol

1

Measured by the standards of *Architectural Digest*, the place was gauche. A snide columnist would probably christen it "Taco Chic" or some other such clever insult. To the people over whom it towered, it was the epitome of taste and lavishness. By any objective standard it was huge. The buildings themselves weren't that tall, but the compound sat on a low hill, its thick, reinforced steel walls coated with clay-colored concrete to simulate adobe.

Six feet high at their lowest point, the walls undulated around the hilltop, rising and falling with the contours of the hill, sometimes reaching a height of twelve feet where the land dipped beneath them for a few yards. It wasn't pretty, but it sure as hell was impressive. Inside the walls there was less in the way of pretense. The rambling buildings, connected by tiled *ramadas* to keep the brutal sun off the flagstoned walks, were two stories high for the most part. All tinted glass and stucco, they were as faceless as the desert that stretched away to the north.

A huge fountain, its water tapped from hundreds of feet below the desert floor, burbled softly. Thick greenery, full of colorful birds and lazy lizards, shrouded the kidney-shaped pool surrounding the gentle arc of water. On a small island in the center of the pool a statue of a man wearing a serape and a tacky Hollywood sombrero added its own meager stream of water. There was something contemptuous in the statue's face and in the obscenely offhand manner in which its disdain hissed into the pool.

Inside the largest building the man who had built Casa La Paloma cracked thin heels on the hardwood floor. He reached the head of the stairs, stopped for a minute and pulled absently at the ends of a scraggly mustache. His coal-black hair was unkempt, the curls more tangled than usual. Thin and tan, he looked fit. Hard muscles, as taut as cables, quivered just under the skin.

Finally, as if he had decided a difficult question, he smiled and resumed his descent to the basement. A huge man, fat as only a Mexican Buddha would be, shifted in his chair at the foot of the steps. Dressed in denim and hand-tooled boots, he might have been a ranch hand. In a way he was. Across his ample lap was an Uzi submachine gun, the only discordant note in the otherwise tranquil surroundings.

"Good day, Don Calderone," he said.

Calderone nodded but said nothing. He was too busy for pleasantries this morning.

A huge mahogany door stood half-open at the far end of a long, wide hallway. The parquet floor, runnered in thick Persian carpet, gleamed in the soft, indirect light from recessed ceiling fixtures. When he reached the door, Carlos Calderone stopped, his hand on the gleaming brass knob. He ran the fingertips of his hand slowly across the wood, admiring its smooth surface, then raised his fingers to his nose and sniffed the sweet fragrance of lemon oil.

Pushing the door open wide, he stepped through, then closed it behind him. Two men, talking softly, sat at an elaborate console built into one wall. Above them several screens, each alive with its own swarm of winking electronic ants, cast a green-and-amber glow over their faces.

Calderone watched them for a few moments. If they had seen him enter, they gave no sign.

Busy at clicking keyboards, they summoned screen after screen of data, scrutinized it, then passed to the next. Calderone was proud of himself. Computers were alien to him. He understood little of how to use them and less of how they worked. But this roomful of the latest in high-tech equipment belonged to him. He knew that you didn't have to understand anything as long as you could afford to buy those who could. And Carlos Calderone could afford to buy anything, even an army of men to help him to obtain whatever his heart desired.

Finally breaking the silence, he asked, "So how is your new toy working, Alfredo?"

One of the two men at the console spun in his swivel chair. In the dim light Calderone was little more than an outline. Alfredo exaggerated his smile, hoping the man could see it. "Very well. Fantastic even. Better than I hoped."

"And can you do what you said you can do?"

"Yes, Don Carlos. The intercepts work perfectly. We can track anything on the rail system in the entire southwest. All we have to do now is figure out the rest of the coding. It's not at all complicated, more like learning a new language than solving a puzzle. It should be relatively easy."

"I hope so, Alfredo. Your toys aren't cheap."

"I know. But they'll be well worth it. The railroads are controlling everything by computer now. Once we have access to the scheduling data, we can figure arrival and departure times as well as points of origin, destinations and intermediate stops for every freight and passenger car in the system. That ought to be useful information in and of itself. But we also have the ability to enter the system and change logging. You can send a car anywhere you want, and no one will think anything of it."

Calderone grunted. "We'll see."

"It will work. I can guarantee it. The dry run is scheduled for tomorrow."

"I'll have a flock of chickens for delivery near Tucson. Can you be ready for that shipment?"

"No problem."

"I hope you're right."

"Don't worry about it, Don Carlos. We will have everything in working order in a few hours. I have already made a few simple destination changes, tracked the cars through their altered routes. No glitches."

"Glitches I don't know about. If you say it works, I believe you . . . until I have reason not to." Calderone walked to the console and ran his fingers over one of the screens. For a moment he imagined the creeping letters and numbers were alive. It made him feel good to see them. It felt like God must have felt on the seventh day.

He said something under his breath, but Alfredo didn't quite catch the words. "You said something, Don Carlos?"

"It is good."

Alfredo was pleased with himself. He smiled.

SAN CARLOS WAS just large enough to be called a town. Its buildings ranged from dilapidated to ramshackle. On the edge of town a tall smokestack belched dense black clouds into the air. The thick smoke seemed to hover over the mouth of the stack just long enough to realize it was too heavy to float, then slid sideways and thinned out, sifting down like black snow over the nearby houses. The streets, little more than packed dirt, were littered with everything from Coca-Cola cans to yesterday's newspapers.

Gangs of barefoot children played noisily, their thin legs a blur as they ran up and down the streets, ducking between unpainted buildings and dodging broken glass and ragged, rusty cans. Their dark eyes glittered in flat, emotionless faces. Their laughter was forced and tinny, almost strident, in the hot afternoon.

San Carlos had one church, no school and a dozen cafés and cantinas. But what set it apart from the surrounding towns and villages was its bus station. The single strip of asphalt for miles around passed through its heart and once every day, heading north or south on alternate days, a bus came...if it was running. And because of the bus San Carlos had more than its share of visitors. Farmers visiting family wandered in on foot, as well as others, more transient, eyes darting nervously at every passing face. No one knew who they were, but everyone knew *what* they were...*pollos*, chickens, people desperate to cross the border. Most planned only to work for a few weeks or a few months at most, just long enough to scrape a few dollars together, enough to keep them and their families fed for a year.

And where one found chickens, one also found coyotes.

Hard men wearing expensive shirts and cheap jewelry wandered in and out of the cantinas. Alongside the farmers they looked sophisticated, like men of the world. And so they pretended to be. Merchants of an unusual kind, trading in an expensive and perishable commodity, they cruised the side streets, looking for too furtive an eye, sudden haste as their cars drifted by.

As often as not an old Chevrolet, fenders rattling against rusty bumpers, blared loud disco music from elaborate tape decks. Inside, the cars were as garish and glamorous as they were decrepit outside. In the dirt parking lot behind the San Carlos bus station, it wasn't uncommon to see two or three such cars at a time. Their drivers, hair modishly long, slicked back with a little pomade, silk shirts smelling of cheap cologne and heavy sweat, circled the station like bloated hawks, their talons all but hidden in thick flesh.

There was nothing new in the hunt. It was as old as the border. But under the surface, things were changing. The coyotes themselves were now among the hunted. They had as little to fear from the police as ever. A few pesos in a furtive palm still bought the same unofficial license. But someone had decided that centralization, corporate organization and the efficiency of coordination were long overdue. Unlike most of the people they preyed on, the coyotes had a choice: they could go along with the new program, they could find another line of work, or they could take a ride into the desert, lie down and bleed to death in the sand.

It was a choice because Carlos Calderone was a reasonable man—to a point. In an age of corporate mergers and vertical monopoly, it made sense to him to consolidate. Smuggling was no longer a crime; it was a science. It was economics at its most refined. There was a demand for cheap labor north of the border. South of the border was a plentiful supply. Enterprise and common sense suggested that a man who could control the supply and establish contact with those making the demand could make himself not only rich but indispensable.

Many of the growers in Arizona were no less reasonable than Carlos Calderone. What they wanted was quick hands and strong backs, the quicker and stronger the better. The price was negotiable, within reason, and if someone was willing to handle the logistics—and the headaches—it made good business sense to cut a deal. Once that had been established to the satisfaction of both sides, the rest was a simple tactical exercise. Starting small was fine. Staying small wasn't in the cards.

Felipe Mendoza was about to find that out.

Parking his 1977 Camaro behind the bus station, Felipe listened to the end of a Donna Summer tape, his left arm keeping time on the hot black metal of the driver's door. When the tape finished, he listened to the hiss for a few seconds, then clicked off the tape deck. He climbed out of the car just as a battered blue Buick slipped in beside his Camaro. He glanced at the three men in the vehicle, then closed the door of his own car. He didn't turn back, even when the hard prod of something small and round slammed into his lumbar vertebra. He knew better.

A thick hand grabbed the keys dangling from Felipe's fingers, the hot breath in his ear smelling of jalapeño. "Get in the back, Mendoza. Then slide over."

Felipe did as he was told. He climbed into the Buick as the rear passenger slid over to make room for him. In his lap, pointed vaguely in Felipe's direction, was the biggest pistol he had ever seen. He had dreamed of such a gun, but never expected to see one. The front passenger was already in the driver's seat, and Felipe watched as the third man climbed into the Camaro and started its engine.

Smiling broadly, his thick, wide teeth a yellow smear under his mustache, he said, "Nice stereo, my friend." Then he backed out of the parking space and nosed out into the street. The Buick lurched after it. Felipe watched his captors nervously. He wanted to make small talk, maybe exchange anecdotes on the oddities of the job. But something told him he'd better not.

The sun was almost straight ahead as the Buick chased the Camaro into the desert. The blue-white of the horizon looked like a knitting scar where someone had sewn earth and sky together. After an hour it was no closer to healing. The cars were well off the road by now, their suspensions creaking as they tracked over the barren earth. Since the compliment to his stereo, no one had said a word to Felipe.

When the Camaro's brake lights flashed, Felipe inhaled deeply. He watched his fingers in his lap, which wriggled like a ball of snakes no matter how hard he tried to keep them still. When the Buick braked behind the Camaro, the drivers of both cars got out, the man in the Buick walking around to Felipe's door. He opened it and jerked a thumb. Felipe climbed out slowly.

He looked at the man in the rear of the Buick, who still held the pistol, its chrome finish glinting in a blade of light slashing through the windshield. It was truly a beautiful weapon, Felipe thought.

"So, Felipe, how's business?" the man with the thick teeth asked. "Good?"

Felipe shrugged. "I'm out of business."

"No, Felipe, no, no, no. That isn't true. You are *supposed* to be out of business, my friend. But you aren't."

Felipe turned slightly, looking for the shiny pistol. If he had to die, and there was now no question that he had to, it might as well be with such an exquisite pistol. He watched the man holding the big gun. The man noticed him watching the pistol and smiled slightly. He raised the muzzle a bit and smiled more broadly.

Felipe crossed himself, and the man with the gun grew somber, as if not wanting to desecrate such a moment. Then, when Felipe was done praying, he smiled again, this time with an easy radiance. Felipe watched the pistol, his attention totally absorbed by the glittering weapon, its finish flashing small bits of fire as it moved in the sunlight. It was almost hypnotic.

He didn't feel the wire as it was slipped around his neck. Not at all.

2

Mercy Hospital wasn't the sort of high-tech institution Ronny Sipe was used to. On the other hand, there was little choice in ten thousand square miles. If you needed medical attention, you went to Mercy. If you couldn't make it to Mercy, regardless of the reason, either you didn't really need help, or no amount of help would do you any good.

Sipe padded across the lobby, the soft rubber soles of his desert boots squeaking on the clean but faded asphalt tile, squares of black and white alternating in a pattern as old as greasy spoons. He stopped at the desk to ask where the new arrival was being treated, thanked the young nurse who answered him absently before turning back to her crossword puzzle, and walked down the hall to the elevator. The hospital was only three stories high, and had one elevator that served both visitors and patients alike.

Sipe pressed the button to call the car, then listened to it rattle on its cable. The doors groaned open, and he stepped onto the pebbled metal floor and pushed the button for the third floor. As the doors closed, the car had already begun its climb, swinging gently from side to side. Sipe hadn't felt that queasy twinge of motion sickness since his first—and last—Ferris wheel ride.

On the third floor the night nurse sat behind an oaken fortress of a desk directly opposite the elevator. He told her who he wanted to see, and she explained, with that mixture of patience and exasperation that must be taught in nursing school, that the patient was not to be disturbed for any reason whatsoever. Besides, which, she informed him, he was under guard.

"Then tell the guard Ronny's here," Sipe said, smiling.

Slapping her crossword onto the scarred oak, she rose with a rustle of starched cloth and walked down the hall. Her practical shoes squeaked with every step, and she glared over her shoulder to discourage either his following her or optimism that he might get to see the patient. Probably both, Sipe realized. He sucked on an old filling while he waited.

She was back in two minutes, her confidence badly shaken. "The officer says you can come down," she snapped. Then, as if to taint his victory, she warned, "You can have five minutes. No more."

"Thank you," he said, leaning forward slightly to read the name tag on her crisp lapel, "Nurse Martinez."

She snorted her contempt and sat down.

Sipe walked quickly down the hall and backed up a step when he almost missed the open door. The room was backlit by a small bulb in a wall sconce, its pale fan of light splashing up the wall and across the ceiling. Randy Carlton slouched in a low-slung chair next to the bed, his hands folded across his belt. He'd changed from his uniform to a pair of jeans and a checkered shirt.

"Ronny," Carlton said, shifting his weight in the chair. "Thought you'd be by sooner."

"Yeah, well..."

"Don't matter, though. He hasn't been awake yet. Doc says he may never be." Carlton stood up, his six-foot-six frame towering over the slender figure huddled under a single sheet, its crisp white broken only by a faded black stencil.

"I was hoping maybe I could ask him some questions."

"What for? Nobody gives a damn, anyway."

"I gave a damn. So do you." Sipe stepped into the room and closed the door behind him. Its hollow core echoed the bright snap of the brass latch.

Carlton walked to the single window centered in the far wall. The lace curtains were open, and they hung limply in the breathless night air. He looked out and up, watching the stars for a long second. The moon was almost full, and the shadowy silhouette of an owl darted across the nearly round disk.

Without turning to Sipe, he said, "This has got to stop."

"I know that. But I don't know how to stop it."

"Think of something, dammit!"

"You make it sound so easy."

"I know it's not easy, Ronny. But it can't be so damn hard as we make it. It just can't be."

"Get me something. Something I can use, Randy. A name, a place, hell, I don't know...a license plate number."

"You want to hear something funny?"

"What?"

"Captain Dickerson says it's their fault. He says they just screw up. They try to sneak in and they blow it. Isn't that funny?"

"Shit. This is six in the past two months, half on the Mexican side. And all strangled with a wire. How the hell does he explain that?"

"He says he doesn't have to. He says explaining things is *your* job."

"I can't explain squat if he won't ask a few questions. I need an investigation, for God's sake. I need information, witnesses, dates, places. I need wiretaps and photo surveillance. I can't get staff, and I can't handle all that on my own."

"He says we're shorthanded, see. He says we got maybe fifty men to cover a thousand miles of border twenty-four hours a day, seven days a week. Hell, Ronny, I don't know... maybe he's right."

"That's a crock, and you know it. Everybody's shorthanded, but that's no excuse. You can't just sit back on what hands you got and do nothing."

"Don't you think I know that? Shit, Will and I have been working overtime, off the books and off the record, for four months. We still don't have anything we can use."

Sipe walked to the side of the bed and looked down at the unconscious man. "Any ID on him?"

"Sure, and he had a bankbook and two grand in traveler's checks." Carlton started cracking his knuckles, as if he wanted to punish his own body for the frustration he felt. "You know, Ronny, when this guy wakes up—if he ever does—we'll still know absolutely nothing about him. He'll be scared stiff. If he has any idea who gave him that skinny necktie, he won't tell us. And the funny thing is, after we ship him back to Mexico, he'll probably pay the same guy to smuggle him back up here. If I didn't know better, I'd swear there was some kind of pipeline."

"I think there is, Randy. But I can't prove it."

"Why do you think so?"

"How else can you explain it? It runs like a top, nobody ever gets nailed. Unless I miss my guess, somebody's cut a deal with some of the big farmers up here. They run these poor bastards in, use 'em up, then ship 'em back."

"You got any leads?"

"Nothing much. And what I do have wouldn't stand up in a kangaroo court, let alone the appellate court. Even if I managed to get a conviction, which I doubt I could do, I'd be laughed right out of Arizona on appeal."

Randy seemed uncertain about something. He looked at Sipe thoughtfully, as if debating whether to raise an issue he wasn't all that clear about himself. Finally, with an off-hand wave, he dismissed whatever reservations had been holding him back. "You know, Ronny, there's something I've been wondering about."

"What's that?"

"I'm not sure. I mean, it's just a guess, so if it's crazy, just shut me up."

Sipe watched him closely. "Go ahead."

"Well, I'm not so sure this guy is a run-of-the-mill illegal." He stared at the bed as if expecting confirmation from the unconscious man. "I mean, we've only seen four of the six, but something doesn't seem right. They don't look like farm workers. Not to me, anyway. Their clothes are too fancy. Their hands are soft. Hell, they look like they *eat* regularly."

"So, who do you think they are?"

Carlton spread his hands helplessly. "I don't have a clue. Told you it was crazy."

Sipe leaned back in his chair. "I don't know. Let me think about it. You might be onto something."

Carlton sat back down, this time tilting his hat far back and fixing his pale green eyes on Sipe. "You want any help?"

"Uh-uh. Not yet."

"You'll let me know?"

"Sure. Listen, I've got to be going. You give me a call when he wakes up, all right?"

The other man nodded, then folded his hands across his midsection. As he slid down in the uncomfortable chair, his eyes drooped and his hat fell forward. Sipe closed the door gently.

Stroking his chin thoughtfully, Sipe walked slowly toward the elevator. He nodded absently to the night nurse as he punched the call button for the elevator, then stood facing the scratched wood of its doors. When it arrived, he stepped in almost unconsciously.

The street was deserted, and the few lights threw shadows in every direction. A two-story rooming house stood across the street from the hospital. Its sickly green neon sign was only partially lit, and the illumination flashed on and off halfheartedly. Glancing at his watch, he realized there was no point in driving home. The office was full of interesting puzzles, and since he had nothing better to do, he decided to catch up on some paperwork.

Sipe crossed the street and stepped into the alley between the rooming house and a hardware store. Behind the latter a square of compressed clay served as a municipal parking lot. His government-issue Ford was the only car in the lot. Sipe unlocked the car, then hesitated before getting in. He walked to the front of the car and sat on the left fender, pulling a pack of cigarettes from his shirt pocket as he wriggled himself into a comfortable position.

Away from the flickering signs on the street, the sky was dark enough for him to see quite a few stars. It was rather hot for being so late, and he was conscious of his damp shirt as he lit a cigarette, then leaned back to lie on the hood. The smoke spiraled straight up, undisturbed by a breath of air. He closed his eyes and found himself staring into the sallow features of the unconscious man across the street. Even in comatose repose, there was something affecting about them. The mobility of pain seemed to flicker just under the skin, as if the placid face were a thin mask under which a contorted parody lay hidden.

Running over the day's events, he wondered why corporate law had seemed so unappealing. It paid so much more, and offered a thick layer of insulation from reality. Even if your masters were responsible for human suffering, you never saw it, were protected from it in a hundred ways. There was something to be said for that, not to mention the perks that came with that insularity.

But he didn't have to think about it for very long before he knew the reason he had chosen as he had. The internal argument was one he had committed to memory, and lately it had been argued more and more frequently, with increasing passion on both sides. And every time he ran through it, he expected something different, as if he might yet discover some loophole in the logic on either side.

But the bottom line, as he very well knew, was that logic had nothing to do with his choice. It was a decision made out of passion, and money was no antidote for that. He cared, he knew he cared, and he told himself that that made all the difference. Yet there was no smugness in the declaration, and no self-congratulation.

The analytical intelligence that made him so good at what he did also made it painful for him to do it, because he understood only too well that the choice would never make him rich, and never satisfied. The world was too full of people only too willing to take advantage of others who were less intelligent, or weaker, or less fortunate than they. A crusader's work, like that of a woman, was never done.

Flicking the cigarette away, he watched it arc through the darkness, outlined against the sky like a meteor. He hopped down from the hood and climbed into the car. It started right away, catching him by surprise. He clicked on the lights and eased down the alleyway to the street, not bothering with his seat belt.

The dozen blocks to his office were completely deserted. Most of the shops preferred not to bother with illuminated signs, and there were no streetlights. During the short drive, he began toying with what he knew that might be relevant to the case, and realized that almost everything could be and that possibly nothing was. Smuggling was just too profitable, and those who took the risk were likely to smuggle anything from drugs to aliens.

By the time he had parked his car on the street below his second-floor office, he had decided to ransack his files, starting at *A* and checking every case in the bulging drawers that might conceivably relate to the recent rash of killings. He hadn't wanted to say anything to Carlton, but he'd already made a few inquiries. As with the border patrolman, there was something that didn't sit quite right with him. He'd begun to wonder whether he was getting paranoid, whether the endless stream of misery was sucking him under. Now he wasn't so sure.

He opened the glass door to the lobby of his building, then shuffled across the marble floor. He'd never been able to decide whether he was fortunate or cursed to have so much work, but it was too late to consider any other arrangement. It came with the turf.

The stairway seemed higher than Everest, and he realized he was exhausted. Another night on the office couch seemed like a certainty. The long corridor seemed even longer than it was, and he dragged himself toward the front of the building, finally stopping in front of the frosted glass that was his only defense against the world. And like so many defenses, it let him see very little and protected him not at all.

Once inside, he sighed, walking to the refrigerator with the uncertain step of a condemned man reluctantly negotiating his last mile. There was some V-8 and an open can of diet ginger ale. He opted for nutrition and opened the juice. It was salty, and he knew he'd regret it later, but there was plenty of water in the cooler.

The fourteen filing cabinets that contained his current paperwork occupied one short wall of the outer office and spilled over into the rear office. He clicked on the overhead light to browse through the first drawer. Flipping through them, he paused now and then to yank a file free of the paper squeeze until he had a stack nearly eight inches thick. Tilting one file at an angle to mark his place, he hefted the stack and walked over to drop it onto the vinyl-covered sofa.

Sipe turned on a floor lamp and shut off the overhead fixture. Dropping onto the sofa with the first file, he realized it was going to be a long night. He riffled through the papers of the first folder but kept staring at his office door. It was now lit only by a small brass lamp, its green shade tilted at a forty-five-degree angle to let the sixty-watt bulb throw its light a little farther into the shadows.

Several hours later he got up with a sigh and walked in to sit at the desk. He flipped idly through the thick black phone index open on his desk. Then, as if struck by an idea, he flipped backward, this time with purpose.

Finding the page he wanted, Sipe picked up the unsharpened pencil he used to dial and tapped it, eraser down, on the open page. The steady rap of the rubber joined with the metallic tick of a Seiko quartz clock on the wall. Together they weren't enough to drown out the sound of a dropping pin.

Sipe sat back in his chair and folded his hands behind his head. The pencil was still clutched like a single chopstick in the fingers of one hand. He stared at the ceiling, knowing that what he was about to do was at best unorthodox, and at worst illegal. But, he reminded himself, you know what they say about desperate times.

He tilted forward with a thud and tugged the phone and phone book toward him into the center of the light. With a shrug, he jabbed the pencil into the rotary dial and began to spin it. The phone rang twice, seemed to hesitate, then rang twice more. A nasal voice, more Bronx than Washington, answered just as the fifth ring began. "Justice Department..." To Sipe, it sounded as much like a question as an identification. "May I help you? Who do you wish to speak to?"

Sipe told her and tilted back in his chair while she put him on hold. He listened to the not quite silent line, a thousand whispers crissing and crossing in the jungle of cables into which both he and the Justice Department were plugged. He wondered whether, after all, Muzak might not be a bad thing, instead of being teased by scraps of conversation, almost familiar voices fading in and out, names, famous and unknown, bouncing around the cable network like so many electrons.

The sudden click put an end to his philosophizing. He listened to the abrupt greeting on the other end, trying to visualize the woman who now spoke to him. Was she a blonde or a brunette, did she have long legs or large breasts? Or both?

When the mystery woman stopped speaking, he identified himself, told her who he wanted to speak to and why, then felt himself slide back into electronic limbo. Another teasing interlude of crackling whispers was almost immediately terminated. His party was finally on the line. "Mr. Brognola. My name is Ronald Sipe. I'm an assistant U.S. Attorney in Arizona. We met a couple of years ago. On your turf."

"Yes, Mr. Sipe, I remember you. How are you?"

"I need help."

Ronald Sipe's office was dark. Mack Bolan put his hand on the knob, and the half-open door swung all the way in. Something didn't seem right. He leaned forward and let his combat senses take over, probing the darkness. When the soldier had ascertained he was alone, he stepped through the doorway and slipped to one side, pulling the door closed with one hand and opening his jacket with the other. Even in the early heat, the butt of the Beretta felt cold.

Bolan skirted files and a low sofa that were more appropriate to a dentist's office than the office of a U.S. Attorney. His legs brushed the vinyl, denim scraping against the network of crazed lines where the vinyl was just beginning to peel. Footsteps in the corridor outside froze him in his tracks, and he held his breath as a bulky shadow stopped momentarily in front of the pebbled glass. A rattle of keys echoed tinnily from the hall, then the shadow moved on, its owner humming to himself in a nasal baritone.

Stepping to the inner doorway, he pulled out his big .44 Desert Eagle and snicked off the safety. The weight of the pistol gave him some reassurance, and he began to move more quickly. Through the open door he could see the left wall of the inner office, which was lined with filing cabinets in a tight rank, their tops littered with stacks of office supplies and bulging folders waiting to be put away. As he

moved to the left, Bolan could see more of the office, which
seemed to be as deserted as the outer room.

One corner of a scarred wooden desk came into view,
and Bolan leaned to the left, dropping into a crouch. The
back of a tall leather chair, canted to the right, towered over
the desk. The chair faced the window behind the desk, but
a shirtsleeved arm draped over the armrest told Bolan the
chair was occupied. The sleeve was rolled up to the elbow,
its cuff hanging loose.

Bolan held his breath. Dashing across the doorway, he
peered into the right side of the office, but nothing seemed
out of place. He moved through the doorway, his gun held
tightly in one hand, drew a bead on the center of the tall
chair back and catfooted forward until he was inches from
the desk. All he could see of the chair's occupant was the
left arm.

The warrior stepped cautiously around the desk and spun
the chair halfway around. The man in the chair remained
motionless. His left arm—an inhuman, fish-belly white—
slipped off the armrest and dangled toward the floor. Bolan noticed a thick brown band under the flapping cuff, and
just below the elbow, a slight trickle of nearly dried blood
curled over the forearm and disappeared. A disposable hy-
podermic dangled obscenely at its source, its shiny plastic
reflecting a narrow band of sunlight that slipped in through
the gap in the draperies.

Bolan put the .44 into its holster and knelt beside the man
in the chair. Using a sheet of typing paper, he removed the
needle. Then he released the thick rubber tubing knotted
just under the shirt cuff. The flesh under the rubber was
wrinkled and whiter than the rest of the arm. The warrior
leaned forward and placed his head on the man's chest. A
faint heartbeat, like an impossibly distant drum, thumped

intermittently, pausing each time as if to gather its strength for another try.

The man's chest barely rose and fell with his shallow breathing. Bolan stood and tugged the man to his feet. When the deadweight threatened to slip away, the Executioner propped him on the edge of the desk and slapped his cheeks.

"Wake up. Come on, wake up."

The man groaned, but it was a groan of protest. He seemed to resent being disturbed, as if where he was was so much better than where Bolan was. The warrior tried to force him to walk, but the man's legs were made of rubber. They buckled as soon as Bolan slacked off his own support.

A small bathroom stood in the far corner, but Bolan knew without looking that there would be no tub. The room was too small. He dragged the nearly unconscious man to the doorway and saw a small shower stall in one corner of the tiny bathroom. Bolan reached in and turned the cold on full blast. The stream of water pulsed and stuttered, but it was going to have to do. He propped the man against the doorframe, bracing him with one knee, then stripped off his jacket and draped it over the small sink. He tugged his weapons free and placed them on top of the jacket.

The man started to slip, and Bolan grabbed him. Like a stevedore manhandling an obstinate crate, the warrior pushed and shoved his resistant burden under the cold spray, then stepped in after him to hold him upright. He slapped the man's cheeks several times, trying to force him awake. The cold water poured down around them, and the man groaned again.

Bolan cupped the man's head in both hands and tilted his face toward the cold water. It pooled in both closed eyes and filled the man's nose and open mouth. He choked and spluttered, shaking his head in an indifferent effort to escape the water, then gagged as his throat constricted. Bolan knew what was coming, but there was little chance to avoid it. He slipped to one side, and the man began to vomit, choking and gasping.

Bolan turned the man again to force him to face the stream of water, and he could feel the man's entire body begin to shudder. He shook his head from side to side, once bumping the back of his head into his savior's face and cutting his lip. With the initial danger past, Bolan allowed the gasping man to slump gently to the floor of the shower. He stepped out, leaving the water on full blast.

Grabbing his Beretta, he walked to the outer office, intending to lock the door. He stopped abruptly in the center of the room. The frosted glass in the outer door was dark. As he began to move again, the shadow moved and he heard the rattle of the doorknob. It was too late to lock the door. He sidestepped and took cover behind a row of cabinets.

The knob squeaked and the latch clicked open. Crouching behind the metal cabinet, he shifted the Beretta to his left hand. It was tempting to shoot first, through the glass, but until he knew who was trying to enter the office he had to hold his fire. It could be anyone, from a cleaning woman to a burglar. There didn't have to be a connection between the man in the shower and anyone who tried to enter the office.

The door swung open slowly, its hinges squeaking like an old radio sound effect. The large shadow was broad enough to cover the entire panel of glass. When the door finally opened wide enough, the shadow split in two, and one man stepped through. His right hand was extended, and Bolan caught a glimpse of an automatic pistol with a suppressor threaded in place before the interior darkness swallowed both the man and his gun.

A second man, taller and slimmer than the behemoth who led the way, slipped in and closed the door behind him. The frosted glass now glowed softly again, the overhead fluorescent in the hallway ceiling bleeding through and throwing a pale block onto the tiled floor.

In the near darkness Bolan watched while the two men huddled together. Their whispered conversation was too soft for him to hear, despite the closeness. The lead shadow lifted a small walkie-talkie to his lips, and Bolan heard a sharp burst of static.

"Looks like you're overreacting again. Nobody's here. I'll let you know for sure in a couple of minutes." The big man thumbed the walkie-talkie off and tucked it into his shirt pocket.

The slender man passed in front of the glass, and a click filled the room with light. Bolan blinked away the sudden glare, and the big man froze. He shouted something as he swung around his automatic. His reactions were good.

But Bolan's were a little better.

The Beretta chugged twice, the suppressed whisper like thunder in the sudden silence. Two bright red blotches exploded on the big man's denim shirt, and he looked at the holes in his chest as if he didn't believe they were really there. Then, in a slow second that seemed to take an eternity, he looked back at Bolan, his mouth frozen in a silent O.

He seemed to stumble over the pattern in the tile and pitched forward. A spasmodic contraction jerked his trigger finger once, then again, the slugs slamming into the floor as he fell.

Behind him, now suddenly exposed and still uncertain what was happening, the tall man stuck out his tongue as if thinking. He reminded Bolan of a chess player caught off guard by an unexpected maneuver. He spotted the warrior in the same instant and dived to the floor, landing on a shoulder and rolling toward the wall. He slammed into the legs of a lounge and tried to rise, but his boots slipped on the slick tile and he landed hard on one elbow.

The pistol in his other hand wavered, and he fired one shot while trying to regain his balance. The slug ripped into the plaster just above Bolan's head, sending a shower of dust and fragments sifting down over the Executioner's wet skin.

He was exposed in the corner, but his opponent was just as vulnerable. Still lying on the floor, the thin man rolled to his right, his feet slipping under the lounge and hampering his movement. He fired again to buy himself some time, but this shot went wide. Bolan took careful aim and fired a single shot, catching the prostrate gunner in the shoulder. The bullet slammed down through the collarbone of his gun hand, and the arm went limp.

Reaching for the pistol with his other hand, the hard guy rolled back just as Bolan fired again. This time the shot was dead on. The 9 mm stinger splintered bone as it bored through the man's skull, and he jerked like a landed trout for a second or two, then was still forever.

Bolan scrambled to his feet and ran to the door. This time he locked it, pressing his ear to the glass. The hallway outside was quiet. He heard a door open and close at the far end of the hall, a mumbled conversation, then silence. He checked the two men on the floor. Neither had a pulse. As he stood after checking the big man, a burst of static crackled and Bolan, startled, turned to the door.

Then he heard a voice, thin and reedy, almost a whisper. "Alonzo, you there? Come on man, answer me. Alonzo?"

Bolan reached into the big man's pocket and yanked the walkie-talkie free. He held his hand over the mike and pressed the send button. "Hang on," he mumbled, deepening his voice to approximate what he assumed the dead man had sounded like.

"Everything all right up there?"

"Yeah, yeah."

"All right. Look, if you don't need me, I'm gonna go ahead. Okay?"

"Okay, okay. I'll see you later."

Bolan tossed the walkie-talkie onto the floor and walked back to the inner office.

4

Randy Carlton punched the time clock with more than his customary violence. The mechanical jaws in the clock's inner workings chewed at the stiff cardboard, chomping several square bites out of the edge of his time card and stamping 7:03 four times before he yanked it loose. The whole partition on which the clock was mounted rattled its Plexiglas windows.

Will Ralston, his partner, eyed him from the other side of the coffee machine. Carlton slammed the card back into its slot in a battered metal rack, which had seen better days. The metal panel on its front was creased and dented, its khaki paint chipped and peeling in several places, betraying at least three earlier paintings.

He joined his partner at the coffee machine, breaking two Styrofoam cups as he yanked them from the dispenser. The third, miraculously, held together. Carlton dumped sugar into the white cup without looking, then opened the petcock on the coffee machine, watching the watery brown fluid dribble until the cup was half full. He churned the coffee and sugar into a viscous mess with a plastic stirrer, then added milk. After downing the lukewarm slop in the two gulps, he crumpled the cup in a large fist, ignoring the goo oozing out of the ruptured Styrofoam and seeping through his fingers.

With a sardonic smile, he flipped the cup behind his back and watched it hang precariously on the lip of a plastic wastebasket. When it finally teetered in, he raised his right arm triumphantly, shouting "Yes! And it counts." He cupped his hands in front of his mouth and simulated the buzz of an adoring crowd.

"You finished, or is it just halftime?" Ralston asked, tilting his Stetson far back on his head to reveal the broad forehead of a prematurely balding man.

His partner ignored the taunt. "You see those dorks from Arizona last night? Jeez, how the hell do you blow a fifteen-point lead in eight minutes? Wildcats, my ass. Pussycats is more like it."

"I guess they miss a certain power forward. Of course, he's a little long in the tooth, and I'd bet my next check his jump shot ain't what it used to be."

Carlton groaned. "Here we go again. You never give up, do you? Well, old buddy, I'll bet you *my* next check I can still wipe the court with your raggedy ass. How about lunchtime we play a little one-on-one."

"What'll you spot me?"

"Two baskets."

"Shit! You outweigh me by forty pounds and have a six-inch height advantage."

"Yeah, but I'm gettin' old. Isn't that what you just said? That ought to be worth something."

"All right, all right. We'll talk about it later. What's in the hopper for this morning?"

"Same old shit. Check the rail yards. Run down to the border for a nice leisurely ride."

"Great, just what the doctor ordered. It's supposed to get up to a hundred and five today. Too damn early in the year for that kind of heat."

"Shouldn't bother you. You grew up around here. I come from Flagstaff. It's human weather up there, not lizard weather."

Ralston finished his own coffee and tossed the cup, intact, into the wastebasket. "You ready?"

"No."

"Good! Let's roll, then."

The two men signed out, Ralston noting their itinerary on the assignment log, and stepped out into the early morning. The light was intense, but the temperature, at least, was still in the low eighties.

Ralston led the way to the Bronco cruiser, his boots clacking on the asphalt of the parking lot inside a wire fence. At an even six foot he would have been imposing except for his partner's half foot advantage in height. He had brownish hair, and Carlton loved to tease him about the premature streak of gray at each temple. Ducking under the doorframe of the 4x4, he knocked his hat off, as he did at least twice a week. Carlton had unmercifully kept a running tally since their first day as partners.

"Three twenty-seven. You're right on your average, Will."

Ralston took a swipe at him, catching the taller man in the shoulder as he climbed into the passenger seat.

"How come the rail yards? We were just there two days ago."

"I know, but Ronny Sipe got a hunch. Says we ought to give the place another look."

"Fine by me." Carlton eased back in the seat to give his head a little clearance in the compact vehicle. The roads were okay, but the rail yards were potholed and lumpy, tearing up Broncos and drivers with equal indifference.

Ralston pumped the accelerator, turned the key, then waited for the engine to settle into a smooth rumble. He kicked it into gear and backed out of the parking place, spun the wheel and darted through the chain-link fence.

Out on the street he cruised along slowly. Each man swept his side of the street with practiced casualness. The job had honed instincts to a sharp edge. Despite the regular patrols and the occasional tips about coyote runs, they made nearly half their collars in broad daylight on the streets of district towns.

The border seemed to have some sort of mystical influence over the illegals, and they treated it as if it were possessed of magical power, as if mere passage across it rendered them invisible, or at least superficially legitimate. For some of the Border Patrol officers, it did. Ralston and Carlton were more concerned with the predators charging exorbitant rates for smuggling workers across the border. If you had been south and seen what most of the workers were leaving behind, it was hard to blame them. An occasional blind eye hurt no one, and helped ease consciences still a little thinly skinned.

Not everyone felt the same way, however. Some of the officers eased their own guilt by aggressively pursuing more of it. Rough treatment, even brutality, wasn't uncommon. There was an unwritten rule among the southeast Arizona detachment that business was business, and each man had his own.

The rail yard was a tangle of spurs, sidings and low sheds. Baked under the desert sun 360 days a year, it looked more like a moon base than a train yard. The sheds, all peeling paint and corrugated metal, occupied one side of the yards, each pair separated by a freight dock and siding. Once through the sagging gate, Ralston swung the Bronco in a wide half circle, then killed the engine.

Both men jumped down and loosened their side arms, which they carried in western-style holsters. Some of the characters they'd encountered were about as close to illegal as you could get and twice as ornery. An angry hobo had less to lose than an illegal alien, who at least had hopes of a surreptitious entrance and six months' worth of work before slipping back over the border. The bums, on the other hand, didn't give a damn about anything as mundane as a job.

Ralston had taken twenty-five stitches and a hairline skull fracture when he had attempted to wake a sleeping hobo. The man came awake with an eighteen-inch lead pipe in his hand and caught Ralston across the forehead before the lawman knew what was happening. The attacker claimed later that he'd thought he was being robbed. Ralston thought that was plausible, and didn't blame the guy, but his head ached for two months all the same.

They started at one end of the row of freight sheds, checking each open car, sometimes climbing up into a boxcar or tugging a canvas bonnet loose to look up into a pyramid of concrete culverts. Worming their way down the rows, they talked in loud voices, kicking and banging against anything handy to make as much noise as possible. They were less concerned about catching anyone hiding in the yard than they were replaying Pete O'Brien's last day on the job...and on earth.

O'Brien had peeked into a flatbed stacked with twenty-four-inch oil pipe, and staring down one of the long tubes he found himself also staring into the considerably smaller mouth of a sawed-off 12-gauge. The hiding man, spooked by the sudden burst of sunlight, had squeezed off both barrels. There wasn't enough left of O'Brien's head for the undertaker to work on.

While Carlton checked the first few cars in each row, Ralston explored the freight sheds and a couple of cars on the end of each line. The sheds took a little time, and Carlton gradually pulled ahead of his partner.

The first three rows turned up no living thing but a pair of rats nesting in the manure-filled straw of an empty cattle car, and the usual complement of flies, their glistening green turning an assortment of cowpies into a surrealistic bed of living emeralds.

Carlton noticed the smell first as he worked his way down the fourth row. He couldn't place it at first, but he couldn't avoid it, either. By the time he reached the fifth row of boxcars, he refused to confront what he already knew. In aisle six the smell turned to stench, and the hum, like a high-tension line ready to blow its transformer, filled the space between two rows of cars.

"Will? Can you come here? On the double."

"What's the matter."

"Just come here, will you?"

Carlton pulled a large checkered handkerchief from his back pocket and wrapped it across his mouth and nose. He walked forward cautiously, like a man entering a bear's den, just the toes of his boots touching the baked clay beneath them. He heard Will Ralston behind him, but he didn't turn around.

"What the hell . . . ?" Ralston stopped suddenly, sniffed and almost gagged. "Jesus H. Christ!" He coughed, then cleared his throat, fighting back the surge of bile. He yanked out his own handkerchief and smothered the lower half of his face with it, taking shallow breaths. He stepped to his partner's side. "My God, what an awful stench."

"Yeah, isn't it?" Carlton stepped forward now, one foot at a time. He reached the sliding door of the next car in the row. "It's locked," he said, nearly choking. "Get me something to rip it open, Will."

"I saw a crowbar in one of the sheds. Be right back."
Ralston, as if glad to get away for a moment, sprinted back
down the aisle, then disappeared around the corner of the
last car.

While he waited for Ralston to return, Carlton backed
away from the boxcar and, feeling slightly ridiculous,
knotted the handkerchief over his mouth and nose, tucking the pointy end in under his shirt to keep it snug. He felt
like a bad guy in a Clint Eastwood spaghetti western, and
for a second, almost smiled. Then he remembered why he'd
done it.

Ralston sprinted back, a three-foot crowbar in his hand.
He passed it to his partner and stepped backward a few
paces to knot his own handkerchief in place. It was eight-
thirty, and the heat had already begun to rise. As he hefted
the crowbar, Carlton looked up at the sky, its blue all but
bleached away by the rising sun, and watched the shimmering air rising from the roofs of the rows of cars. Three
black specks curled in place high above him, gradually
growing larger, like a trio of eight balls rolling down a spi-
ral staircase. He watched them for a moment, but didn't
have to guess what they were. He already knew.

Slipping the straight end of the crowbar under a heavy
padlock, he leaned into the bar, but had virtually no leverage. He tried pulling up, but couldn't reach high enough to
exert any real pressure. He dropped to one knee, then
crawled under the car to grab a couple of creosote-spattered
two-by-fours. He felt something hot and wet drip onto his
back and dampen his shirt.

Crawling back out from under the car, he swiped one big
hand across his shoulders, felt the sticky moisture and
brought his hand back. Raising the damp fingers to his
covered nose, he took a shallow whiff, then hastily wiped
the hand on his uniform pants.

Stacking the two-by-fours against the door of the box-car, he repositioned the crowbar, pinning the lumber about midway along its length, then leaned into it. With the wood as a fulcrum, he was able to pry the padlock latch away. The bolts started to give, creaking in the old wood, ripping splinters out of the door, then popping, one by one. When all four had come free, the latch sprang back against the door. The rusted bolts rattled in the latch mount as it swung back and forth.

Carlton tossed the bar to one side and reached for the door handle. He gave it a shove, and the door, protesting at first, rolled back and slammed into its block. A wave of noxious air swept over both men like a hot liquid, and Ralston dropped to his knees and ripped the kerchief from his face. The splatter of vomit made Carlton's stomach churn, and he turned away, trying to block out the sound.

He turned back to the car while Ralston, still choking, got to his feet. Pulling a heavy flashlight from his belt, he clicked it on and played the beam around the inside of the car.

"Oh my God!" he said, swallowing hard and turning away from the dark interior of the boxcar. "Will, run and get the yardmaster. Forget the radio. Use his phone to call in. Then call Ronny Sipe and tell him to get his ass over here."

Carlton, vaguely aware of his partner's feet pounding on the hot earth, backed away from the open door. He reached up and yanked the kerchief away.

Then he threw up.

5

Bolan hauled the still-groaning Sipe out of the shower. He was conscious but groggy. Bolan shook him, and the man tried to wriggle out of his grasp. He took a wild swing, but the fist sailed harmlessly past the warrior's shoulder.

"Hold on a minute, friend. I'm on your side."

"What are you doing in my office?"

"You've had a lot of unexpected company tonight, haven't you?"

Sipe narrowed his eyes and tried to fix Bolan with a piercing stare that kept fading in and out of focus. He reached for his left arm and rubbed it absently, kneading the flesh just below his elbow. He hit a sore spot and yanked his cuff out of the way, nearly tearing it from his sleeve. Like a crystal forming in time-lapse photography, understanding began to transform his face, the stuporous slackness replaced by bafflement.

"Who are you?" he asked.

"You sent for help."

He nodded. "Yeah, I did. You from Brognola?"

Before Bolan could answer, Sipe slid down the wall to sit on the floor, his back against the shower stall. "I don't feel too good."

"Why don't you tell me what happened?"

Sipe rubbed his face with both hands, chafing the skin of both cheeks. Then he screwed his knuckles into his eye sockets. He tried again to stand, and this time managed to get halfway up before he lost his balance and slipped back to the floor. He looked up at Bolan and tried to smile, but his features tumbled over themselves, and he settled for a weak grin. Extending his right hand, he said, "Help me up, would you?"

Bolan grabbed the hand and pulled, and Sipe bounced to his feet and leaned against the shower stall for a long moment. He started to walk, and nearly fell. Bolan caught the attorney under the arms and half dragged him into the inner office.

When they were within leaning distance of the desk, Sipe shook Bolan off and caught the edge of the desk with both hands. Like an old man, he shuffled his feet, the soles of his shoes scraping on the tiled floor. When he got close to the chair, he smiled like a man reaching the peak of Everest, then bent to swing the desk chair around. He toppled into it with a shuddering sigh.

"Okay, let's start all over. Who did you say you were?"

"I didn't."

"Well, do you mind telling me who you are?"

Bolan tilted his head slightly to one side. A shadow of a smile formed on his lips, but he let it go no farther. He had to hand it to Sipe. The guy had guts. Half dead, maybe more, twenty minutes ago, he was already scratching his way back to some semblance of control.

Bolan stood up and walked into the bathroom, returning with his jacket in hand. Sipe noticed the two guns for the first time as Bolan casually sat down, reached into his pocket and pulled out a small leather case. Tossing it across the desk, Bolan watched as Sipe opened it, looked at him, then back at the case.

"Mike Belasko. That you?"

"That's right."

"And you say Brognola sent you?"

"I'm helping him out. Let's just say I'm from Justice, okay?"

"Did he give you the details?"

"He said you could handle that part of it."

Sipe shook his head, rocking slightly in the big chair. "Yeah, I guess I can do that."

"Before you do, why don't you tell me what happened here?"

"Not much to tell. I was working late, reading some papers. I called Washington and must've fallen asleep. I'm not sure. Anyway, the next thing I know, I'm looking into the wrong end of a pistol. These guys were standing—"

"Hold on a minute." Bolan raised a hand like a traffic cop. "How many guys?"

"Two, I think, maybe three. I'm not sure. It all happened so fast. Anyway, I tried to get up. My gun was on the filing cabinets. That's where I always leave it. You wouldn't believe how uncomfortable the damn thing is when you have to sit at a desk for four or five hours. I got slugged, and that's all I remember. Until I woke up in the shower, that is. I guess I forgot to thank you for that."

Bolan waved it away. "Did you get a good look at the men?"

"One of them. The others not so good."

"Ever seen any of them before?"

"I don't know. I think maybe, yes, but . . . for some reason I could swear I'd seen this one guy before, but I don't know where."

"Would you recognize one of them if you saw him again?"

"The one guy, hell, yes. No doubt about it. In fact, I hope I do see the son of a bitch. I—"

Sipe stopped when Bolan stood up. "Come on out here a minute, will you? Can you manage?"

The attorney shook his head and stood up. He tottered for a moment, then edged around the desk, holding himself up with one hand. He walked unsteadily to the doorway. Stepping to one side, Bolan pointed to the two bodies on the floor.

"Good God!" Sipe mumbled, then fell to the floor with a damp thud.

Bolan knelt beside him, slapping Sipe's cheeks to wake him up. The man groaned, then raised himself on one elbow. "Sorry. I don't know what happened. I just..." Then he remembered why he'd fainted. His eyes kept drifting past Bolan's shoulder to the nearer of the two dead men, then back to Bolan's face. The pallor of Sipe's cheeks had grown even more ghostly under the bright red prints of Bolan's hands.

"Either of them look familiar?"

Sipe didn't answer immediately. He stared at the behemoth on the floor, twisting his neck to an uncomfortable angle. He inhaled deeply, then let the air out in a long, slow whistle. He nodded. "Yeah. The fat bastard is one of them. I won't forget him for a while."

"What about the other one?"

Sipe shook his head. "No, I don't think so. I'm not sure, but he doesn't look like the other guys I remember. I just don't know. What the hell happened here, anyway?"

"I'm not sure," Bolan said. "I came here straight from the airport. When I got to your office, it was dark, but the door was open. I wasn't here long when the Welcome Wagon showed up."

"You mean they followed you?"

Bolan shook his head. "I don't think so. They were probably waiting outside and saw me come up."

"You mean they know who you are?"

"Not necessarily. Probably just paranoia. They knew what happened to you and had to be jittery. They were waiting to make sure you croaked. An unfamiliar face made them nervous. Either that or they just wanted to double-check."

"It's a good thing you got here when you did." Sipe collapsed back to the floor, breathing in short, shallow drafts. His chest moved spasmodically, and he pressed against it with both hands, trying to reestablish control. "Christ almighty," he whispered. "I must have really touched a nerve."

"Looks like it. Now all we have to do is figure out whose."

"I'm gonna have to call the sheriff about my late friends here."

Bolan nodded. Sipe got to his knees, then using the doorframe to hoist himself up, he climbed to his feet. Bolan offered a hand, but the attorney waved it away. He gritted his teeth, his clenched jaw muscles bulging under the white skin. Upright again, he walked slowly toward the bulk of the fat man, stepped around to the dead man's feet and stared into the still surprised features. "That's him, all right. The bastard."

He turned and walked over to look at the second body. After a long minute he shook his head, slowly at first and then definitively. "Nope. Never saw this guy before." He started to walk back toward Bolan, then stopped.

Bolan tossed him the walkie-talkie. "They had a friend outside."

Sipe turned to look at the door, as if he expected another man to burst through it.

"Don't worry. He left."

"Then these guys have a car downstairs somewhere."

"Maybe."

"Want to take a look?"

"I think you should get these two taken care of first. Then we'll see what we want to do."

"I'll make the call." Sipe walked back into the inner office. His legs were steadier now, and he seemed to be shaking off the grogginess. He stepped around his desk and dropped into the big chair. "After I call the sheriff, I think I'd better get you up to speed."

Sipe reached for the telephone, but it rang before he lifted the receiver. The noise startled him, and he dropped the phone as he snatched it from its cradle. Peevishly he bent to snag it from the floor. He watched Bolan thoughtfully as he lifted the receiver slowly to his ear. "Sipe," he snapped.

"Where? When?" He knitted his eyebrows in a tight frown. "I'll be right there." He let out a long breath as he replaced the receiver. "Jesus!" He stood up.

"What's wrong?"

"Come on. I'll tell you on the way over. I hope you don't mind riding in wet clothes."

"I've done worse," Bolan replied. "Where are we going?"

Sipe grabbed his snub-nosed .38 Police Special from the top of the filing cabinets. "You'll see. I think you may have gotten here just in time." He slung his jacket over his shoulder and ran toward the door.

6

The rail yard was clotted with emergency vehicles from as far away as fifty miles. Ronny Sipe paced back and forth at one end of the aisle. Mack Bolan, after a cursory introduction, had slipped to one side. He watched the controlled chaos with a dispassionate eye, more interested in the chemistry of the living than the dead. Will Ralston directed traffic in front of the open boxcar, but Randy Carlton was someplace else. With his Stetson tilted forward, he leaned against another freight car, his legs crossed at the ankles. His arms were folded across his chest, but his big hands just wouldn't keep still.

Sipe and Bolan had been the first to arrive, followed by an intermittent stream of police. They all waited for the medical examiner and the crime photographer. The heat dried their clothes quickly, leaving them wrinkled, but no one seemed to notice anything unusual. It was just one more footnote in an already convoluted story.

No one seemed to feel like speaking. Instead, they just leaned against the ends of the boxcars or wandered in tight little circles, avoiding one another's eyes. When the photographer finally arrived and began his work, even Bolan was overwhelmed by the bizarre flashes issuing from the open mouth of the boxcar. The incessant clicking and small bursts of light had swallowed all other sights and sounds.

Randy Carlton seemed to take it the hardest, first stalking up and down the aisle like an enraged beast, then, as the aisle grew crowded, collapsing in a heap in the closed end of the aisle, his back to the boxcar. Bolan watched the rangy patrolman with interest, recognizing in him some of the same passion and outrage that had shaped his own life. It wasn't often he came across a lawman who carried in his gut that white-hot flame that burned without consuming or being consumed.

Most lesser men, if they were aware of it at all, tried to ignore it or, if that wouldn't work, to quench it. Drinking was a common hazard for cops, anything to numb them, to let them get through the day without feeling too much. It was impossible to understand the sensory overload of a day on the job unless you'd been there.

Bolan understood.

He drifted closer to Carlton, as if drawn by an invisible cable slowly tightening, its silent ratcheting slowly but steadily narrowing the gap between them. He stopped about ten feet away, knowing it was the longest ten feet in the solar system, and knowing that Randy Carlton knew it, too.

As the word spread, the law-enforcement crowd continued to grow. Arizona Rangers, border patrolmen and the county sheriff with three deputies all mingled in the restless crowd as paramedics began removing the bodies. Wearing surgical masks, they were forced to check each one to make sure there was no sign of life. And one by one they wrestled each lifeless corpse into a black body bag. The angry rasp of each heavy zipper cut through the low buzz of conversation, and Carlton shuddered every time.

Sipe stopped pacing for a moment and slipped down to the end of the aisle. He nodded to Bolan, then planted himself in front of Carlton, staring at him for a quick eternity. Finally he bent forward to rest his hands on his knees, and in a hoarse whisper he asked, "You okay, Randy?"

"No, I'm not okay and I will *never* be okay again." His jaw snapped shut.

Sipe resumed his pacing. He stopped once and looked at Bolan, either for help or sympathy, then, as if he knew there was no help and that sympathy was useless, he shrugged and walked away.

He stood with his back to the crowd, and Bolan could see by the tight set of his shoulders that it wouldn't take much to send him teetering over the edge of the same precipice Randy Carlton had already fallen over. Muffled shouts echoed between the railroad cars, and Sipe turned, then took a few steps forward just as the milling crowd began to surge back toward him. Like boiling soup overflowing a pot too small for it, the crowd burst out of the mouth of the aisle and spread away on both sides, squeezing in between the cars and the loading dock at one end and bubbling into the open at the other.

Two paramedics pushed through the last remnants of the crowd and sprinted toward an ambulance. Sipe recognized Marty Sanfilippo from the EMT unit at Mariposa Hospital. He watched Sanfilippo and the other paramedic open the back door of the ambulance and yank a wheeled gurney through it. He was almost mesmerized by the flashing red and blue lights all but invisible in the harsh sunlight. The paramedics rushed back toward him, and Sipe fell in behind them as they slowed to maneuver the gurney through the crowded aisle.

"What's going on, Marty?" Sipe puffed.

"We got a live one," Sanfilippo said.

"He going to make it?"

"How the hell do I know, Ronny? He might not even want to." Sanfilippo didn't elaborate. He didn't have to.

The paramedic squeezed through a tight ring of lawmen, which closed behind him like an airlock. Sipe turned sideways and started to follow, when an elbow caught him in the ribs. The border patrolman who'd blocked his passage didn't bother to turn, and Sipe grabbed him by the upper arm and tugged. The larger man spun his head, ready to argue, until he saw who it was. "Shit, Ronny, why didn't you say something?"

"Forget it, Buck. I didn't recognize you, either. Just let me through." Sipe didn't really mean it, and Buck Allenson knew it. The two men had had more than one run-in, and each knew there would be others.

Sipe slid through a narrow gap and entered a semicircular clearing around the yawning boxcar door. Flies buzzed in and out of the doorway, and the lawmen gathered there swatted absently as the insects landed on their sweating necks and arms. Reluctantly Sipe walked toward the boxcar and poked his head into the shadows. An overwhelming nausea surged over him, and he doubled up, banging his forehead on the floor of the boxcar. He vomited onto the railbed, and the twinges in his gut seemed as if they would never stop. Long after his stomach was empty, involuntary contractions racked him, and it was several minutes before he could straighten up.

"What's the matter, Ronny," someone in the crowd asked, "don't like Mexican food?" The smattering of awkward laughter died before he turned.

"Who said that?" Sipe stared at each of the lawmen in turn, but no one said anything. "Who the fuck said that?"

The men squirmed as Sipe walked toward them, but they kept their silence. Finally Roy Harrison, one of the deputies, said, "Hell, Ronny, it don't make no difference who said it. It was just a joke."

Sipe shook his head like a teacher at the end of his rope. "A joke? You think that's something to joke about?" He flung one hand back toward the boxcar.

Harrison cleared his throat. "No, not especially. But, damn, you got to keep a sense of humor. You know that. Hell, you know what we see on this job. How can we get anything done if we let it get to us?"

Sipe shook his head again. He turned away, took a step back toward the open door, then swung back. "I'll tell you one thing, Roy. If I find out who's responsible for this, he'll wish to God it was him in that boxcar. I guarantee it."

"Come off it, Sipe," Buck said. "It don't mean nothing. Hell, for every dead Mex in that train, there's a million more ready to take his place. And take his chances, too. They accept it. Why the hell can't you?"

Sipe said nothing. He looked at Allenson a long time, then, with a wave of his hand, he turned back to the boxcar and hauled himself up through the open door. Inside, the stench was even more overwhelming, but his stomach was empty now and his anger took control.

Marty Sanfilippo and his partner were just lifting a frail man, who appeared to be in his early fifties, onto the gurney. A third paramedic stood to one side, an IV bottle held over his head in his right hand. Several coils of clear plastic tubing dangled from his left hand, and he tapped them nervously against his left knee.

Sipe clapped Sanfilippo on the shoulder. "Marty, you got to save him."

The paramedic turned with a stiff mask in place of his usual smile. "You mean keep him alive long enough for you to question him, don't you? That's all you're really interested in."

"Marty, what the hell are you talking about? You know I—"

Sanfilippo nodded his head at the unconscious man.
"That could be my father, or one of a dozen uncles. How
the hell do you think I got here? Ronny, get out of my way.
I'm gonna save him—if I can—but not for you. Not for
him, either. I'm gonna save him so I can find out who's responsible for this. And then I'll take care of it. *My* way."

"You can't do that. You—"

"Watch me, Ronny. Just stand back and watch me. It
shouldn't be too hard. You're already pretty good at it."

"Marty, I—"

"I gotta go. This man needs to be in the hospital." Sanfilippo turned away, shrugging off Sipe's hand. He backed
toward the doorway, then set the end of the gurney on the
boxcar floor while he jumped to the ground.

Sipe watched Sanfilippo's partner jump down, and the
two men hauled the gurney off the car floor, releasing col-
lapsible wheels as they did so. A moment later they were out
of sight. The attorney walked to the doorway and watched
them maneuver through the crowd. Not until the gurney
was lifted into the ambulance and Marty had followed it in,
ahead of the closing door, did he turn back. For the first
time he saw the row of body bags, the wrinkles in the shiny
black plastic filled with pulls of brilliant sunlight. He
walked across the open doorway and peered over the
shoulders of the lawmen.

Moving a mental finger from bag to bag, he didn't stop
until he reached twenty-three. And beyond the row of bags,
now so overwhelming in their number they might as well
have been a gargantuan course of strange, iridescent bricks,
Randy Carlton, hat still tilted far forward, leaned against
the end of the boxcar. For a second Sipe thought maybe
Carlton could stop the row from reaching any farther. Then
he remembered the knot of bodies still in the corner and
knew that wasn't possible.

It was too late for that. Way too late.

RONALD SIPE SAT in his office, staring at the telephone. There was something about the instrument that frightened him. As often as he'd used it, as much as he was inclined to take it for granted, when he really thought about it, the telephone seemed to be a miracle. The ability to send a few numbers through a wire and talk to someone thousands of miles away seemed like presumption.

His grandfather had never used a phone, wouldn't even allow one in the house. The old man never tired of telling him how unnatural it was. He used to say, "If God wanted us to talk to people that far away, he'd have given them bigger ears and us bigger mouths. Most mouths is too big by half already."

The old man wouldn't argue. He'd just state his case, then stop listening. Any attempt to change his mind was wasted air. Sipe himself didn't believe in so parochial a view, but whenever he was faced with the prospect of phoning on a serious matter, he'd pause, partly in fear and partly in wonder. Now, waiting for a phone call from Ray Conlan, the county sheriff, he wondered why in hell he didn't move east and look for something less nerve-racking to do.

It was midday, but heavy draperies pulled across the double windows blocked out the sun. The bloodstains on the carpet were little more than dark shadows, and the childlike scrawl of the body outlines seemed almost phosphorescent on the rug, glowing a little from the ambient light. Finally he shook himself free of the depression that threatened to overwhelm him and looked at Bolan.

"Randy will be here any minute. Maybe the three of us can make some sense out of this mess. Now we have two potential witnesses, and neither one of them is able to tell us anything. I guess it'll be up to us."

"Start at the beginning, and we'll see where that takes us."

"Shit, Belasko, I don't even know which end is up. You think I can tell where it all starts?"

Bolan said nothing. To keep the silence from eating at him, Sipe rapped a pencil on the desktop, the rhythm slowly swelling until it filled the room. Finally, stretching his arms above his head, he leaned back in the chair. "Here goes..."

7

There was no water for as far as the eye could see. The Sonora Desert, like an abandoned movie set, stretched from one arid corner of the horizon to the other. The dry soil, flaky and sandy in some spots, hard-baked like ancient tile in others, was nearly colorless, what tone there was shading from pale beige to yellowed ivory.

Randy Carlton loved the desert and hated it with equal conviction. Its beauty was undeniable, but its hostility was implacable. The plants, a hundred kinds of cactus sporting every conceivable form of spine and needle, and gnarled shrubs, twisted as an arthritic grandfather, offered little relief from the colorless monotony. Their greens, mostly dark, and all covered with a pale layer of gritty dust, might just as well have been brown or black.

He was fascinated by the cloudless sky, its blue bright enough to hurt the eyes, and paler than any blue on earth, seemed to press down as if it were made of glowing metal. Its weight added to the overwhelming desolation and accentuated the inhospitable impression to an unbearable degree.

Far to the south the purple smear of the San Antonio Mountains seemed the only thing holding off the weight of the sky. The peaks gave the impression of having been blunted, as if by bearing the weight of heaven far too long, they had been compressed. They shimmered with an illusory unreality, their substance boiling off in the heat, bleaching as it rose and surrendering its color to the sun.

Carlton always felt alone in the desert. The world seemed to revolve around him, and he shrank in his mind's eye to insignificance, no more substantial than a geometric point. Reduced to one dimension, he served no other purpose than that of a pivot, a tiny jewel in a colossal watch, everything whirling around him.

To the west, hundreds of miles away, lay the waters of the Pacific, so alien in the desert it seemed a sin even to think of them. To the east, more hundreds of miles of desolation, the barrenness reaching out, stretching itself to the filmy thinness of beaten gold until finally it fell almost prostrate, nearly exhausted, at the feet of the warm waters of the Gulf of Mexico. And to the north, confident of its impregnability, lay the agricultural wealth of the greatest country on earth.

And it was that richness, more than anything else, that made him angry. He didn't begrudge anyone anything they owned. But he couldn't understand the single-minded avarice that would enrich itself at the expense of those who had nothing at all.

Through the heart of hell meandered the Rio Grande. At once, the sluggish river was an invitation and a barrier. For thousands of Mexicans who would be Americans, to cross it meant a chance at a new life or, as often as not, something far less lofty—new clothes for the kids, an operation for an ailing grandmother.

But in Arizona there was no certainty, nothing like the luxury of a visible boundary between having and needing. The Rio Grande was too far to the east to help him here. Instead of the sluggish river he had to patrol an imaginary line.

Skittering like crabs, creeping like snakes or running flat out, like the mustangs high in the northern mountains, they came in waves, a tide of flesh as endless as the swells of the ocean. And to stop them, come hell or high water, the most powerful country the planet had ever seen sent a handful of men, most of whom couldn't care less what brought the intruders in the first place. And those who did care had no choice but to try, regardless of their sympathy or compassion.

The main roads were few, the secondaries just as scarce, as often as not dwindling down to a pair of shallow ruts baked hard as any pottery. Dry wash and arroyo crisscrossed the barren land like the veins on an old woman's hand. The paths of least resistance were many for the little rain that fell. Points of stone stabbed at the sky like accusing fingers, their layered skins a map of ancient history.

Mesmerized by the stubbornness of nature, he wondered at the saguaro and prickly pear, which seemed almost human, bristling against the fate that had condemned them to such a hell, grabbed on to any patch of earth deep enough to hold them and hung on for dear life. And Randy Carlton, almost as shallowly rooted, held on for dear life to the notion that what he did could make a difference. What kind of difference, and to whom, was something he didn't dare consider.

Scorpions and spiders, lizards and snakes all kept to the shade, preferring to move at night, if they had to move at all. They were too wise to the ways of the desert to stir even at the harnessed thunder of an engine.

Randy Carlton, one muscled arm dangling against the scalding steel of the driver's door, rocked sideways as the Bronco chewed at the pebbled sides of a shallow gully. "You sure we're heading right, Will?"

"I guess. Over the next rise we ought to be able to see the border."

"I haven't seen a sign of life. Nothing's passed this way for months, as far as I can tell. Hell, I haven't even seen a soda can or a cigarette pack."

"All I know is what the guy said. Three miles east of Santa Cruz," he said. "Twin towers, one brown and one red."

"That could be any damn pair of chimneys out here. Hell, how will we know we got the right place?"

"Your guess is as good as mine. What time you got?"

"Nine-fifty."

"Well, we still got time. Let's get on over this rise and see what happens."

The younger man shook his head, but he shifted down and pushed the vehicle up the steep slope. At a branch in the gully, he gunned the engine and climbed up and out, slipping between two tall saguaros.

"Damn, I get the creeps out here," he mumbled.

"You city boys are all the same."

"City, my ass. I didn't know what a city looked like till I got to Tucson."

"Ruined you forever, that did."

"Got me an education."

"When's the last time you used any of it on the job?"

"Hell, I took some psychology. Use it all the time. That's the main reason I don't blame you. See, I *understand* you. That's why I have sympathy."

"Fuck you. Drive." Ralston laughed. He reached into the back and hauled a soda out of the Styrofoam cooler behind his seat. He cracked open the can of Coke and took a long pull. "Want a swig?"

"Naw. Us city boys can handle the heat."

"You're just a long drink of water. That's why you don't get thirsty."

The surface of the slope was smoother, and the Bronco didn't bounce as much, but Carlton had to maneuver in and out among the saguaros. The plants were protected by law, so even if he was inclined to drive over them, he couldn't. Besides which, as he well knew, the larger plants were pretty sturdy, at least the healthy ones. And the sick ones were even more of a problem.

It was a hobby for drunken cowboys to shoot hell out of a big saguaro, law or no law, but it wasn't as uneven a match as it sounded. Carlton still had a clipping on his kitchen wall about a drunken rancher who'd banged away at a thirty-foot plant. The trunk gave way, and when it toppled the rancher was too drunk to get out of the way. When they found him, he was flat as a sieve and had as many holes in him. There was a kind of justice in the incident that appealed to Carlton's sense of fair play...and of humor.

From the crest of the hill a broad valley spread out below them to the south. The downward slope was steep but flattened out quickly, descending almost imperceptibly after the first three hundred yards. The floor of the valley, nearly a mile away, was dominated by two enormous chimneys of rock, towering three hundred feet over the surrounding country. Behind them, two miles away, a scattered group of low mesas broke the horizon into a series of postcard snapshots, each almost perfectly framed. And beyond was the ominous purple of the San Antonio range, its peaks obscured in a yellow haze. Instead of the limitless expanse of earth and sky, the world seemed to be compressed in a wide, flat space no higher than the mountains themselves. The sky itself threatened to press down until the third dimension was squeezed out of existence.

Ralston drawled, "Well, well, well, what have we here?"

"Looks like your man knew what he was talking about, Will."

"Sure does."

"I gotta tell you, though, I don't like it."

"Why not? What have we got to lose?"

"Tell me again what he told you."

Ralston sighed. "Dammit, Randy, we've been over this already."

"Let's go over it again, all right? Humor me."

"Said he had some information for me, information I would find quite interesting. He said if I wanted to know who was responsible for the 'dead cows' in the railroad yard, he could help me. Dead cows, that's what the son of a bitch said. Damn! Then he told me to meet him here."

"You didn't recognize the voice?"

"Nope. And it didn't sound like he was trying to disguise it, either. He was sort of whispering, like he didn't want anybody to hear him or something. But that's all."

"Sounds like a setup."

"Sure it does, but what else can we do? I wasn't about to tell anybody else. Besides, if we know it's a setup, then it ain't one, is it?"

"Sure as hell hope not." Carlton threw the emergency brake on and snagged a pair of binoculars from a coat hook screwed to the roof of the Bronco.

The desert was hotter than he imagined. Despite having the window open, the heat hadn't bothered them. The hot breeze funnelled through the moving car had cooled them a bit. But on the roasted sand of the hilltop the air was motionless. The pressure of the sun on his arms, chest and thighs felt like lead weights.

Randy scanned the valley floor from end to end, slowly sweeping the glasses back and forth in overlapping bands.

Through the binoculars it looked even more lifeless than to the naked eye. The arid beauty was lost as individual cacti and the small tangles of brush swam in and out of focus like a filmstrip of the Martian surface.

Carlton paid particular attention to the base of the chimneys, scanning them to eighty or ninety feet above the valley floor. There was no sign of life, and no indication that anyone was or had been into the valley since the dawn of time. He brought the glasses down and squinted into the sun for a moment before turning back to the Bronco. He tossed the glasses into the rear, then climbed in.

"See anything?" Ralston asked.

"Nope. Nothing."

"Guess we might as well go on down, huh?"

Carlton didn't answer right away. When he finally spoke, he was nearly whispering, as if he feared someone might overhear him. "I got an idea, Will. You drive." He jumped down to the ground and walked around the front of the Bronco, resting his fingers lightly on the burning hood.

Ralston climbed out of his bucket seat, banged his head on the roof and dropped in behind the wheel. Carlton yanked the passenger door open and climbed in. His partner looked at him sideways, bafflement barely concealed under the faint smile. "What the hell are you up to now?"

"You'll see. Just go slow."

Ralston shrugged. "Whatever you say, sport." He released the handbrake and nudged the Bronco up over the crestline. The front wheels fell sharply, and he braked until the big tires caught on the packed soil under the sandy veneer. He threw it into neutral and let it roll, pumping the brakes to keep their speed down.

Finally on the floor of the valley, Ralston watched their path, weaving in and out among the saguaro. In the rearview mirror he could see the narrow band of dust hang in the air behind them. With no air to disperse it, it just hovered, straight as a contrail, then gradually sank back to earth. Carlton kept dodging and weaving, his hat in his lap, trying to check the sky, and the terrain to left and right.

"We supposed to do anything when we get to the chimneys? Some kind of signal?"

"Nope," Ralston said. "Just wait. He said he'd find us. Funny, though, he mentioned your name. Wanted me to be sure you came along."

"That's strange."

"That's what I thought. But it can't be somebody we know. I mean, it's one thing not to be seen with us—I can understand that—but if it's somebody we know, we'll recognize him as soon as he shows up."

The chimneys were about a half mile away now. "Time to go to work," Carlton said. "Whatever you do, don't stop. Just keep on to the chimneys." He crawled out of his seat into the rear of the Bronco and cranked the rear window down into the door.

"What the hell are you up to, Randy?" Ralston yelled over his shoulder.

"I don't like the smell of this. I'm gonna cover our asses. See you later." He draped a canteen over his shoulder and grabbed a Winchester carbine from a rack on one wall. Leaning through the open window, he pushed off with his feet and then he was gone.

Randy lay flat for several seconds, watching the Bronco bounce away through the saguaro. Using the cloud of dust for cover, he scrambled up, pitched forward into a small clump of Joshua trees and lay still.

He glanced at the sky, and the sun stared back at him, unblinking like a deformed eye, its iris burned away by its own fire.

8

The black Cadillac was dusty as it pulled into a long, narrow lane. On either side ranks of orange trees marched off like good soldiers as far as the eye could see. The driver of the Cadillac kept his eye on the dusty lane. In the rearview mirror he could see the cloud kicked up by his passage linger in the air, turning the air behind him a thick beige.

The man in the back seat fitted a slender cigarette into a long black holder. Thin as a whip but heavy, the holder was made of rock-hard ebony with an amber mouthpiece and gold seat. The length of the holder was roughly etched. At a distance it would appear to be covered with random geometrics. Up close the intricate filigree of densely engraved Aztec figures demanded close attention.

Carlos Calderone acknowledged that the cigarette holder was an affectation. He would also admit that he had been quitting smoking off and on for two years. Until he did, he figured, he might as well smoke in style. The Aztec motif was a recent addition to his arsenal of pretensions. In idle moments he fancied himself the last link to a bygone era. How else, he wondered, could one explain his extraordinary good fortune in so short a time?

He pressed a button on the thickly padded armrest of the Cadillac and raised his voice slightly. "Go slow, Juan. Slow." The driver shook his head, but if he said anything, Calderone didn't hear it. He had already clicked the mike off. The big car slowed noticeably, and Calderone pressed his face against the tinted glass. The aisles between the ranks of trees seemed to stretch out to infinity. The foliage crowded in to block off his vision way out at the edge of the world. This particular orange grove, he knew, was one of the largest in the state, and that was a good thing.

Calderone had never seen this grove before, but he had seen more than a few in recent months, and though one was much like another, he had begun to fancy that each had its own personality. The way the light filtered through the trees, the fixed color of the sky when viewed through the leaves, the texture of the soil in the aisles, even the crunch of tires on the endless lanes from highway to headquarters. He sometimes thought he could identify each if he was brought blindfolded in the middle of the night, as long as he was permitted to see the sun in midmorning.

"Stop!" he snapped, forgetting the microphone was off. He switched it on and barked again. When the car skidded to a halt, he ordered the driver to back up a few yards. Far to the west, like figures in a dream, a small band of tiny men drifted toward him, ladders hoisted on one shoulder. The stark angularity of the ladders was unmistakable. Invisible at this range, but no less certainly present, were the cloth sacks, each probably doubled now and draped over one shoulder to protect it against the scrape of the aluminum ladders.

Calderone watched the tiny figures scurry into the trees and disappear. For a long moment he sat motionless, his face conscious of the coolness of the glass inside the air-conditioned car. Finally, when he realized the men would not soon return to the aisle, he rapped on the glass partition and the car moved on.

He had been looking forward to the morning's meeting for a long time. Waywayanda Farm was one of the three largest growers in the Tucson area. If he could convert its owner, a man noted for the shortness of his temper and his general contempt for organization of any sort, he would be well on his way to dominating the traffic in illegal labor. That he would be able to do it eventually, Calderone had no doubt. But the sooner he managed it, the happier he'd be. And the owner of Waywayanda, Jim Tyack, Big Jaime to friend and foe alike, was a crucial link in the chain.

The grove came to an abrupt end and the interminable lane suddenly burst into a broad clearing. To the left, huge barnlike buildings towered over the clearing. Refrigerated storage barns and sorting sheds open to the weather on all sides shouldered one another for dominance. Calderone could see the sorting conveyors churning in infinite loops, the sorters hefting the heavy crates to dump them into the feeder bins at one end. Others danced back and forth, closing the wire loops on full crates of sorted oranges and lugging them to low flatbed trailers where they were stacked for transport to the refrigerated storage barns.

Even through the closed windows of the Cadillac, he could hear the hum of the engines and the clank of the conveyors. Calderone knew the mind-deadening racket firsthand. He'd spent more than a few years nipping back and forth across the border, taking what work he could find, for what pay the growers were willing to give him. More often than not, there had been little enough of either.

Exploitation was a strange thing, Calderone thought. It was like a tunnel, and once in it, it seemed endless. All a man could think about was getting out. It pressed in on you, squeezing the air in your chest, making you gasp for breath. It was dark and it was terrifying. No matter how long you were trapped inside it, you never forgot there was something else, a world outside the tunnel. You might surrender any hope of ever seeing the light of day again, but you never forgot it was out there somewhere.

Carlos Calderone was no fool. He knew that the more money you had, the less likely it was that you'd be sucked back into the tunnel. He'd be damned if he would let that happen, no matter what the cost to anyone else.

Opposite the work buildings stood a monument to the rightness of his choice. A huge white house, porches running the length of the front on both first and second floors, stood on a slight rise. A circular driveway of crushed blue stone looped away toward the house then curved back toward the lane. A half-moon of the greenest grass in Arizona filled the inside of the driveway. Tyack had turned his back on the local fashion of cactus gardens, choosing to spend a little precious water to prove just how little the desert intimidated him.

Behind the house, ten thousand acres of cotton basked in the sun. As Calderone got out of the car, he could see several bright yellow machines, like Martian insects, lumber across the cotton fields, throwing plumes of dust high into the air where they merged and cast a thin shadow like that of a coming storm across the harshness of the sunlit fields.

A big man with a beard stood on the first-floor porch in front of double glass doors. The man wore coveralls and a checkered shirt, its sleeves rolled up past his elbows. Tipped forward against the sun, a straw hat, carefully shaped into a cattleman's roll, completed the studied portrait of country bumpkin. But Jim Tyack was anything but. A shrewd businessman, he was content to let others react to the image, then caught them off guard and cut their legs out from under them. It had made him a fortune and a legend at the same time.

He watched Calderone approach, stroking his chin with one huge hand and chewing on an unlit cigar. The Mexican climbed the steps, painting a brilliant smile on his face as he reached the top stair. He extended a hand, which Tyack examined without interest. When Calderone realized his host had no intention of shaking hands, he let it drop, wiping the damp palm on his white cotton pants.

"Nice to meet you, Mr. Tyack."

"That remains to be seen, doesn't it?" The big man didn't smile, and Calderone wondered whether he had made a mistake in coming. "Guess you might as well come in, since you come all this way."

He turned and opened one of the tall doors and stepped inside, holding it wide for his visitor, then flipping it closed with his wrist. Without a word he led the way into the interior of the large house. They passed through a high-ceilinged living room, which was furnished simply but comfortably. Calderone noticed the Indian artifacts with some confusion. Woven rugs and blankets hung on the walls, and a huge rug bearing a thunderbird design occupied the center of the room.

Tall bookshelves occupying one full wall bore an assortment of art books and a large collection of native American poetry. Calderone commented on the pottery and Tyack shrugged. "That shit belongs to my daughter. I make the money and she spends it, is how it works out. A pot's a pot to me. Far as I'm concerned you only need one to piss in."

Calderone smiled. Tyack didn't return it.

The big man veered left and led the way into a large office that still managed to feel claustrophobic. It was cluttered without being messy and was dominated by a large metal desk of the kind the Mexican had seen in government offices. The walls of the room were bare. One wall was glass and looked out over the sorting sheds, while another was lined with filing cabinets of the same scarred gray as the desk.

Tyack walked to a refrigerator, opened it, yanked a couple of cans from their plastic web and slammed the door. Sitting down behind the desk, he unceremoniously tossed a beer at Calderone and gestured to a pair of chairs on the other side of the desk. He snapped the tab open and took a short sip of the beer. "Now, what can I do for you, Señor Calderone? You were kind of mysterious on the phone."

"Not really, Mr. Tyack. It's just that I have found it better to discuss matters of business face-to-face. It reduces the possibility of misunderstanding."

Tyack grunted. "That'll be the day. I haven't seen a business meeting yet didn't have its share of misunderstanding. Sometimes I think that's all business is, sortin' out confusion that shouldn't have been there in the first place. But go ahead, it's your nickel."

"May I ask you a few questions?"

"Sure. If I don't want to answer, I don't have to."

"How many people do you employ?"

"Depends. Anywhere from twenty to about three or four hundred during peak harvest."

"How much do you pay them?"

Tyack looked sharply at Calderone, then took a long pull on his beer. When the can was empty, he slapped it down on the desk and stood up. "I don't want to hear any union bullshit this morning. This meeting's over."

"This isn't about unions, Mr. Tyack."

"No, then what the hell is it about? And make it quick."

"How much do you pay your pickers?"

"Forty-five, fifty cents a box."

"How would you like to pay less?"

Tyack looked at the ceiling. He half closed his eyes and fixed Calderone with a suspicious stare. "What's the catch?"

"No catch. I supply the men. You pay me thirty cents a box, and I pay them. I handle all administration. No headaches, no paperwork. All very neat."

"You telling me you can cut my labor cost nearly forty percent and you still make a profit? I don't believe that."

"What have you got to lose?"

"I already got my crews for this year. I don't like messing around this late."

"That can be handled. You don't have to worry about a thing. I'll take care of everything."

"Tell me a little more. I might maybe could give it a try, you persuade me a little."

"Persuasion is my business, Mr. Tyack."

9

Carlton eased to his feet, the glasses dangling from his neck. He could no longer see the Bronco, but the plume of dust had stopped rising, so he knew Will had stopped. He scanned the area immediately ahead with the glasses, then sat and waited patiently for several minutes, hoping to catch a flicker of reflected sunlight, or some other indication that the 4x4 was under surveillance. He listened patiently but heard nothing.

Keeping low, he used the sparse vegetation as best he could, dodging from saguaro to cholla to Joshua. He felt like a botanist in hell, bouncing from one thick-skinned plant to the next. The heat was still rising as the sun climbed higher in the sky. Beyond the chimneys he noticed the haze burning off. The purple of the San Antonio Mountains was brighter, almost incandescent, throwing the bright light off with what seemed like increased energy.

He stopped for another survey with the binoculars at the base of a huge saguaro. Above him he heard a soft rustle and an inquisitive hoot. He looked up into the face of an owl peering down at him from a hole in the cactus about fifteen feet off the ground. The bird won the staring contest, and Carlton turned his attention back toward the chimneys.

Just ahead was a wide area with no cover. Before chancing it, he wanted to make certain he and Ralston were

alone. The objectives of the binoculars were covered with
a layer of fine dust, which splintered the sunlight and
rimmed his view with a rainbow glare. He tilted them back
and blew at the dust, which seemed to cling as if magne-
tized. He wiped at it with the tail of his shirt, then blew
again, watching the bulk of it puff away and disappear.

The view was sharper now, and he checked both sides of
the chimneys. Wider at the bottom, they seemed to grow
from a common base. For no apparent reason, he wondered whether they were the remnants of some ancient vol-
canic activity, and made a mental note to read up on the
geology of the desert. He was only a quarter mile from the
base of the rocks now, but still couldn't see the Bronco.

He dropped the glasses and leaned forward into a crouch.
Sprinting into the open, he kept one eye on the sky and
zigzagged toward the next cover. He hadn't seen a sign that
indicated they weren't alone, but it was better to assume
they weren't. Just as he reached the next line of greenery,
he heard something that sounded like a distant thunder-
clap. He strained his ears, but it wasn't repeated. Carlton
dropped to the ground and swept the glasses up the chimneys. Then he heard the steady, unmistakable sound of a
helicopter. A moment later a McDonnell Cayuse swept
around the left column of rock, swooping in a circle like a
gigantic bird of prey.

Swinging the glasses up, he nailed the chopper. Three
men were visible through the Lexan bubble windows of the
cockpit, sitting almost motionless, like figures in a paper-
weight, as the chopper swung its narrow tail in his direction and spiraled to the ground. The men were obscured by
the tail for a moment, and Carlton cursed. "Turn around,
dammit. Turn the hell around."

The chopper suddenly pivoted on its axis, and the bubble was once again facing him. The pilot was busy with the

controls and talking into a headset. The other two men sat behind him, each holding an automatic rifle.

Randy got up to run toward the chopper, but it dropped suddenly straight down. The sliding windows to the rear of the cockpit bubble were open, and the passenger on the right side leaned forward as the pilot banked while swinging the chopper in a tight circle.

The hammer of the rifle was just audible over the pulsating *whup-whup* of the chopper, magnified as it bounced off the solid rock of the chimneys and echoed across the valley floor. Dropping to his knees, Carlton swung the Winchester around and sighted through the scope. The chopper was slipping back and forth now, like a pendulum on a short line. Both passengers were busy firing at the ground.

Timing the cycle of the chopper's undulations, Carlton counted down and squeezed. The bubble glinted in the bright sunlight for an instant, then the chopper swung back. Through the scope, the young patrolman saw one of the shooters doubled over, his right arm across his chest, the hand clasping the opposite shoulder.

He sighted in a second time as the second passenger looked around nervously. This time the pilot made a big mistake. Instead of climbing until he could figure out where the shot had come from, he hung in the air, nearly motionless. Carlton fired again and the chopper suddenly swerved. It started a downward plunge, pivoting on its rotor shaft, then slipped sideways like a piece of cardboard in a stiff breeze, skipping on the current of hot air rising along the chimneys.

Carlton grabbed the glasses and tried to pin the chopper in the center of his field, but it kept slipping away. In fitful glimpses he saw the pilot slumped forward over the controls. The uninjured passenger had dropped his rifle and struggled to shift the pilot to one side, then the helicopter was gone again.

Letting the glasses fall, Carlton watched the spinning chopper as it began to wobble. Without the binoculars he could see nothing in the bubble. Bright blades of sunlight stabbed out into the desert as the chopper swung back and forth into the zone of sunlight between the two columns of rock.

It started to rise, still out of control. The passenger must have made some headway, but not enough, and not nearly soon enough. Like some metallic bug, drunk on its own motion, the chopper staggered between the chimneys. Its tail spun to the left and slammed into the shaft of reddish-brown rock. The antitorque rotor buzzed with a whine, sending a brief shower of white sparks cascading down along the chimney as it tore itself to pieces.

The slender tail snapped in two. A small orange bud appeared at the broken end, seemed to skitter along the tail and suddenly blossomed into a huge orange flower wreathed in thick black leaves. Then it was gone. A smoky black cable rose between the chimneys, as if the crippled helicopter had sent out a lifeline, hoping to hook the flat top of the chimney and haul itself up to safety by main force. The cartwheeling fragments spiraled and flashed for an instant, splinters of shiny metal turning over and over, their motion slow, almost stately, like the slow-motion replay of someone overturning a drawer of cutlery. Then Randy heard the boom and realized the certainty of what he'd seen. The chopper had gone to perdition, taking its three inhabitants with it.

"YOU SURE YOU KNOW where we're going?" Bolan asked.

"I sure as hell hope so," Sipe answered. "Carlton and Ralston could be in big trouble."

"It could also be a setup."

Sipe nodded grimly. "I thought of that. But what choice do we have?"

"No more than usual." Bolan lapsed into silence while Sipe watched the road. The attorney's Renegade was tightly sprung, and every ripple in the highway tossed them into the air. He hung a hard right, slipping onto a narrow asphalt strip, the black band stretching out ahead, its width slowly diminishing to a point.

For more than a half hour they hadn't seen a car. There was no one behind or ahead of them, and they hadn't been passed by anyone heading in the opposite direction.

"Sometimes I wonder who built these roads and why they bothered," Sipe muttered. "All the things we have to do in this country, and the goddamned highway lobby gets whatever they want."

Sipe wrestled the Renegade off the road and stopped. He took a pair of field glasses from the dash and scanned the horizon, moving the glasses slowly, as if he were looking for something specific. To Bolan's naked eye, it was a seamless fabric of beige and blue. The attorney grunted and handed the binoculars to his companion. Pointing with a thin finger, he guided Bolan's eye.

"What am I looking for?"

"See those two points about eleven o'clock?"

"Yeah."

"That's it. That's where they were headed."

"How do you know that?"

"Buck Allenson said they got a call to meet somebody there. That's all I know."

"Well, we came this far. There's no point in turning back now, is there?" Bolan reached into the back for a compact leather case and placed it across his knees. Sipe reengaged the gears, and the vehicle jumped forward, transmission grinding.

Bolan opened the case and hastily assembled the rifle it contained while Sipe watched him out of the corner of his eye. "That's really something. What is that ugly thing?"

"A Weatherby Mark V, modified a bit."

"You're not going to need that, you know."

"Maybe not. But it doesn't take long to break it down."

Sipe began to whistle, his breath hissing between teeth and through compressed lips in a nearly tuneless stream. When Bolan was finished assembling the rifle, he checked the scope and mounted it.

"I suppose it's beautiful in its own way," Sipe said. "The rifle, I mean."

"I take it you don't like guns much."

"You could say that."

"They're tools, just like any other."

"I don't get nervous when a man opens a toolbox."

"Maybe you should."

Sipe laughed. "You might have something there. My old man always wanted me to learn a trade. He said plumbers were never out of work."

"Neither am I." Bolan stared through the windshield in silence for a few moments, then reached for the glasses. He twiddled the focus knob, then shouted for Sipe to stop.

"What is it? What did you see?"

"I'm not sure. It was just a flash of light, a reflection of some sort, high up alongside one of the columns. There it is again."

"Any ideas?"

"None that I like. Can you think of any reason a helicopter might be out here?"

"Only two. Border Patrol or smugglers. This is no-man's-land. Nobody else has any reason to be out here."

"Step on it."

The terrain in front of them was rough; small hills and sharply etched gullies interlaced in the valley floor already had Sipe wrestling with the steering wheel. As he stepped on the accelerator, the jouncing Renegade became almost unmanageable. He tried to say something to Bolan, but his teeth snapped together with a sharp crack and he bit his tongue. He wiped a small trickle of blood on his sleeve.

The Executioner kept the glasses trained on the top of the chimneys, but he saw nothing else. Suddenly a plume of oily smoke appeared between the rock towers. Bolan rolled the window down, but the roaring engine and whining gears smothered all other sound. He tossed the glasses into the back and cradled the Weatherby across his knees, the muzzle toward his door. Unconsciously he took the safety off with his thumb.

The smoke rose about halfway up the chimneys, then seemed to hit an invisible ceiling. The oily rope flattened into a small cloud, seemed to balloon out, then dissipated.

"I don't like the looks of that," Sipe managed to shout before his jaws banged together again.

Bolan kept his eyes on the flat cloud. As they labored up a gradual incline, he could see that they were only a couple of miles away from the chimneys. When they crested the hill, Sipe braked to a skidding halt. The warrior noticed tracks to his right and pointed to them. "Somebody's been here recently. I can't tell whether they were coming or going, though."

Sipe rolled his window down and leaned out with the binoculars. Without having the dusty windshield in his way, he was able to see more clearly. Tracking the oily smoke back to its origin, he spotted the wreck of a helicopter in the saddle between the two chimneys.

10

Randy Carlton scrambled to his feet and began to run. The oily smoke of the destroyed helicopter filled the gap between the chimneys. Against its backdrop, he noticed another, paler smoke, its slender tendrils twining upward and slowly dissipating in the dry air. The desert was suddenly silent, except for the crunch of his boots on the sandy soil. He still couldn't see the Bronco, but as he drew closer it was apparent that it was the source of the pale smoke.

He called to Ralston in a voice that was half shout and half whisper. He stopped to listen for an answer, and when none came, he increased his speed. The roof of the Bronco came into sight, a thick green line broken by the arms of clustered saguaro. As he got closer, he saw the roof line broken by odd marks, then realized they were bullet holes, the paint chipped and broken around them, raw metal scars glinting in the sunlight.

He was aware only of the slap of the glasses around his neck and the canteen at his waist. His feet felt leaden and the ground seemed to stretch out and away from him, as if the faster he ran the farther he had to go. Then he broke through into a clearing, and stopped dead in his tracks. The window frames of the Bronco were nearly vacant, yawning at him like the mouths of dead men, black and motionless, lined with sets of jagged glass teeth.

The shattered glass was strewn on the sand, sparkling like cheap jewelry tossed away in disgust. Carlton called to his partner again, and heard nothing. He began to walk forward cautiously, shifting the Winchester nervously in his hands. Approaching the vehicle from the rear, he couldn't see anyone inside. He backed away a bit and circled to the driver's side, moving forward on tiptoe. The steering wheel had been shattered, its hard plastic reduced to a pair of splintered spikes jutting up like antlers, the broken ends as ugly as raw bone.

He tiptoed to the door and leaned in. The seats were full of broken glass, but the Bronco was empty. The side windows were gone, too; chunks of glass covered the rear floor. Bright spots of sun spilled through the bullet holes in the roof and sparkled on the litter. Small rainbows refracted by the rough edges of the glass winked and flashed as he turned his head from side to side.

"Will? You there? It's me, Randy. Will, where are you? You okay?"

The passenger door was open, and Carlton walked to the other side of the vehicle. A few drops of blood, already dried by the sun, half soaked into the sand, dribbled toward the base of the chimneys, and he began to follow them. Several feet from the Bronco, they stopped. The soil had been disturbed, and he walked faster, following the tracks.

A sudden crash sent him diving to the ground, until he realized it was the chopper wreckage shifting as it burned. He looked up at a saddle-shaped notch, about thirty feet off the ground, and saw part of the still-flaming shell, its paint peeled and metal blackened.

Climbing to his feet, he caught a glimpse of the familiar green of the Border Patrol uniform. He scrambled through some tangled brush and found Ralston lying on his left side.

As Carlton bent down, he already knew it was useless. Ralston's shirt was soaked with blood. A small crusty patch of sand beneath his partner's crooked left arm glistened dully. A few small insects crawled across the dark patch and disappeared.

Ralston's eyes were open but glazed, his chest motionless, his open mouth slack. Carlton bent his ear to the bloody shirt, but his partner's heart had stopped. He straightened up and closed the man's eyes with a rough thumb and stood to look at the burning wreck of the chopper. He raised a clenched fist and shook it, but didn't have the heart to curse the flaming hulk and its dead occupants.

He walked back to the battered Bronco and opened the driver's door. He brushed the broken glass from the seat and climbed in. The radio mike lay on the floor, its case shattered and wires sprouting like the springs of an old mattress. The key was still in the ignition. He turned it, and the engine sputtered, then caught. Steam began to spurt from under the hood, and he shut the engine off.

Climbing out, Carlton popped the hood release and walked to the front of the Bronco. One bullet hole in the hood seemed to be the only damage to the engine compartment. He spotted the source of the steam almost immediately. A gaping hole in a radiator hose leaked coolant. A small greenish pool had collected in the sand under the engine, at its center a deep depression where the slug had buried itself in the ground. With a little luck and a little gaffer's tape, he should be able to patch the hose long enough to get back to a main road.

A distant buzz seemed to be tugging at his consciousness as he opened the tool chest in the rear of the 4x4. It whined and snarled, and finally unable to ignore it any longer, he turned to see a cloud of dust rushing toward him.

He climbed onto the running board and saw a Jeep, four men on board, racing directly at him.

Carlton jumped onto the ground and grabbed his carbine. He backed away from the 4x4, peeking over his shoulder to make sure he didn't impale himself on a cactus. He ducked down behind a fat prickly pear and watched the Jeep approach. The vehicle skidded to a halt alongside the crippled Bronco, and a tall thin man jumped out of the passenger seat.

The man seemed to be made of old leather, and the garish clothing he wore made him look like a scarecrow in some disco version of *The Wizard of Oz*. On his head he wore an elaborately feathered Stetson with a snakeskin band, the rattle clacking as he moved. The fabric of his purple shirt, large white polka dots sprinkled everywhere but on the puffy sleeves, glistened in the sun, shimmering as he moved. White bell-bottom pants and black boots completed the costume. A droopy mustache, Pancho Villa style, waggled as he said something over his shoulder to the men in the Jeep, but the patrolman couldn't make out the words.

Carlton started to back away, but slipped and fell. A cactus spine embedded itself in his left wrist, and he cried out involuntarily. The scarecrow turned, reaching for a pistol on his hip. The other men jumped out of the Jeep, and Carlton ran.

As he raced toward the base of the chimney to find some solid cover, the first spray of automatic rifle fire zipped overhead and slammed into the rock. He took one in the shoulder and stumbled, scrambling forward on hands and knees. Working backward up the slippery pile of rock, Carlton ducked into a small cleft and waited.

Bracing his carbine against a ledge on a boulder, he drew a bead on a polka dot, dead center, and fired. The scarecrow fell slowly, like a collapsing balloon. The other three men, right behind him, ran for cover. Carlton caught the squat Mexican in blue denim in the upper arm, and he pitched backward. The remaining men cut for the Jeep, while the patrolman got to his feet and tried to steady his aim as he fired a third time. The shot missed and the fleeing men reached the Jeep just as Carlton squeezed off another round. The men dived backward, an M-16 flying to one side.

Then Randy heard another vehicle.

"YOU'RE RIGHT. There's a chopper there. It must have crashed."

"How?" Bolan asked.

"What do you mean?"

"I mean, how did the pilot get so close to those rocks? What the hell was he doing in that tight?"

Before Sipe could venture a guess, Bolan pointed to a new cloud, a ball of dust sweeping around the base of the rocks from the right. The young attorney passed him the glasses, and Bolan opened his door and stood on the running board.

"Two four-wheel drives, six or eight men, and they're shooting at somebody." He ducked back into the Renegade and closed the door. Sipe kicked the vehicle into gear and plunged over the crest of the hill.

Zigzagging in and out among the gargantuan saguaros, the Renegade roared and skidded as Sipe worked the clutch and brake. Even in four-wheel-drive, it was all he could do to keep the vehicle upright and headed in the general direction of the rocks.

"You got a gun?" Bolan shouted.

"A .38, why?"

"You're going to need it."

"We don't know that. We don't even know who those men are. They might just be a bunch of kids raising some hell."

"Folks around here usually do that when a chopper blows up?"

Sipe didn't answer. Bolan was right, and he knew it. They were on the valley floor now, and the sound of gunfire came in sporadic bursts. As they charged into the clear, Bolan spotted the Border Patrol 4x4, its hood up, and Sipe screeched to a halt alongside it. Both men jumped out, Bolan racing to the front of the abandoned vehicle. He noticed its missing windows and poked his head inside, seeing nothing but scattered glass in the seats and rear, a smear of blood.

"Look around here, Sipe. I'm going to go after those Jeeps."

"You'll need help."

"Come on, then. But watch me. Don't go off half-cocked. Understand?"

Sipe grinned and gave him a thumbs-up, twirling the pistol on its trigger guard. Bolan shook his head, then sprinted toward the sound of gunfire. The deep bark of a carbine gave him hope that at least one of the border patrolmen was still alive.

The warrior dropped to a crouch and moved forward carefully, picking his spots before darting from cactus to shrub to whatever passed for a tree in the desert. The firing ahead had abated somewhat. He couldn't tell, and didn't want to guess, whether that meant the patrolman was holding his own or was out of luck.

Suddenly he was in the clear. The two Jeeps were parked near the base of the wall, but both were deserted. The sharp report of the carbine echoed across the desert floor, magnified by the silence and the hard face of the rock. Bolan crouch-walked to the rear of the nearer Jeep, then dropped to one knee. Both engines were running.

Quickly he crept forward, turned off the ignition and pocketed the keys. He did the same with the second Jeep. He spotted a rifle in the front seat and tossed it to Sipe. The blood-smeared corpse, its tongue already lolling thickly, lay on its back in the sand. Bolan felt a little better, knowing the odds had been cut.

The firing had stopped altogether. Bolan could hear a conversation in harshly spoken Spanish drifting through the sparse growth. Edging ahead, he spotted three men crouched behind a huge, blocklike boulder. One of them was pointing up the face of the left chimney, and Bolan followed the man's extended arm to a shallow notch in the rock face, just behind a cluster of boulders. That had to be where the lawmen were holed up. The other hardmen were nowhere in sight.

Bolan wanted to get a fix on the others before betraying his presence, but time was a luxury he didn't have. He turned to see where Sipe was, but the attorney had disappeared. Suddenly he saw Sipe rise out of a crouch and approach the three men from behind. The pistol in his hand was extended straight out. The man might not like guns, but there was no quarreling with his guts...just his common sense. Bolan raised the Weatherby and drew a bead on the centerpiece of the trio, just as Sipe hollered for them to raise their hands.

The three men spun around like kids caught peeking through a whorehouse window. Sipe took a step forward; the man on the left, partially concealed behind the center gunman, moved his shoulder slightly. Peering through the Weatherby's scope, Bolan missed the motion. He saw the middle man sidle slightly to the right, and shifted his aim. The middle man dropped straight down as Bolan found the gunman on the left. He squeezed the trigger, just as he heard a burst from a submachine gun. The target spun like a broken top as the heavy Weatherby slug slammed into his shoulder, shattering the shoulder blade on the way out.

Looking for his next target, Bolan dropped his aim and found the middle man twisting to one side, his feet digging at the slippery soil. He squeezed off another round, drilling the prostrate gunner in the side. The man bent in two, then jerked like a broken puppet for several seconds. He was still quivering as Bolan swept the scope to the right.

The third man had beat a hasty retreat.

The warrior charged forward. Sipe lay on his side, facing away from Bolan. Kneeling beside the attorney, he grasped the fallen man's shoulder and felt the sticky shirt cling to his fingers. Sipe rolled onto his back with no resistance. A jagged lines of holes crossed his chest from left shoulder to right hip. The shirt was a solid red mass.

Ronny Sipe was dead.

Bolan looked up at the column of smoke, then turned to the mound of scree at the base of the chimneys. Someone shouted in Spanish from a tangle of cactus between Bolan and the rocks. Then a flash of pale blue darted from left to right among the shades of green, and Bolan brought up the Weatherby.

Using his scope, he moved from cactus to cactus, scanning anything large enough to offer some cover, until he found what he was looking for. A patch of faded denim, no more than an inch wide, stuck out from behind a ragged saguaro. Bolan watched, but the man stayed out of sight. Voices echoed from the rocks, and the Executioner knew he didn't have time to wait.

The saguaro was tall, but no more than the thickness of a thigh. Its soft, pulpy interior was no real protection from a high-velocity projectile. Bolan studied the denim for a second, shifted his aim high and to the right, then squeezed. He saw the saguaro explode, and the denim disappeared. If he had calculated right, he had a head shot.

Dead on.

y

11

Bolan worked laterally along the base of the rock. The firing was sporadic now, an occasional shot echoing up and away, soaring into the sky and disappearing like a bird heading south. The jumble of fallen rock gave the gunmen a distinct advantage. He had as little cover for himself as the saguaro had offered his last target.

He still hadn't seen them, and nothing they had done gave him an indication they knew he was behind them. But Bolan was not about to take a chance. Ronny Sipe had already made the mistake of assuming too much. It had cost him his life.

The Weatherby, reloaded, hung from his shoulder by its leather sling. The rifle was fine for selective, long-range fire, but the kind of close-up, rapid fire he would need to take these guys out called for a different kind of tactic. Bolan wanted to be able to sling lead around like a desperate politician slings mud. In this kind of confrontation, how accurate was less important than how much how fast. The Uzi he had snatched from one of the dead men was just the ticket. Two extra magazines didn't hurt, either.

But the biggest unknown in the equation was time. As far as Bolan knew, at least one of the pinned-down border patrolmen was wounded. If both were there, they might both be bleeding to death while he maneuvered. Assuming the worst was a two-edged sword. It made sure there was nothing casual about the approach. But it also meant you might lose your cool unnecessarily.

Angling sharply toward the left, Bolan pressed in toward the base of the chimneys. The entire valley floor around the the red rock columns was a tangle of broken stone, great, flat slabs of rock lying cheek by jowl with boulders, small rocks crunching under foot. The whole mess looked like some psychotic version of Stonehenge. Fixing the gunmen's location by ear, the warrior tried to get as close as he could without exposing himself.

Using tangled thornbush as cover, he worked his way to within thirty feet of the outermost ring of fallen rock. He was close enough to the chimneys to hear the sucking wind of the burning chopper. Its smoke had thinned considerably, but flames still leaped into the air thirty or forty feet above the wreckage. The stone itself had been dyed a deep, sooty black by the rising smoke.

Falling to his stomach, Bolan wriggled forward, darting in among the thorny branches like a fat snake. The inch-long thorns snagged on his clothing and stabbed through to the flesh, ripping and shredding his shoulders and back. The wounds, both scratches and punctures, itched and burned as if the thorns had been dipped in some exotic toxin.

The thin but persistent growth crept right up to the very edge of the fallen rock, and Bolan found himself flush up against the flat red face of a huge boulder. To the left, a narrow gap would just admit him, but he had to bend his body into the thorns in order to slip around a sharp outcrop where the boulder had sheared away from the chimney. A thick slab, split away on impact, lay flat on the ground, and its top edge was as sharp as a razor. One consequence of infrequent rain was the absence of erosion. Knife edges on the rock tended to stay sharp.

Reaching down along a thorny branch, trying to find where it joined a trunk, Bolan grabbed a smooth, dry surface. The bark felt almost silky. He began to work the branch back and forth, trying to crack the bark and rip the branch away. The tough, thick fibers of the branch bent and twisted, but wouldn't give. Letting it go for a second, he repositioned his hand and twisted the branch toward the edge of the rock. Whipping it back and forth against the stone, trying to avoid making a sound, he sawed away, slowing ripping through the tough branch almost fiber by fiber.

After five minutes, during which only one shot had been fired, he finally succeeded in ripping far enough through that he could tear the branch away. The gathering quiet disturbed him. The wounded man hadn't fired in more than a quarter of an hour. If he was out of ammunition, it wouldn't take long for the others to figure it out. It was also possible he had lost consciousness. That, too, would be an invitation for a quick frontal assault.

Either way, Bolan would then lose the edge of the pincer effect. With the remaining gunmen trapped between two points of fire, the advantage was his. Once the border patrolman was out of the picture, it shifted back to the gunmen.

Easing into the niche, Bolan wriggled past the sharp edge of the rock, scraping some skin away, but thankful to be free of the thorns. Even in the shade the heat was oppressive. Every breath made his mouth feel drier. His skin burned, and sweat rolled down his brow and into his eyes. The rips and tears of the thorns felt as if they were full of liquid fire.

The darkness suddenly exploded with a spine-tingling rattle. The brittle sound echoed from the walls of rock around him, and Bolan froze. It was too dark inside to see much, and his body blocked out much of the light. But he didn't have to see anything to know he was in big trouble. An angry rattler, coiled in the shade somewhere ahead of him, was taking exception to his presence. Without seeing the snake, he had little chance of killing it.

Backing out would be difficult, if not impossible, and he would be vulnerable to a strike in any case. Groping blindly ahead was like playing Russian roulette with a fully loaded pistol. Shooting into the darkness would probably not net him a snake, and would certainly give away his location. His only chance was getting some light.

Backing away a little, slowly, he slid one hand under his body and groped in his pocket for a cigarette lighter. The snake rattled a second time, not satisfied with Bolan's failure to heed the first warning. The reptiles were unpredictable, but two warnings were two more than some people got. He concentrated all his attention on the coffinlike confines of the niche, trying to will the rattler into some semblance of patience. The only certain thing was that a sudden movement would get him bitten.

Bolan started to remove his hand from the pocket, holding his breath until he tugged it out from under his body. The sweat poured off him, the hiss of his breath echoed raspily off the rock. His hand was now free, clutching both a cigarette lighter and the Beretta 93-R. He lost all track of time, and couldn't tell whether minutes or seconds had gone by.

His sweaty thumb soaked the ignition wheel, and the lighter didn't catch the first two times. He rubbed the wheel on his shirt to dry it, then used his left hand to thumb it again. He shifted the Beretta tentatively, aiming it in the general direction of the sound. Bolan knew he'd have one chance—the flame was certain to provoke a strike.

The fourth time, a small spark flew from the wheel, but still the flame didn't take. He smelled butane in the enclosed space, its acrid bite tickling his nostrils. The flame darted up on the fifth try, and he saw the rattler, a big diamondback coiled in tight rings, its tail shaking frenetically. The reptile raised its head as Bolan shifted the pistol and squeezed. The 9 mm slug caught the rattler just behind the head, ripping through its spine, and taking the head off. The snake's tight coils quivered as the tail continued to shake for a second or two, then collapsed into the center of the still-wriggling loops.

Bolan let his breath out in a long sigh. His mouth felt dry, and his lips stuck to his tongue. He bit his lower lip gently, then shook himself. The chill in his spine was still there, lingering on like an afterimage on the retina long after a meteor has already turned to ash.

Bolan reached out for the dead snake and shoved it aside with the warm muzzle of the Beretta. He could only hope the snake had been alone in the shadowy niche. Crawling forward, he was forced to curl his body around the face of the boulder on his right, then haul his legs in after him. Another bend, this time to the left, brought him back into the light. Four feet away open air and bright sun waited. It would be a tight squeeze, but he had no choice but to go ahead. The cramped tunnel wouldn't permit him to turn around, even if he wanted to.

Dampened by the rock, the echo of a short burst of automatic weapons fire whined into the niche. He heard angry shouts, and a rush of heavy steps on the loose stone. The mellow baritone of the carbine rolled up and away like thunder, and Bolan breathed a silent prayer of thanks that at least one of the patrolmen was still alive.

Anxious to get out of the claustrophobic nook, Bolan shimmied and wiggled until he felt the heat of the sun on the backs of his hands. He reached back to snag the Weatherby, which he'd been forced to drag along by its sling. It caught on an outcropping of rock, and he jiggled the sling until it slipped free. He had pushed the Uzi ahead of him, and now he had both weapons handy again, the odds seemed a little more encouraging.

Crouched in the mouth of the tunnel, he listened for a minute. The footsteps had stopped, and so had the voices. He might as well have been alone in the desert for all the sound he heard. A slight whistle, barely audible, was the only legacy of the burned-out chopper and the holocaust that had consumed it.

He scanned the jumbled rock in front of him, looking for a place to hide. Tangled vines, their small leaves and thick cords clinging with tiny roots to the flat face of the stone, covered the bottom of the chimneys. They were stiff and brittle, crackling under his feet as he stepped cautiously out and moved laterally along the smooth front of an upended rock.

Another rock, larger, but just as flat, sat with one end buried in the scree, its other end propped by a boulder. Like a daredevil motorcyclist plotting his next run, Bolan inched up the natural ramp until he could see over its upper edge.

He spotted the first two men almost immediately. Crouched in the shade of a huge rock, they pressed against it, peering out along either side. They were totally absorbed in their quarry and left their backs wide open. It was tempting to take them out, but Bolan held himself in check. He wanted to know how many others there were, and where they had holed up. He kept hoping for another shot from the carbine, anything to keep the hunters riveted to their prey.

Bolan waited patiently, the Uzi resting on top of the rock. Something arced through the air from the right, beyond a cluster of boulders, and landed out of sight on some loose scree. Bolan thought at first it was a rock, but when it came bouncing back, he knew better. He ducked just as the sudden crump of a grenade sent splinters of razor-edged stone whirling off in every direction.

Inching back up over the lip, he noticed that one of the two men in sight had fallen to his knees. A splash of red was just visible where he squeezed his left shoulder with his right hand. A quick burst of fire, apparently from two guns, erupted from the same patch of boulders the grenade had come from. That was all Bolan needed to know.

He swept the Uzi in a broad semicircle, his finger loose on the trigger. Satisfied, he brought it back around, this time squeezing. The SMG chattered noisily for a moment, then went dry. He dropped down and changed clips, tossing the empty down the slope behind him. Easing back up, he saw the wounded man leaning against the rock, his weapon on the ground to his right. The second man lay flat and was now staring back in Bolan's direction.

Tucking the Uzi in his belt, Bolan crouch-walked down the flat rock and slipped the Weatherby off his shoulder. The big Mark V felt solid in his hands. Dropping to his stomach at the foot of the rock, he cradled the rifle across his elbows and crawled fifty feet to his right. Peeking around a boulder, he could just make out the second man, who swiveled his head back and forth, still uncertain where the shots had come from and less certain what he should do about it.

Dressed with all the style and taste of a circus clown, the man looked out of place in the shadow of the desert chimneys. He seemed bewildered. Bolan eased the scope to his eye, settling the cross hairs for a moment on the man's left temple. The head kept bobbing like that of a frightened bird, and the warrior slid the sight a little to the right, opting for a more stationary target.

The crack of the big rifle bounced off the faces of the chimneys. The reverberating sound had a sharp edge, like metal tearing or like that first terrible instant after a lightning bolt when the sky splits open. The high-velocity slug found its mark, entering through the top of the shoulder and sliding down along the backbone until it came to rest over the right hip.

Before the body stopped jerking, Bolan was on his feet. He slipped the Weatherby back over his shoulder and hauled the Uzi from his belt, charging straight ahead.

Two men, their faces frozen in surprise, watched him for an instant before reacting. By the time they'd recovered, it was already too late—Bolan emptied the magazine of the machine pistol. Both men fell backward, landing in a heap at the foot of an upright slab of bluish-brown rock. He tossed the empty magazine away, rammed the last one in place and listened. He could hear nothing.

Looking up at the towering chimneys, Bolan tilted his head far back. His voice echoed eerily from the stone. "Ralston! Carlton!"

When no one answered, he began to run.

12

The moonlight filtered down through the orange trees. The breathless air still carried a trace of the afternoon heat. An occasional breeze hissed through the branches, shaking the leaves, but the four men moving along the aisle weren't interested in the weather.

Up ahead, a small clearing marked a crossroads in the heart of the grove. The men moved easily, even confidently, talking and joking. It was Friday night, and each had a week's wages in his pocket, still in a pay envelope. They had opened the envelope to count the bills, then folded them carefully and returned them to the safety of the crisp white paper.

At the crossroads, they stepped into a dusty lane and stopped. The van wasn't there, but it was early, and there were a lot of farms to be serviced. Their turn would come, if they were patient. Passing a half gallon jug back and forth, they worked on the cheap wine, trying hard for a party mood. The wine helped, but the women would help a lot more.

Roberto Miercoles sat on the rough grass at the edge of the clearing. He tucked the jug into the crook of his elbow and hoisted it to let a thin stream of third-rate burgundy trickle down his throat. The wine burned a little, but it was better than what they usually drank.

The others stood over him, chatting sporadically and keeping an eye on the wine. In the moonlight the wine looked almost black, its surface glittering like coal as it slapped against the sides of the jug. When he tried to put the jug down, it hit a rock and dropped into the sand. The others held their breath until Roberto felt the bottom to make sure it hadn't cracked. Eighteen miles was a long way to go for a jug of wine, even on a Friday night. The women would have some to sell, but it would be watered down and three times as expensive.

Roberto lay back on the grass, letting the stiff blades tickle his neck. Like the others, he was all bone and wire, his leathery skin little more than a tight brown sheath holding the moving parts together. Unlike them, he was new at picking. His shoulders ached, and his thumb and fingers were blistered from the constant friction against the rough skin of the oranges.

He would get the knack of it, if only he could hang on for another two or three weeks. The big gringo who rode around on the tractor had been pushing him all week. Six days in a row he had picked the least, but luckily it was a bumper crop, and getting the fruit in was more important than busting chops. In a tight year, the others told him, Roberto would have been handed his walking papers.

Fruit picking was Darwinism at its most brutal. If you were slow, you got a little slack, but not for long. If you couldn't keep up, you were sent packing. Two, three days, and he would either make the team or get sent away. And the word traveled fast. Once you were cut, God and all else holy had to smile on you before you got another chance at some other farm.

And you had to be careful. If you went too fast, too soon, you got hurt. If you got hurt and couldn't work, God wouldn't smile on you. He couldn't help you, either.

Gordo Gonsalves, nicknamed for his girth, and the nominal leader of the small group, kicked the soles of Roberto's feet. "You sleeping, Roberto? You don't want to miss all the fun, do you? Wake up."

Roberto laughed. "I don't know whether I'm in any shape to party."

"Oh, my friend, don't say that. You see these women, you change your mind. You better be ready. Dead men will come out of the trees to get in line. I myself will take two or three turns."

"Two or three?"

"Yes . . . with each one. Gordo needs to charge his batteries. It is a long week with no women."

The smaller of the other two laughed wickedly. "Is Gordo a man? I think he must be a vibrator. I myself need no batteries to make a woman smile. Sometimes they even pay *me*."

"Sure, José. You are used to taking money from women. Even your mother gave you ten pesos to run away from home, no?"

"That's not true, Gordo," the fourth man chimed in.

"It isn't?"

"No. It was twenty pesos." The men laughed easily, but the good-natured kidding skirted dangerously close to insult. Because of the circumstances, the men seemed willing to tolerate a little more than usual. They all expected the women to give them the chance to disprove even the most scurrilous attacks on their virility.

The three standing men continued to joke, poking one another in the ribs with bony elbows. Roberto lay on the grass, too tired to join in. He was debating whether to get up and go back to the tent when lights exploded at the far end of the lane. The twin spears bounced wildly, and the snarl of a decrepit transmission rose and fell as the approaching vehicle bounced over the bumpy lane.

Gordo walked into the middle of the lane, spreading his arms in welcome. The bright beams of the headlights heightened the garish colors in his Hawaiian shirt. The outline of the approaching vehicle gradually sharpened into the silhouette of an old Volkswagen van. Gordo stepped aside, his arms still extended, and shouted hello. The van stopped, rocking on ancient springs that continued to creak for several seconds. Gordo walked around the rear of the rusty van, leaning forward at the waist and puckered his lips in a grotesque parody of a kiss.

The rear door swung open, and Gordo, eyes closed, inhaled the cloud of cheap perfume that seemed to overwhelm the more subtle scent of orange almost immediately. The door banged against the side of the van, and a woman almost as large as Gordo climbed down with a labored sigh.

"Rosita," Gordo bellowed, "give me a kiss!"

The big woman adjusted the folds of her tentlike dress, the flesh on her upper arms moving independently, like thick, pale turkey wattles. "Hold your horses, Gordo. Rosita has to catch her breath."

"Didn't you miss me?"

"A blind woman couldn't miss that shirt, Gordo."

The woman laughed heartily, and the sound was not unmusical, although her voice was deep and rough-edged. The driver's door banged open and two more women, less bulky than Rosita and several years younger, tottered to the rear of the van on spike heels. The soft soil kept giving way under the sharp heels, and the women walked with an odd gait as if they shared a strange deformity.

"Girls, I have a real treat for you," Gordo promised. "Where's Roberto?" He turned to look at the others, and they stepped back into the shadows and hauled the man to his feet. He'd been dozing, and he shook his head groggily as he was shoved forward into the red glare of the van's taillights.

Gordo wrapped a heavy arm around Roberto's neck, hugging the much smaller man to his massive chest and rubbing his knuckles vigorously into the man's hair. "A real tender chicken, this one." He laughed. "You should pay *me*. Anna, take him under your wing. Young chickens should stick together."

A slim, dark-haired young woman, her face prematurely lined, black eyes slightly sunken in sallow cheeks, staggered tipsily toward the fat man. She paced back and forth in front of Gordo, who was still holding Roberto around the neck, and rearranged her body parts, cocking her hips and thrusting her breasts forward in a distant echo of a Hollywood vamp strutting her stuff.

Gordo let go of Roberto, and Anna leaned toward the young man, taking his chin in one bony hand and tilting his head up. Her dress was bright red and low cut, ready for a daring fifties prom. She reached up and slipped one tattered spaghetti strap from her shoulder and tugged the bodice of her dress suggestively.

"You want to help Anna with this?" she said, leering.

Roberto stammered, and Gordo slapped him on the back, pushing him into Anna's arms. She clasped the young man around the shoulders and fell over backward, laughing uncontrollably as he struggled to free himself from her clutches. Between bursts of brittle laughter, she gasped, "Gordo, your chicken doesn't seem to like women. Maybe *you* should take him for a walk, eh?" She sat up abruptly, dumping Roberto onto the ground. With brutal efficiency, a gesture devoid of any hint of seduction or sensuality, she tugged her dress down to her waist and pulled him to her chest.

"Make up your mind, sweet one. Anna has to make some money." She climbed unsteadily to her feet and sat on the rear bumper of the van. Roberto looked past her to the ragged ticking of a mattress crammed into the back of the van, and darted a glance at Gordo almost helplessly, but the fat man was already walking into the trees, whispering into Rosita's ear. He looked at Anna, and the young woman saw his uncertainty. Taking the bull by the horns, she tugged her red dress all the way off and watched as it drifted to the ground. She lifted her spike heels carefully through its folds and tugged her panties off before sitting on the mattress and sliding back into the van. Roberto shrugged, then climbed in after her. This wasn't what he had expected, but then nothing he'd yet seen in America had failed to surprise him.

"Should I close the door?" he whispered.

"What for?" Anna mumbled, raising her arms over her head. He lay beside her, his head on her shoulder, and listened to his heart, her heart and the rumble of the still-running engine.

Roberto felt repelled and attracted at the same time. He hadn't been with a woman in weeks. It was something he thought about almost constantly, but this wasn't exactly what he had in mind. It was too direct, too commercial. There was no finesse involved, no courting, no flirting. He had imagined that the subtlety he preferred would redeem almost anything, even the separation from his family. It would be possible to pretend, even if only for a few minutes, that he was in command of his own life. He would pick a woman; she would pick him. Together they would decide what to do and when. But this, this was...

Roberto sat up. Anna, still lying back on the mattress, didn't seem to notice. He reached out and touched her thighs, sliding his hand over the skin. It wasn't as soft as he was used to, but then neither was the woman herself. His palm rasped on her dry skin.

He leaned back, resting his weight on one elbow, and circled her breasts with tentative fingers. Anna grabbed his wrist, forcing his hand back between her thighs, and hoisted her pelvis. Roberto withdrew his hand altogether. She spread her legs, and he crawled between them on his knees. He couldn't decide what to do, and Anna shifted her hips impatiently.

It was then he felt the sharp jab in the middle of his back. He reached back idly, expecting to hear the buzz of an angry fly. Instead, his fingers bumped against cold steel. Slowly he shifted his weight back onto his haunches and started to turn, the steel jabbing him again.

"Don't turn around, amigo," a rough whisper ordered.

Roberto froze. Anna seemed not to notice anything. She continued to squirm, showing less and less interest.

"What do you want?" Roberto asked.

"Nothing. I don't want anything." The whisper was more insistent, but no louder. "Go back to Mexico, understand? You don't have a job here anymore."

"But why...?"

"Shut up! You're not wanted here. Mr. Tyack has other plans."

"Can I just get...?"

"You don't get nothing. You don't need nothing. You want to walk, do it. You want to die, give me an argument."

Roberto turned slightly, and the blade flicked at his bare back. "Don't turn around, I said. I mean it."

"Gordo? Is that you? Come on, man... quit it."

The young man turned then, and the blade caught him in the side, slipping in between two ribs. It slashed sideways, and slipped out. Anna felt the warm splash on her thighs, and laughed. "Baby," she said, "couldn't you wait to get it in?"

Roberto pitched forward and landed on her chest, pinning her to the mattress. She smacked his rump, but he didn't move. She pinched him, and he didn't respond. She heard a soft flutter, and a piece of paper landed on her chest as she slid out from under Roberto's deadweight.

She snatched at it, crunching it in her fist as she pulled her legs free of her john. Then she realized the warm sticky fluid running down her legs wasn't what she had imagined. She screamed.

And she didn't stop screaming.

Gordo, his loose belt flapping around his waist, rushed out of the trees to the van. Anna, still naked, stood beside the van with her hands covering her face, the blood, black in the moonlight, slowly thickening on her bony legs. Footsteps pounded behind him as he stepped to Anna's side. As he tried to pull her hands away, the crumpled paper slipped from her fingers.

The other men had joined him, and Gordo bent to pick up the paper, unfolding it carefully with his thick fingers and pressing it flat in his open palm.

"What is it, Gordo? What happened?"

He extended the palm, the paper fluttering slightly as his hand shook. "A pink slip. I have heard about this. We better get the hell out of here. Tyack is dealing with the devil."

When he crossed himself, he was already heading for the highway. Anna's screams continued to ring in his ears, though her mouth was closed and she was already attempting to wipe away the blood on her thighs with handfuls of sand.

13

Mack Bolan entered the hospital with some reluctance. Over the years he'd seen more than his share of human suffering. It was one thing to see it on the battlefield, where it was the only logical outcome. It was another to see it on the home front. He wasn't naive, and he wasn't a dreamer, but there was still something unsettling about the increasing frequency with which innocent people, and those whose job it was to preserve that innocence, found themselves looking down a deep well with a gun at their backs.

Waiting for the elevator, he wondered what it was in the collective heart of mankind that made it not only tolerable, but more and more often desirable, to use brutality as an instrument of self-enrichment. Impatience with reality was part of it, maybe, raised expectations leading to frustration and ultimately to violence. But that wasn't the whole picture. It couldn't be.

There had always been haves and have nots. The haves, more often than not, had been willing to keep what they had by violent means, just as those who had nothing were willing to resort to violence to get a slice of the pie. Cavemen had been violent men in a violent world. Some scientists even speculated that Cro-Magnon had waged a successful war against Neanderthal, the classic example of the upstart kicking ass to claim his place in the world.

But that was a simpler time, and the violence, almost by definition, was simple. There was nothing inherently wrong in warriors wreaking havoc on other warriors. That was, after all, what warriors were for. But lately, it seemed to Bolan, there were too many warriors, and far too many innocent people caught in the middle.

With a heavy sigh, Bolan entered the elevator and punched the button for the third floor.

The hallway was empty as he stepped off the elevator. The desk opposite was vacant, and Bolan walked past it to check the number on the nearest door. The next door bore a higher number, and he turned to head back in the other direction. Room 8 was the second on the right. The door was open and a dim light was on when Bolan poked his head in.

A soft blue flicker from high on the wall washed over the two beds, one of which was empty. In the other, Randy Carlton lay propped on a pair of pillows.

"I was wondering when you would stop by," he said. "Maybe I should have said 'if.'"

"You had a pretty rough time of it."

"Yeah, I guess so. I'll be all right in a couple or three days, though, soon as I get my strength back." The patrolman pointed to an empty chair between the beds. "Sit down and watch my alma mater get whipped."

Bolan eased past the foot of the bed, ducking to avoid blocking the picture on the television high up on the wall. "You played basketball?"

"Yeah, four years, U of A. That was a long time ago, though. It seems like it must have been in a different life, or something. I remember all those lectures from the coach, how team work and cooperation were the key to success. How they could be used in the real world, once you left the boards behind. All that Knute Rockne and Gipper stuff.

Seems like every coach, regardless of the sport, thinks the same. It's all crap, too. Teammates are brothers you know, working for a common goal, all that shit. But it doesn't last longer than the uniform.''

Carlton turned his head away. When he spoke again, his voice came as if from a great distance. It sounded sluggish, almost as if he were underwater. ''Will Ralston and I were partners. Almost four years. You know what that's like?''

''Yeah, I do.'' For a moment Bolan flashed on some of his own memories, the scars still fresh, as if a careless prod would start them bleeding all over again. ''Yeah...''

''I'm sorry, Mr. Belasko, I guess I...''

''It's Mike. And you have nothing to apologize for.''

Carlton struggled to sit up, groped around under the pillows, finally finding the controls. He pressed a button, and the top of the bed began to sink, stopping its descent when the upper half of the bed had risen high enough for him to face Bolan comfortably. ''I guess I wouldn't even be here if it wasn't for you.''

''You were holding your own when I got there.''

''What about those bastards? Did you get a good look at them?''

Bolan nodded.

'''Cause I'll tell you, as soon as I get out of here, I'm going to look for them. You can take that to the bank.''

''That won't be necessary.''

The patrolman sat up a little, his eyes searching Bolan's face in the flickering blue light.

''What we have to do is find out who sent them, and why. That'll be a lot tougher, I'm guessing,'' Bolan told him.

''How'd you know where to find us, anyway?''

"Ronny Sipe and I stopped at your headquarters. One of the officers there told us where you went."

Carlton's face went dark. He seemed to be puzzling his way through a sudden mystery.

"Anything wrong?"

"I'm not sure. You said somebody told you. Do you remember who it was?"

"Ronny talked to him, but he was hard to miss. A big guy, about six-four or so. Buck Allenson."

"Allenson! That bastard..."

"What's the matter?"

"You're sure he told you where to find us?"

Bolan leaned forward. "Certain. Sipe said Allenson told him you'd gotten a call and had gone to meet the informant in the desert. Why?"

"Because he couldn't have known. We didn't tell anyone about the tip. Will and I talked about it and decided not to. We were afraid of a leak, and we knew some of the guys aren't above sending us on a wild-goose chase. A lot of them don't give a shit about the job, and they keep ragging us about how serious we are...were. We wanted to cover our asses, either way, you know?"

Bolan was quiet for a long moment. The younger man watched him carefully, as if he could read the conflicting emotions that were racing through Bolan's mind and were reflected on his face. "Then he must have known about the ambush. Not only that, he deliberately sent me and Sipe out there..."

"Figuring you two'd get iced as well."

"Did you have any idea that Allenson was on the pad?"

"No. I didn't like the guy, but that was just personal. And we knew somebody had sold out, but...jeez! We figured it was just taking a few bucks to look the other way. Maybe even feed information about patrol patterns, so the coyotes would have an easier time of it. But setting four people up for murder, no way did we think that."

"What do you think now?"

The patrolman chewed on the inside of his lower lip for a while before answering. "I don't know. What else can I think? Unless somebody told him, and he just passed it on to you. That's possible, isn't it?" He shook his head. "I don't know what to think. I can't believe he would go that far. But somebody did. At least the bastard didn't get away with it, whoever it was."

"The last time I looked," Bolan said quietly, "five hundred wasn't a bad batting average."

"Five hundred? You mean...? Ronny, too?"

"Yeah. Ronny, too."

Carlton sighed. His shoulders shook for a moment, then he closed his eyes and fell back onto the pillow. "We better keep an eye on those two guys down the hall," he whispered.

"What two guys? I know about the guy from the boxcar, but he's still in a coma. There's another one?"

"Yeah, there's another one. Not from the boxcar, but Ronny and I think...thought...there was a connection. They found him in the desert with a wire around his neck. He's been here a couple or three days."

"Did he say anything yet?"

"No, he was in a coma, just like the other guy. But, hell, one of them will wake up. He has to. Otherwise..." He held his hands out, palms up. He didn't have to elaborate.

"Is there anybody here you can trust?" Bolan asked.

"Ray Conlan."

"The sheriff?"

"Yeah. He's not crazy about illegals, but he's an honest man. You can trust him."

"I think I better go see him in the morning. Tonight I'll just hang around here."

"You have to sleep sometime, you know."

Bolan stood up. "I'll be back in a minute."

"Where are you going?"

"Just to talk to the nurse a minute. Be right back. You get some rest."

Bolan stepped out of the room, conscious of the blue light flickering behind him. The nurses' station down the hall was still empty, which seemed odd, and he walked quickly to the desk. The office behind it was dark, and the door that had been open earlier was closed. He rapped on the door with his knuckles, but heard only the echo of his knock. He turned the knob, but the door was locked. Turning to the desk, he rifled through the drawers until he found a set of keys.

The warrior unlocked the door and clicked on the light, the bright flash of the overhead fluorescents filling the room with a harsh glare. The night nurse lay trussed and gagged in one corner, a bright white strip of adhesive tape covering her mouth. Bolan knelt beside her and felt for her pulse. She was unconscious, but still alive.

Bolan stood and ran to the door, drawing the .44 as he slid through the doorway and out into the hall. He sprinted toward Randy Carlton's room and was relieved to find him still watching the basketball game. Bolan slipped the Beretta from its sling and tossed it to him.

"What the hell's going on?" the patrolman demanded.

"Those two men, what rooms are they in?"

"I don't know. Down the hall a few doors, I guess. Why?"

"Wait here, and keep your eye on the door."

Bolan bounded out of the room and started a door-to-door search. The first room on the right was vacant. The next was occupied by an old man, fast asleep with the television still flashing away. Slipping across the hall, he tried the first room on the left. Both beds were occupied by children. A young woman, her head on her chest, slept awkwardly on an uncomfortable chair between them.

The next room was dark, but its door was open. As soon as the light went on, Bolan knew he had found one of the men he was looking for.

Too late.

The stark white of the sheet was splashed with bright red, a trail of red leading to the edge of the bed and down its side. The red pool on the floor was occasionally broken by ripples as another drop of blood splashed into it.

Bolan ran to the door of the next room, turned the knob gently, then banged the door with his shoulder, sending it crashing back into the wall. In a combat crouch, he stepped through the door, the Desert Eagle held in front of him in a two-handed grip.

A single bed occupied the center of the small room. By the metal headboard, a man with a startled look on his face was frozen in the act of turning toward the door. He moved slowly, like ice thawing under a winter sun, gradually bringing around a suppressed Uzi toward the intruder.

Bolan fired once, then again. The startled hit man flew backward into the edge of the bed, blood from his massive wounds trickling down the wall behind him. The assassin slipped from the bed, dead before he hit the floor.

A slight scratch behind Bolan caused him to whirl around, seeking a target. He jerked his weapon upward when he saw Randy Carlton, Beretta in hand, leaning against the doorframe.

"We need to get some protection for this man, fast." Bolan indicated the still-unconscious patient. "He's the only witness we have now."

"I'll call Ray Conlan. Then I think I'd better make some arrangements for myself. I don't think I like the quality of care in this joint. I think it's time to check out."

14

The fat man looked at his boss through hooded eyes. The broad brown face, eyes slightly angled over prominent cheekbones, gave more than a hint of his Indian ancestry. But there was nothing primitive about the surroundings, or about the submachine gun on the table by his elbow. The boss, as usual, was pacing back and forth, whirling at one end of the table and marching back in the other direction, like a bear in an electronic shooting gallery.

Finally Carlos Calderone stopped at the center of the table and leaned forward, taking the weight of his upper body on stiff arms propped on the polished wood. He stared hard at the fat man, and Tomás Sanchez was getting uncomfortable. He was also getting angry, and that was something he couldn't afford to do.

"Tomás," Calderone hissed, making no attempt to conceal his exasperation, "you keep fucking up. Everything I tell you to do, you say not to worry. I ask you how it went, and you tell me it went fine. Only later do I find out it *didn't* go well, and that it's *not* fine."

Sanchez shrugged his shoulders. "Don Calderone, you tell me to act like a businessman. 'Don't do it all yourself, Tomás,' you say. 'Delegate, Tomás,' you say. So I delegate. Can I help it if you give me faulty tools for a complicated job? Do you fix one of your computers with a bulldozer?"

Calderone turned his back on the man, letting the edge of the table take his weight as he leaned back. Sanchez stared at the expensive linen jacket, admiring the fineness of its weave, and waited for the next insult, which he knew would not be long in coming.

Inhaling deeply and holding his breath for a long time, Calderone tottered slightly, and Sanchez wondered whether his boss was not, after all, no more than the spoiled child he seemed sometimes to be. He wondered, too, whether Calderone would turn blue and black out, falling to the floor in a dramatic gesture like the women in the television *novelas* did. He was still smiling at the notion when Calderone whirled again to face him.

"One," Calderone snapped, "I tell you to get rid of Mendoza, and he is still alive in the hospital." The first finger waggled suggestively, and Sanchez stared at it as if transfixed.

"But, Don Calderone, I—"

"Wait, Tomás, please wait. You will have your turn." The hand moved slightly and, as if by magic, a second finger joined the first. "Two, I ask you please to supervise the railroad test, make sure the chickens get to their destination without a hitch, and instead they end up a pile of dead meat in a railroad yard. That is not fine. That is not things going well."

"I already told—"

"Three—" and a third finger appeared "—I ask you to take a stone out of my shoe, to get rid of those nosy border patrolmen. It goes very well. They show up where they are supposed to. At the time they are supposed to. We even get a bonus with that attorney and his friend, and what happens?"

He paused to let Sanchez have his say, but the fat man knew it was still too early. If he was going to fire back, he'd better save his ammunition until he had a better target.

Calderone bit his lower lip before continuing. "I'll tell you what happens. What happens is I lose a two-million-dollar helicopter and eight men."

"You got rid of the attorney and the border patrolman."

"And you left two witnesses, no, Tomás? Did you not?" Calderone dropped his voice to a soft purr. He added a fourth finger. "Then, I ask you very simply to clean up the mess you have already made, and you make a mess of that, too."

"How did I know there would be somebody on guard at the hospital?"

"That is not the question, the question is, why *didn't* you know, or why didn't you at least make allowances for the possibility?"

Sanchez shrugged. He'd give Calderone a point. He screwed up, plain and simple on that one.

Now waving a full five fingers at the man, Calderone concluded his litany. "I ask you to make room for our people at Waywayanda Farm, and there is still no room. You make me look like a fool in front of that madman Tyack. I tell him I can handle everything. I tell him no problem for me, and no headaches for him. And what is happening, eh? Nothing. That is what is happening. Nothing at all."

"I'll take care of it, Don Calderone."

"You'd better, Tomás. You'd better do just that. You have been with me a long time, and I like you. But this is business, and businessmen can't afford mistakes. If you are getting old, if you lose a step or two, it is time to retire, maybe, no? And in this business, when you retire, Tomás, there are no gold watches, eh?''

"No gold watches. I understand. I'll take care of it myself.''

"Okay, my friend, I'll be waiting. Soon, eh? This Tyack is unpredictable.''

DOWNTOWN TUCSON WAS QUIET. Tomás Sanchez drifted through the night streets listening to the sand hiss under the wheels of his van. He wasn't at ease with himself, or with the job he had to do. False papers in his pocket—acquired at great expense, and meticulously supported by all the appropriate files and documents in the usual government data banks—testified to his legitimacy. But he didn't feel legitimate. And that made him nervous.

He carried all the proof anyone could ever want that he was precisely what he seemed to be, just another Chicano making a buck or two, hustling to keep up with the rent and the cost of living. No longer a stranger in a strange land, at least as far as the papers went.

But he felt as if he were a stranger, and all the paper in the world couldn't change that. And Arizona would always be a strange land. He wondered whether it was strange even to the tall, bearlike Anglos who could drag out a family tree with two-hundred-year-old roots and maps of the family trek from Kentucky and Missouri. Somehow, clinging to life on the very edge of the desert had to be at least a little bit strange, even for them.

Strangest of all, though, was the way he made his living. That it was better than life in Guerrero, where his family had fought off starvation with a stick, was unquestionable. But whether he had somehow lost something of himself in the process was less certain.

It wasn't a question of ethics, exactly, and it wasn't a guilty conscience. What it was he wasn't sure, but it was there, all the same. It was more like some vague premonition that he had purchased something without asking its price. Someday, when he least expected it, the bill would come due, and the price would be high.

He knew all that, and that wasn't what bothered him, either. What really gnawed at him was the knowledge that whatever the price, he would be willing to pay it. And knowing that, he also knew that he was no longer a free man.

As the van cleared the heart of the city and moved out into the outskirts, more like a cluster of separate small towns than the suburban sprawl of a big city, he watched the moon, now a day or two past full, gliding just above the mountains. It seemed to stare at him, not with malice, not even with interest, but with a sort of benign indifference. It was the eye of a creature that saw him and didn't care whether he was there or not. It was like being invisible.

The village of Los Gatos lay a few miles to the south. With the radio thumping away, the heavy bass echoing from the rear speakers, Sanchez covered the distance without realizing it. Keeping time on the wheel, his foot to the floor, the black van almost an extension of him, he cruised easily and effortlessly, pulling off the road into a sandy lot beside an off-brand gas station to wait.

The others were there almost immediately, pounding on the driver's window and waking him out of his reverie. He opened the door and hopped down, moving gracefully despite his bulk. He unlocked the rear of the van, and the three men quickly loaded four five-gallon cans of gasoline, then climbed in. Sanchez closed the rear door and got back behind the wheel. He didn't know the men in the back and didn't want to know them. They were a dime a dozen, and fifty bucks would buy them for the night. That's all Sanchez needed. They even supplied their own gasoline.

He eased back onto the highway, falling in behind a blonde in a red convertible. Ten minutes later the blonde and her car had dwindled to a pair of taillights, and they, too, vanished a few moments later. Under the moon the desert was pale silver, everything but the saguaros taking on the subdued color of the moon. The saguaros themselves stood black and silent like shadows made flesh.

The desert suddenly disappeared, the endless sand now replaced by row upon row of orange trees. Sanchez slowed down, looking for some telltale sign among the trees. He noticed a hundred tiny replicas of the moon, sparkling in the pools of water at the bottom of the irrigation ditches, miniature versions winking back from other, smaller skies. Waywayanda Farm was now the only place on earth.

An orange smear flashed by and Sanchez hit the brakes. The van lurched a little as it backed up, and he watched for the orange light off to the right. It was small, and winked on and off, but there was no doubt in his mind he'd found what he was looking for. He jumped the vehicle ahead a few yards, pulling off the road into a weedy patch between two orange trees.

The first lesson had been wasted on all but a few men. Now it was time to speak more softly, and deliver an indisputable lecture. He climbed down from the van and walked to the rear. When he unlocked the door, his three acolytes tumbled out, lugging the heavy gasoline cans with them. Sanchez hauled the fourth can out and set it down, then gathered the men around him.

Hurriedly, in a whisper, he explained what he wanted them to do, then gave each a loaded shotgun. The guns, he stressed, were to be used only in self-defense. All that was necessary was to make certain their message was understood. The three men, little more than shadows under the thick foliage of the trees, nodded vigorously and walked back the few yards to the end of the aisle where he had seen the orange light.

Sanchez led the way among the trees, watching the light wink on and off, and finally realized it winked because someone was passing back and forth in front of it. When they got within thirty yards, he whispered to them to put the cans down and follow his lead.

The outlines of nearly two dozen tents were clearly discernible among the trees, their grommets reflecting the firelight in a hundred small flashes. There would be somewhere in the neighborhood of fifty men in the camp, maybe more. Sanchez listened to the music of an acoustic guitar for a moment, trying to place the tune. When he couldn't, he shrugged his shoulders and stepped out. Moving quickly, he approached the camp fire at a near trot. He was almost upon the camp before someone noticed him, and the music suddenly stopped.

"*¿Señor...? Buenas noches.*" Sanchez returned the greeting, then motioned this three henchmen to stand beside him.

"You men are no longer wanted here," Sanchez told them. "Mr. Tyack wants you to leave."

"But he—"

"No argument. Just hit the road."

"Who are you? You don't work for Mr. Tyack. Why doesn't he tell us himself if he wants us to leave? Most of the crop is still unharvested. We have just started." The man who argued was older than most of the others, and was obviously someone they respected. Sanchez felt rather than saw the pickers closing ranks in a tight semicircle behind their spokesman.

Before Sanchez could respond, a blast rent the air and the old man went spinning off to one side and fell on his back. It was several seconds before the reason for it registered on Sanchez, and then his brain almost immediately went numb. One of his fifty-dollar gunners had fired his shotgun.

No one moved.

Another blast from one of the shotguns, this one angled over the heads of the pickers, suddenly sent them running in every direction. The night exploded with blast after blast from three shotguns, and the air stank of cordite. When the firing stopped, all the workers had vanished.

The three hired guns rushed into the trees and were back a moment later with the cans of gasoline. They unscrewed the caps on two of the cans and walked among the tents, splashing the volatile liquid on canvas after canvas. The second pair of cans was opened and soon the smell of cordite was gone, replaced by that of the fuel. The four empty cans were tossed onto the fire, where their fumes ignited with dull booms as they spurted tongues of flame.

"Can we take anything?" one of the goons asked, tugging on his sleeve.

"No, you asshole, you don't want the police to be able to connect you to this."

The man shrugged, then grabbed a burning brand and casually walked among the tents, swinging the branch from side to side. Each tent went up with a soft whoosh. When all the tents were ablaze, Sanchez backed away, his own eyes locked on the staring face of the old man and the roaring flames dancing in the cold, dead eyes.

He led the way back to the van and hustled the three men into the rear. They stacked their shotguns on the floor, and he closed the door after them. Climbing into the driver's seat, Sanchez slipped his own shotgun onto the passenger seat beside him. As he cranked up the engine, he spotted the moon, a little higher in the sky now, and swung around and headed away from Tucson, out into the desert.

He wondered if the men in the back remembered his was now the only loaded gun. It was funny in a way. But he didn't feel like smiling.

Not even when he stopped the van and reached for the shotgun.

15

The headquarters of the Bisbee County Sheriff was a madhouse. Mack Bolan wormed through a crowd around the water cooler, and asked the way to the sheriff's office. A deputy pointed down a dim hall and told him to look for the last door on the left. Bolan slipped through the last pair of deputies and into the corridor. The hallway smelled of new paint, but the institutional cream and white might as well have been a decade old. There were no dirty handprints or graffiti on the walls, but the colors were timeless.

The last door on the left was open, and a burly man in a gray uniform and Sam Browne belt sat behind a desk barely able to conceal the generous mound of his stomach. He looked up as Bolan rapped on the doorframe, eyebrows knit in a quizzical arch. His leathery cheeks had that welter of fine wrinkles usually found on skin that has seen more than its share of sunlight, and his corona of fine white hair fanned out in every direction.

"Can I help you, sir?" the sheriff asked.

The warrior stepped through the door and extended a hand across the battle-scarred desk. "Randy Carlton called you about me, I believe."

The sheriff's face creased in a genuine smile. "Oh, yeah, Belasko, isn't it? Randy said you'd be dropping by." He grabbed Bolan's hand and shook it firmly. "Ray Conlan's the name. What can I do for you?"

Bolan looked around, found a chair and indicated it with a nod of his head.

"Oh, hell, yes, sit down. Damn, I nearly forgot my manners. The old lady would kick me in the shins for that. I got some scars...."

Bolan closed the door, sitting down while the glass panel still rattled. "Did Randy tell you anything?"

"Just that you had a few things you wanted to talk about, sort of hush-hush, I gather. That right?"

"Yeah."

"Well, I'll tell you, I don't know what I can do for you, but I'd do just about anything to help that boy out. I swear to God, I never saw anybody take his job so serious, not since I was his age, anyway. I like him, and I'd sure as hell like to get hold of the son of a bitch who tried to shoot him. That what this is about?"

"Partly." Bolan had taken an instant liking to the gruff old man. He was one of a dying breed, and he seemed to know it. Rather than wearing it like a badge of honor, ossifying in his sense of himself, he seemed rather to have no ego at all. He was his job, and vice versa. That was a precious kind of lawman, precious like platinum was precious, and for the same reason—both were extremely rare.

"Hell, I ought to shut my face and let you tell me what you want. Belasko, you go ahead and ask me whatever you want to know. I'll tell you what I can. If I talk too much, just tell me to get on with it. No offense will be taken, I can guarantee." He smiled again, even more easily.

"What have you been able to learn about the two men who tried to kill Ronny Sipe?"

"Not much. We haven't got a ripple on their prints. They had no identification on them, and the weapons were sanitized. Blind alleys everywhere we turn. You want my opinion, though, they were Mexican nationals. Unlikely we'll get any help from the *federales*, but we're trying."

Bolan mulled over what he knew and what he suspected, not sure yet that he wanted to paint a full picture for the sheriff, no matter how cooperative he seemed to be. "I imagine it was the same with the gunners who killed Will Ralston?"

"You imagine right. Same mold, I'll bet you. They seem to have a factory down there in Me-he-co, can turn those bastards out on an assembly line, just like old Fords. These guys were a little cleaner than most, though. I don't know if that means they drank from the same well, or not. I'd bet on it, but not the farm."

"I suppose you came up just as empty on the hit man from the hospital?" Bolan knew without waiting for the answer that he was right. Conlan knew he knew, and didn't bother to respond.

The sheriff tilted back in his chair, folded his hands across his belly and propped his high-heeled boots on a corner of the desk, ignoring the pile of papers perched precariously on the edge. "Let me sketch something out for you. I don't know how much Ronny had a chance to tell you, but him and me had a couple of long heart-to-hearts over a pot of coffee. Funny thing, Belasko, but when you get old and feel like you're coming to the end of it, you can't sleep much. Just like when you're young, and the world's your oyster. Seems to me like there ain't much difference between lookin' for the pearl and knowin' for sure there ain't one. You know what I mean?"

"I think so," Bolan said.

"Well, Ronny and me, we was both ends of that pipe, and there was something got its claws into both of us. Neither one of us knew what to make of it, but we sure as hell chewed the leather up pretty fine."

The sheriff leaned forward to press a button on his phone, then picked up the receiver. He covered the mouthpiece with a thick palm for a moment. "You want a coffee?" When Bolan nodded, he added, "How you like it?"

Uncovering the phone, he said, "Two coffees, black, Milton, and knock before you bring them in, all right? Thank you, son."

He placed the phone back in its cradle, a thoughtful expression on his face. "I think what we got here is two archaeologists working the same dig. I got some pieces of pottery and so did Ronny. We was both trying to rebuild the pot, without knowing whether we had the whole thing, or bits and pieces of two or three, or maybe even more. Then, when we got to talking about it, things started to fall into place. I think now, and incidentally, Ronny did, too, what we got is one big mother of a pot. I don't think we got all the pieces yet, but what we do have sure as hell fits."

Bolan waited patiently while the old man hummed to himself, turning over his next statement a few times before resuming. "Now the funny thing is, when you're an archaeologist, you got one blind spot."

"What's that?"

"I'll tell you, it's—" He stopped when a sharp rap on the door signaled the arrival of the coffee. "Come on in, Milt."

The door opened, and a young deputy shouldered his way in, a cup of coffee in each hand. "Milt, this here is Mr. Belasko." The young man nodded as he placed the coffee on the desk, pushing one toward Conlan and leaving the other within reach of Bolan's chair. "Milt is my nephew, but don't let that fool you. He's gonna be a good lawman, soon's he gets a couple of years under his belt." He smiled at the young deputy, then dismissed him with a wave of his hand. "That's all for now, son."

When the door closed behind the deputy, Conlan picked up where he had left off. "Like I was sayin', the thing is, when you're an archaeologist, most of the time you find what you're lookin' for. You're lookin' for old pots, that's what you dig up. It never occurs to you to wonder just how old it is, because you already think you know."

"Then you think maybe there's something going on that hasn't been seen before?"

"There you go, son. That's *exactly* what I think. I didn't pick it up right away. Even an old-timer can be made a fool of hisself, he tries hard enough. But that's what I think now."

"Why?"

Conlan slapped the desk. "Precisely! That's the question, ain't it? And the answer comes from in here." He thumped his chest with a blunt finger. "It's somethin' I feel, not somethin' I can prove. But it's so, all the same."

"Where does Waywayanda Farm fit into the picture?"

"You know about that already?"

Bolan sat forward in his chair. "Know about what?"

"Waywayanda."

"All I know is that name was on a slip of paper. It was in the pocket of the sole survivor of the boxcar."

"Now, Ronny never told me that."

"Well, what are you talking about, then?"

"I'm talking about the death of one Roberto Miercoles at Waywayanda a day or two ago, for no apparent reason, at the hands of a person or persons unknown. I am also talking about the murder last night of an old feller at the same place, and the attack on a camp full of harmless fruit pickers. Burned to the ground, every last tent. Just the one dead, though, thank the Lord."

Bolan leaned forward to take a sip of the coffee, still steaming on the edge of the desk. "And have you managed to put the pieces all together yet?"

"Nope! That's a tall order, and I ain't even sure we *got* all the pieces yet. But I can tell you one thing. You find who killed Will Ralston and Ronny Sipe, and you damn sure will be a whole lot closer than you are now. One thing you got to understand about this neck of the woods, Mike. Down here, labor is cheap, but it ain't cheap enough, not for most of these big-ass farms we got nowadays. The boys that run them places are interested in only two things . . . gettin' as much fruit as they can, and payin' as little as possible to them as picks it. See, you can't use machines to pick oranges, lemons and grapefruits. You got to use people, but people cost money, what with unions and all. Now, you find somebody who don't care about that stuff, and he works cheaper. But you can always go another step, see? If you can find somebody who don't even belong here, who can't go to the law if you push him too hard, and who don't call the NLRB if he gets his hand caught in a conveyor belt, then you *really* got somethin'. What these here growers would like most is trained monkeys. Most of 'em don't see no difference between monkeys and Mexicans anyhow, and that's a fact."

"You sound like you're talking from experience, Sheriff."

"Pretty near, son, pretty damn near. My daddy come out here from Oklahoma in the thirties. Wanted to go to California. Only thing was, when he got to the border, there was already too many Okies in lotusland. They had deputies at the border, and worse. Vigilantes who'd string you up sooner'n let you pass. So Daddy come on back this way. There wasn't but a few citrus farms back then, and a hundred hands for every orange needed pickin'. It was hard times, I don't mind tellin' you. I seen it firsthand. My heart goes out to them people.''

"What's the connection?"

"Dammit, son, it's sittin' right there in front of your face. You don't see it, I can't help you none."

"Can I count on you if I need help?"

"Bet your ass. You for damn sure can. But you got to get me more'n I got now before I can legally do anything. You want my advice, you start at the other end, out there." Conlan waved his hand vaguely. "The other side of the border is where you ought to be lookin', son. We maybe got some mean sons of bitches over here willing to exploit people, even sit on their hands while some folks get pushed around. But them coyotes is a whole other kind of poison. They slit throats 'stead of goin' to the movies on a Saturday night." Conlan smiled grimly. "But you find this one, he's got a head too big for his damn hat, I'll bet you a buck. And one more thing. That boxcar?"

"What about it?"

"It wasn't supposed to be here. It was supposed to be in Yuma. I don't know what that means, but I'd bet my ass it means *somethin'*."

"You mind if I take a look at Tyack's place?"

"I don't, but he might. You be careful out there, and don't let nobody know who you are or why you're there. He's a strange man, and he's got some real hard asses workin' for him. There's a lot I don't like about that place. I don't know what's going on out there, but I'm gonna. Bet on it."

16

Bolan sat in the Renegade, his hands on the steering wheel, white knuckles glowing like small jewels around the rim. What he knew now wouldn't fill a shot glass, and he had no idea where the bottle was.

Somehow there had to be a connection between the murders at Tyack's Waywayanda Farm and the boxcar, and those behind both were somehow responsible for the ambush and murder of Will Ralston and Ronny Sipe. The warrior knew that with a cold certainty, but proving it was another matter. Following the connection back to its source would be harder still. He was convinced that whoever had engineered the alteration in the boxcar's route had also set up Carlton and Ralston, but he didn't know why. If he could answer that question, he might be able to figure out who. Motive was the great unknown.

The most logical place to start would be at Tyack's. He was curious about the local legend, but it was too early to call on him directly. Looking around a bit, maybe tripping over something, was the best bet. Roberto Miercoles had to have friends. Maybe someone had even seen what had happened. The illegals lived in constant fear of being sent back to Mexico. Any white face, as far as they were concerned, was about as welcome as the green vans of La Migra, as they called the INS. Bolan knew some Spanish, but he couldn't do anything about his complexion. What he needed was a link, an illegal who could front for him, someone to convince the others to talk to him, to tell him what they knew. That wouldn't be easy, but he'd have to think of something.

Kicking the Renegade, he headed north on Route 19, toward Tucson. As he drove, he kept mulling over what he knew, arranging and rearranging the pieces, trying to place them in some sort of meaningful chronology. It was the old question about the chicken and the egg. Only this time there were a dozen eggs and he had to decide which one hatched first. The number of chickens was an unknown, so he pushed that question aside.

On a midday morning, the northbound traffic was light, and Bolan was making good time. Low fences, pressed flat in places, altogether absent in some others, lined the highway about twenty yards off the shoulder. There was nothing beyond the fences, as far as he could see—no cattle, no horses—and he wondered what the fences were supposed to do. No signs identified the fenced-in land. Every third post carried a No Trespassing sign, but revealed nothing else.

The highway itself was smooth and seamless, the surface free of potholes and cracks. Unlike the roads in the north and east, the Arizona highways weren't exposed to constant freezing and thawing. There was no seepage to work its way down into minute cracks, then swell up, widening the gap and making room for more water and more expansion. The tires of the 4x4 hissed steadily over the satiny asphalt, the sound accented by a layer of fine sand, a reminder that whenever man was through with this part of the world, the desert was willing and able to reassert itself.

On the horizon a huge brown billow seemed to be crawling across the land far to the right. Bolan watched it as the Renegade kept to a steady sixty-five. It seemed to move

PLAY THE

LUCKY CARNIVAL WHEEL

scratch-off game
and get as many as
FIVE FREE GIFTS...

HOW TO PLAY:

1. With a coin, carefully scratch off the silver area at right. Then check your number against the chart below to see which gifts you can get. If you're lucky, you'll instantly be entitled to receive one or more books and possibly another gift, ABSOLUTELY FREE!

2. Send back this card and we'll promptly send you any Free Gifts you're entitled to. You may get brand-new, red-hot Gold Eagle books and a terrific Surprise Mystery Gift!

3. We're betting you'll want more of these action-packed stories, so we'll send you six more high-voltage books every other month to preview. Always delivered right to your home before they're available in stores. And always at a hefty saving off the retail price!

4. Your satisfaction is guaranteed! You may return any shipment of books and cancel any time. The Free Books and Gift remain yours to keep!

NO COST! NO RISK!
NO OBLIGATION TO BUY!

Guns, Guts and Glory!

America's most potent human weapons take on the world's barbarians! Meet them—join them—in a war of vengeance against terrorists, anarchists, hijackers and drug dealers! Mack Bolan and his courageous squads, Able Team & Phoenix Force—along with SOBs and Vietnam: Ground Zero unleash the best sharpshooting firepower ever published!

If offer card is missing, write to: Gold Eagle Reader Service,
901 Fuhrmann Blvd., P.O. Box 1394, Buffalo, NY 14269-1394

slowly, without turbulence, but kept to a straight line. For fifteen minutes it drew closer, and Bolan had to look farther and farther to the right in order to keep it in view.

Suddenly the land on his right was darker, raked with furrows, and at the far edge of the creeping brown, he saw a huge tiller, its rear end wrapped in a dark brown cloud, shading slowly to light brown, then trailing off in a haze of beige. A moment later the Renegade bored into the remnants of the cloud, the fine dust coating the windshield and forcing Bolan to turn on the wipers.

This was cotton country.

As he drew closer to Tucson, the land changed, got greener. Acre after acre stretched out on both sides. The dark color seemed almost alien, as if the land were afflicted with some plague. Irrigation ditches crisscrossed the greenery and here and there shimmering silver fans of water from elevated poles sprayed out over the crops, each one throwing off a rainbow in the bright sun.

The region represented the southernmost advance of agriculture in the state, and oranges were fairly new here. Most of the groves were farther north, near Phoenix, but in a world where green meant gold, engineering subdued even nature, as long as the price was right.

Bolan hung a left, and suddenly the road ahead was stark and empty. Three miles of flat land gave way abruptly to ranks of trees. The scent of the citrus trees slowly seeped into the air-conditioned Renegade, and Bolan slowed to a crawl. He still hadn't decided whether to talk to Tyack himself, or to take a more direct approach to the laborers. He wasn't sure what to tell the grower, and no one was sure there was even a connection between him and the twenty-nine corpses in the boxcar.

Only a single piece of paper with a name scrawled in wavering letters with a blunt pencil linked the orange grower to the dead men. The Byzantine ways of the illegals, and the invisible web woven by coyotes and growers alike, meant that any man at any given time could have worked for Tyack. Some of the illegals came back year after year. The exploitation was tolerated by the Mexicans because they felt safer. They operated on the theory that it was better to deal with the devil you knew than with the devil you didn't.

For their part, the growers were more than happy to have a regular crew. When that crew was vulnerable, and outside the protection of the law, so much the better. Waywayanda Farm was huge, and Bolan had so far seen no one. The aisles between the trees were deserted. Occasionally a slight glimmer—water puddled in one of the shallow irrigation ditches—would catch his eye, but even the leaves were motionless. Light was the only thing that moved.

After another half mile Bolan pulled over into a small clearing just off the road. The earth was rutted, and thick treads had mauled it repeatedly. He stepped down from the vehicle and looked at the soil for a moment, then realized the tracks were those of a tractor. The clearing must be some sort of staging area or used for transitional storage during the picking.

Bolan cocked his head to listen, but there wasn't a sound. He stepped into an aisle between two rows of trees, grateful for the shade. The oppressive air seemed to cling to him, and every step was like sticking his face into an oven. He was already sweating, and he wondered how the men who made their living scrambling up into the trees could bear it. What must their lives at home be like if they were eager to endure months of this brutal labor?

A quarter mile ahead a wall of green sealed off the aisle. Bolan reached the wall, then realized a hedgerow of some kind had been planted at a right angle to the rows of trees. He stepped over a narrow ditch and stood in the middle of

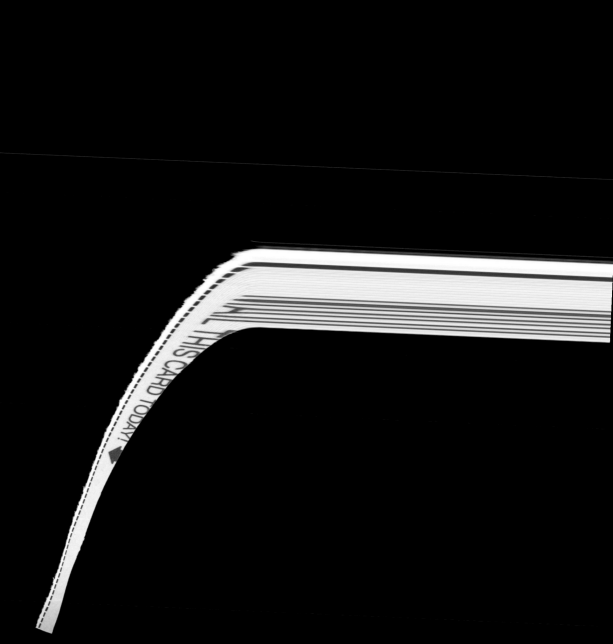

a broad avenue of sand. Looking left and right, he still saw no sign of life. He squeezed into the hedgerow, turning sideways to get through the dense growth.

The hedge was nearly five feet deep, and he peered out through the far side. Beyond the hedge was another avenue, an irrigation ditch, and beyond it, another grove. Bolan slipped out of the hedge and stepped across the ditch. He paused to listen and heard a faint mutter of conversation. It was coming from the left, but it was impossible to gauge the distance.

Stepping back across the ditch, he headed in the direction of the noise, stopping to look down each aisle. After the first three, the conversation stopped, and he began to wonder whether he had imagined it. After checking five more aisles, he still saw no one. The conversation had died altogether. Shaking his head, he walked to the mouth of the next aisle, when an engine exploded behind him.

Bolan turned to see a four-wheel-drive pickup racing toward him, kicking up sand with its oversized tires. Two men sat in the cab, their faces fading in and out of view as the truck raced through patches of sunlight and shade. The warrior jumped across the irrigation ditch and dodged into the trees, the truck fifty yards away and closing fast.

Racing down the aisle, he turned to look over his shoulder in time to see the pickup lurch over the ditch, dipping and rocking as each axle fell into the ditch then climbed out. For a moment he thought about standing his ground, but there was something about the way the truck was charging that told him to forget it. Besides, he told himself, he wanted to keep a low profile until he had a chance to feel his way through the situation.

The truck came on, and he darted to the left, between two orange trees. He was in the next aisle now, and the truck was too large to fit through the narrow gap. It would

have to run to the next turn then come back at him. All he
had to do was stay far enough ahead of them, ducking from
aisle to aisle. He heard the vehicle skid to a halt, and doors
slamming. Glancing back, he saw a sliver of the bright red
truck, which had stopped two aisles back.

The men were on foot now, and although he had a lead
on them, they knew where they were going, and he didn't.
Cutting at an angle, Bolan dashed two aisles over then
sprinted straight ahead. The trees flashed by on both sides
of him, and he kept looking back, to move sure they
weren't behind him. He didn't know whether they were
armed, but had to assume they were, and that they were
willing to shoot.

The light was growing brighter ahead of him, and he realized he was heading for the edge of the grove. If he was
trapped in the open, he'd be an easy target. Bolan skidded
to a halt and listened for a moment. He could hear heavy
footsteps crunching on the sandy soil, but couldn't tell
where the pursuers were.

He squared up, facing toward the sound, and backed up
slowly. He left his guns holstered, unwilling to shoot at men
who, for all he knew, were just doing their job, chasing an
intruder who had no business on the property.

Bolan glanced up at the sun to get his bearings, and cut
off to the left, hoping to make his way back to the Renegade.

He no sooner got his bearings, than one of the pursuers
burst into the clear at the end of an aisle. "There he is," the
man shouted, and the second man burst into the open
about ten yards behind his companion. There was no longer
doubt whether they were armed. Each man carried a pump
action Remington shotgun fitted with a pistol grip.

The warrior ducked behind the nearest tree just in time,
the leaves over his head slicing into hundreds of tiny pieces

and raining down over his head and shoulders. Chips of bark scattered left and right as the heavy buckshot ripped into the tree. Bolan crouched and sprinted to a tree one aisle over.

If these guys were just doing a job, their employer was getting his money's worth. A second and third shot ripped into the trees, the pellets slamming like deadly hail into the trunks, slashing the leaves overhead as the shot spread out.

Bolan glanced up at the thick foliage overhead and grabbed a branch. If he was quick enough, he could haul himself up into the branches. He scrambled, his feet slipping on the smooth bark, and managed to get his legs up just as another blast of buckshot tore through the aisle and chewed at the bark of the next tree over.

Bolan clambered up through the thick leaves, trying to muffle the sound of his ascent. The men had stopped firing, and he could hear them whispering to each other as they worked in closer.

"You think we got him?"

"Hell, I don't know."

"Lucky the bastard didn't have a gun. These damn Remingtons aren't worth a damn when it comes to accuracy."

"With one of these fuckers, you don't have to be accurate, man. That's why we got 'em. You better shut up. How the hell can we sneak up on him if you keep runnin' your mouth?"

The men were just below him now, walking carefully, trying to dampen their steps, placing their feet carefully, one ahead of the other.

The lead man stopped and cocked his head. "Listen, you hear anything?"

The second man followed suit. "No, nothing..."

"You think we got him?"

"I didn't hear anything. Maybe the son of a bitch doubled back on us."

"Who do you think he was?"

"I don't know, but I'll tell you one thing—I'm gonna get on the horn to Calderone soon as we get back."

"What for?"

"What do you think?"

17

"I'll meet you in ten minutes." Bolan hung up the pay phone and walked the half block to Sipe's Renegade. Sitting behind the wheel, he paused for a moment and watched the street behind him in the rearview mirror. It was early, and the pedestrian traffic was light. He started the engine and flipped on the turn signal, then pulled out of the tight parking space. As he coasted to the light at the corner, Bolan noticed a late-model Ford slip into the lane behind him.

When the light changed, he sped through the intersection and slipped into the curb with a sudden jerk of the wheel. The maneuver caught the driver of the Ford by surprise, and he swerved into the opposite lane, then roared by waving an angry fist and glaring at Bolan through the side window. So much for the possibility the guy was a tail. If you were trying to follow somebody, the last thing you wanted to do was call attention to yourself.

Bolan pulled back into the traffic lane and cruised to the next light. The Ford was idling at the same intersection, and the driver turned around when he spotted Bolan in his rearview. The casual finger he flipped over the front seat sealed it.

When the light changed, the Ford laid a ten-yard patch, disappearing in a cloud of burning rubber. Bolan hung a left and covered the eight blocks to Ronny Sipe's office in five minutes. He left the Renegade in the dirt lot behind the building and climbed the stairs deep in thought. He'd been kicking around what Conlan had told him, and it was tempting to think the old sheriff might be onto something. But there was a long way to go from concept to confirmation.

For a moment he wondered whether the wily old man had set him up as a stalking-horse, somebody to go out on a side trail, just in case there was something there. It seemed almost too Machiavellian for Conlan, but Bolan couldn't shake the notion that there was more to the story than the sheriff had told him. At the top of the stairs he turned the corner, then stopped for a minute. The pieces kept rattling around in his head, and he couldn't think straight for the racket.

Reaching into his pockets for the keys to Sipe's office, he froze when the street door creaked softly, as if whoever opened it didn't want to be heard. Flattening himself against the wall, the warrior pulled the Beretta from under his denim jacket, holding it high over his head.

The wooden stairs creaked once, then again. A dull thud, almost inaudible, whispered up the steps. A door opened at the far end of the hall, its hinges creaking so loudly they covered any sounds from the stairwell. The door banged closed, and Bolan glanced hurriedly over his shoulder to see an old man with a cane coming his way.

Bolan brought the pistol down and checked the hallway across from him. Two doors down, chipped gilt lettering identified the men's room. He tucked the Beretta under his jacket and padded across the hall. The door didn't open immediately, and he cursed under his breath. He couldn't risk a shoot-out, not with the old man trapped in the corridor behind him. Instead, Bolan put his shoulder into the door, and the tenuous hold of the thick paint on the doorframe gave way.

The Executioner ducked inside and held his breath. He flipped off the overhead light and worked the door partway open again. Through the crack he watched the old man shuffle past, his rubber-tipped cane patting the floor in an irregular rhythm. A few seconds later a hulking figure strode past the door, but Bolan couldn't make out the man's features. The face seemed somehow familiar, but the bare overhead bulb was behind the man.

The warrior waited a long ten seconds, then started to pull the door open. The screech of protesting metal forced him to stop. The old hinges were too noisy. Pulling slowly on the handle, he painstakingly worked the door back an inch at a time. When he had it wide enough, he pressed his face close to the doorframe and peered out into the hall, just in time to see the denim-clad hulk step through the door to Ronny Sipe's office.

Bolan waited patiently, one ear cocked toward the stairwell. Randy Carlton was due any minute. Another door opened, and he dodged back into the doorway. Footsteps on the hard tile were interrupted by a door slamming, then a jangle of keys. Someone else had left an office, and Bolan let the door ease closed a little, putting his weight on the knob to dampen the squeal of the hinges.

A slender shadow speared across the floor, then stopped, and Bolan heard the sound of a briefcase hitting the floor. The body behind the shadow mumbled something, then scraped the briefcase on the tile as it was picked up. The hatless shadow began to move again, and Bolan thought for a moment the man was heading for the rest room. He let the door close a little more and waited. The footsteps approached in a stuttering rap on the floor, hesitated for a moment, then passed on. Bolan sighed with relief when he heard the sound of feet on the stairs.

Someone in the stairwell said a casual hello, his voice bouncing back up the stairs in a tinny echo. A second later Randy Carlton passed the open crack, and Bolan called to him in a hoarse whisper. The tall border patrolman stopped and turned in what seemed like slow motion.

Bolan yanked the door open and waved him in.

Carlton moved sluggishly, obviously still in pain. "What the hell is going on, Mike?"

"I don't know. Somebody just went into Sipe's office."

"Who?"

"I couldn't tell. He looked familiar, but I didn't get a good look at him."

"Probably just somebody stopping by to say hello. No big deal."

"I'm not sure."

"He come in before you or after you?"

"After."

"Anybody follow you?"

"No, I was careful about that. How about you?"

"I don't think so."

"Then we'll just wait here and see who it is."

"Why don't we go on down and say hello?"

"I thought about it, but I think we might get more out of it if we let him take us to his leader."

The two men continued to talk in whispers while Bolan kept his eye to the narrow opening.

"I sure hope we don't have to wait long. This isn't exactly the most covert surveillance I can imagine," Carlton said dryly. "Sooner or later somebody's gonna have to use the head. Then what do we do?"

"If you've got any better ideas, I wouldn't mind hearing them," Bolan snapped.

Twenty minutes later, there was still no sign of the anonymous visitor, and Bolan was beginning to get impatient. He regretted being so harsh with Carlton and was about to apologize when he heard a squeal at the end of the hall.

He stuck his head out just far enough to peer down along the wall. The hulking stranger surveyed the corridor, and satisfied that it was empty, backed out into the hallway as he pulled the door closed behind him. Bolan pulled his head back, confident that the intermittent light of the bare bulbs overhead had been too weak to betray him. A second later he heard footsteps heading back toward the stairway. This time the man no longer cared about being heard. The warrior eased the door a little wider, the Beretta gripped tightly in his hand. He saw the shadow on the floor bouncing along at a steady clip, the head wobbling slightly from side to side with each step. A second later the man passed the rest room door, and Bolan inhaled sharply. The heavy footsteps began to retreat down the stairs. Now he knew why the features had looked familiar.

"Allenson!" Bolan hissed. "What the hell is he doing here?"

"You sure it was him?"

"No doubt about it. You tell anybody you were meeting me here?"

"No, why?"

"I'd like to know a little bit more about Patrolman Allenson. Are you ready to admit he's in this about as deep as he can get?"

"I still don't understand how he could have a reason to be involved with any of this, do you?"

"Sure. I can name a hundred reasons. And his might not even be on the list."

"I guess I just give people too much credit."

"Maybe so. But I'll tell you what, after the talk I had with Ray Conlan, nothing would surprise me."

"Now wait a minute, Mike. I'm the first one to say I don't like the son of a bitch. He's an arrogant bastard and a bully. but it's still a long way between that and murder."

"You said yourself," Bolan argued, "that you weren't too sure who you could trust. Not even in your own outfit."

"But . . . I mean that was just frustration. Hell, I know some guys turn their backs once in a while, take a little under the table and all, but holy shit—"

"There's one way to settle it."

"Sure. We can catch up to him. 'Nice day, isn't it, Buck? Oh, by the way, just between us . . . you didn't happen to blow away my partner the other day, did you?' And of course he'll tell us. What could be easier?"

"Unless you can think of a good reason for Allenson to be here at the exact same time you were supposed to meet me, I think it wouldn't hurt to be a little skeptical." Bolan waited, and when Carlton didn't answer, he pushed a little. "Well, can you think of a reason?"

"No. I can't think of a reason. But it has to be a coincidence."

"You said you didn't tell anybody. He has no reason to be here on his own. That can only mean he came here because he knew you were going to be here."

"But how?"

"You tell me. You *are* being straight with me, aren't you, Randy?" Bolan flicked on the overhead light, and the small room was suddenly full of glare and harsh shadows.

"What are you suggesting?"

"I'm not suggesting anything," Bolan answered. "I merely asked a question. I'm waiting for a reasonable answer. Unless you have one, then I think we better assume the worst.''

"But I'm telling you I didn't say anything. Not to Buck, and not to anybody else. So he couldn't have known. Unless..."

"Unless what?"

"You said you called from a pay phone, right?"

"Yeah."

"Then...that bastard...somebody's been tapping my phone. How else could he have known?"

"And if your phone's been tapped, then whoever tapped it knew a lot more about what you, Ralston and Ronny Sipe were up to than you had any reason to suspect."

"That would explain how they knew what we were working on."

"And why they got scared. You must have been onto something, something you didn't even realize, and it spooked them. Whatever it was, they must have felt it was just a matter of time before you put all the pieces together."

Carlton grabbed the door handle. "Come on, let's follow him."

"Not yet. We know who to follow, but we have something else to do first."

"Like what?"

"We have to get the files Ronny was working on. That ought to tell us a lot. And while we're at it, we might as well check his office for bugs. Come on."

Carlton reached the doorway as Bolan stepped into the inner office. He knew right away something was wrong. The telephone receiver lay on the desk, its cover beside it. Whoever had taken it apart hadn't even bothered to hide the fact. Without looking, Bolan knew the files wouldn't be there, either.

"I guess that's that," he said. "They must have been through this place with a vacuum cleaner. The files were right there the last time I was here, on top of the cabinets. And Allenson didn't have anything with him when he left here."

"Don't worry about it, Mike. That's why they invented the photocopier. I have duplicates of everything we were working on. I told you we were moonlighting."

"Let's go take a look. I'm particularly interested in two names."

"What are they?"

"Tyack and Calderone."

"Never heard of Calderone. But if he's anything like Big Jaime, he's one mean mother."

18

Carlos Calderone sat on the elevated portico above the garden. Lounging in a lawn chair, he could see the rich green and sparkling water below him, the thick, high wall enclosing the garden, and the desert beyond. Not a drinking man, he sipped leisurely at a tall glass of orange juice, smacking his lips with satisfaction after each long draft.

Turning to the young man on the chaise longue beside him, he smiled. "So, Alfredo, how much longer before everything is ready, eh?"

"A day or two, Don Carlos, no more."

"You are pleased with the toys I bought you?"

"They are not toys, with all due respect, Don Carlos. They are very sophisticated machines. And, yes, I am very pleased."

"Did you think, when you were sweating your ass off in university, that you would land such a fantastic position as I have given to you."

"No, sir, I didn't. It is more than anyone has a right to hope for. I am very fortunate."

"I see you appreciate what I have done for you."

"Yes."

"Then perhaps you can answer a question for me, Alfredo." Calderone drained the last of the orange juice with a long, loud rush of air through the straw, carrying the last few drops from the tall glass. He slapped the glass on a marble-topped table by his elbow, but said nothing.

A moment later a slender young woman, her long black hair in a single ropelike braid down the center of her back, appeared out of nowhere, took the glass in one delicate hand and went back the way she had come. Alfredo stared after her, watching the pendular swing of the thick braid, its undulations alternately revealing and concealing the movement of her vertebrae as she walked. An exaggerated swing of her hips accented the suppleness of the spine, and Alfredo was mesmerized.

When she was gone, he turned back to his mentor, who was watching him curiously. "As I was saying, perhaps you can answer a question for me, eh?"

"If I can, yes, of course." Alfredo stumbled over the words, and felt his skin flush with embarrassment. "What would you like to know?"

"I would like to know when your system will be ready."

"I think in one or two more days. No more than that, certainly. Why do you ask?"

"Because I find that I am surrounded by people who are very good at promises, and very poor performers."

"The test went well, did it not?"

"You got the car where it was supposed to go, of course. That was impressive, but you see, a system cannot be evaluated in a vacuum. All its components must work in concert, no?"

Alfredo started to squirm in his seat. "That is true, but you cannot blame a computer for human error."

"So, you see my problem, Alfredo? Error. Human error. I think I have had enough human error to last me for quite a while."

"I understand, Don Carlos. I will push my men. It will be ready as soon as possible, I prom—"

"No, Alfredo. No promises, please. I have an important meeting this afternoon. I want to be able to give assurances. If I do, and can't deliver, I will look like a fool. That is something I do not wish to have happen. It is something I cannot afford."

"I agree."

"That is all well and good. But do you also agree, Alfredo, that it is something *you* cannot afford?"

Alfredo swallowed hard. This was a side of Don Carlos he had heard much about but never seen. It would be a good idea to watch his step. "Yes, sir, I do."

"It is a hard thing I am trying to do, Alfredo. Very hard. And I am not unaware of your contribution. But American businessmen have a saying. It is one I like because I have no choice but to abide by it. Do you know what that saying is?"

"No, Don Carlos."

"What have you done for me lately? That is a good saying, is it not?"

Alfredo stood up and looked out over the desert. He was beginning to see it in a new light. When he had first come to work for Carlos Calderone, he had seen the desert as a buffer, a kind of insulation to protect him from the intrusions of the outside world. Now he was beginning to understand that impregnability worked both ways. The world could not intrude on him. But he was trapped, a prisoner of his own device. There was no way he could escape, and if he understood the threat implicit in Calderone's oblique little lecture, he would soon regret it.

"I think I better get back to work. We still have to refine the satellite linkage to make sure we are in constant touch with the Comrail system. All of the major components of the system are operational. The only thing that remains to be done is to integrate them and let the computer take over.''

''I don't know exactly what you mean, Alfredo, but I'm sure you do. And I'm sure we will be in constant touch, eh?''

''Perhaps . . . perhaps you could come down later today. I could show you what we have already done. It is quite impressive, actually.''

''I'll think about it. But I must admit I am not accustomed to being invited to visit a room in my own house. That is unusual, is it not?''

''I meant no disrespect, Don Carlos, I—''

Calderone cut him off with an impatient hand. ''I am busy, Alfredo. Later, eh?''

Alfredo walked toward the sliding door across the patio. He watched Calderone's image in the polished surface of the door. It wasn't until he reached for the door handle, and saw a hand raised in a mocking salute, that he realized Calderone was also watching him. He opened the door and stepped inside, chilled to the bone even before he felt the first breath of conditioned air.

Calderone smiled.

Leaning back on the lawn chair, he closed his eyes, enjoying the feel of the heat on his skin. He liked its warmth, and he liked the scent of the sunlight, the way it reacted with his body and changed him. Carlos Calderone was proud of himself. He had come a long way in a short time. Six years ago he'd been scrambling for a living, pushing his ancient Chevy to the limit, making three, sometimes four runs a week, sneaking across the border in the dead of night.

That life seemed so distant now, and it was hard to imagine ever having lived it. He had made enough money to pay the bills, but there was never enough left over. Once the Border Patrol started installing motion detectors in the desert, it became a game of wits. When he caught on, he realized it was a game he could only lose. The detectors were unreliable, but the more of them there were, the riskier each transit became.

Going to jail, back then, hadn't been a problem. There were always ways to deal with that. The world had no shortage of upturned palms, especially *federale* palms, but greasing them was expensive, and took better than half of his earnings. Even if you weren't caught, you had payoffs to make. And if you got in trouble, the cost was high. It reached a point where he realized most of his labor was going to support the expensive taste of corrupt officials on both sides of the border.

That would have been hard enough to bear, but once the self-righteous bastards started playing both sides of the street, milking him for protection, then busting him and hitting his wallet a second time, he had had enough. That had been three years ago.

Now all the bile he had stored, the bitterness of being robbed by those who were supposed to uphold the law, was about to be released. It had been a struggle, but it was going to be worth it. Once he had started hiring coyotes to make the runs, splitting the take while they had all the risks, his bank account had grown dramatically. The richer he got, the easier it was to hire others to do the dirty work. It had gotten finally to where it was a point of pride to be working for Don Carlos.

And as his reputation among the coyotes grew, so did his business. Like a binary star, they circled around a common center, absorbing additional energy from every direction, simultaneously expanding and feeding one another. Now that he was reaching out across the border and starting to organize the growers, there would be no stopping him. At a stroke he could lock up the supply and the demand.

There were problems, of course, but nothing he couldn't handle. It was big time or bust. By the end of the year, he would have the world on a string.

Getting off the deck chair, he walked to the back edge of the portico and looked out over the desert. Already, off near the horizon, he could see small clouds approaching from every direction. In less than two hours he would unveil his master plan. Those who wanted to could buy in. Those who didn't could take their chances.

"GENTLEMEN, I SEE that some of you are not convinced that my little plan will work, even though you do not yet know what it is." Calderone stood at the head of a long table. He looked down the rows, fixing his eyes on each seated man in turn. "Am I right?"

Raul Ramirez, his shaved head gleaming under the indirect light from the ceiling, banged his fist on the table. At nearly three hundred pounds his size alone would have commanded attention. His reputation for bloodthirstiness was merely an embellishment. Ramirez was a careful man, but even so, stories about the swift and merciless revenge he exacted upon would-be welshers were legion. In one case he was said to have killed six men single-handedly, slitting their throats one by one while a henchman kept the migrant workers at gunpoint. When he had finished, he had turned the knife on his own man on the theory that a dead witness could do him no harm.

A can of beer in one huge fist, he rapped the table repeatedly with the other. When the room fell silent, Ramirez stood and walked to the head of the table to stand beside Calderone. "Give me one good reason I should cut you in on my business," he rumbled. "I do all right on my own."

"How much did you make last year?" Calderone challenged. "Tell us all."

"It's none of your damn business, Carlos." The table buzzed at the calculated insult of the first name only. Not even a "Señor Calderone" would have been respectful enough for Calderone's pretensions, but being called Carlos by a slob like Ramirez was insufferable.

Calderone bristled, but he wanted to prove a point. There was no sense ruffling any fence-straddling feathers. Not yet, anyway. "Raul," he said, smiling, "how can I possibly persuade you of the wisdom of my proposal if I have to argue in a vacuum? You don't have to tell me to the penny. A round number will be sufficient." Calderone patted the large man on the stomach. "You are more than comfortable with round things, aren't you?"

Those seated at the table tittered, then when Ramirez cursed good-naturedly, they broke into applause.

"In any case, I should wait until this afternoon when we are all here together. It is not a simple thing to explain, and I would rather do it only once."

"As you wish, Don Carlos." He didn't mean it, and everyone in the room knew it.

19

Randy Carlton was out front when Bolan pulled up. The rangy lawman bent gingerly to pick up a canvas bag and threw it into the back of the Renegade before climbing up into the passenger's seat. He pulled the door closed with a stiff arm, but it didn't catch. He had to reopen it and use the weight of his body to secure the latch.

"The shoulder's still bothering you, I notice."

"Not much. I don't have a good hook shot at the moment, but it's stiff more than anything else."

"You get all the stuff we need?"

"I think so. I got to tell you, though, getting electronic gear out the office without letting on was no easy job. I've been thinking about what you said, and I realize you were right. The thing is, if Buck's in somebody's pocket, you can bet he's not the only one."

"What makes you say that?"

"The easy answer is that Buck's afraid of the dark. A fuller answer is that the only way it could possibly be worth it to some big-time chicken merchant is if he could get everything he needs to know. There's no point in getting dribs and drabs, because the big picture is where it's at. Buck is no fool, but he's also no honcho. He wouldn't have access to everything he'd have to supply, at least not without high-level participation."

"Any ideas?"

"Nothing concrete, but I'm working on it. Anyhow, I couldn't take the chance that somebody might wonder why I need the gear, so I had to run a backdoor play. A couple of head fakes and some fancy footwork and here we are." He reached into the back and patted the canvas sack. "I hope you know how to use all this stuff, because anything with winking red lights and little buttons is beyond me."

"Don't worry about that part of it. How come you're wearing sneakers?"

"The boots were killing me. Every step seemed to rattle my bones, so I dug the old high-tops out of the closet. Pretty tough, huh?" Carlton laughed easily, tilting his head a little and letting it come from the gut.

Bolan started the Jeep. "Let's go see what Mr. Allenson is up to."

Carlton clapped his hands. "All right, show time!" He started whistling "Sweet Georgia Brown," accompanying himself with a catchy offbeat rhythm on his knees and thighs. Suddenly he stopped whistling and sighed.

"God, I love the Globetrotters. When I was little, I was so naive, you know. I mean, they always won, and I never thought anything about it. Hell, they were *so* good. It just made sense they would win. They were the good guys." He shook his head, and Bolan saw the gesture reflected on the inside of the windshield. "Too bad..."

"What's too bad?"

"That life isn't like that. Too bad I grew up. Too bad the good guys don't always win."

"Who says they don't, Randy?"

The patrolman laughed again, the momentary depression already a thing of the past.

He directed Bolan through a complicated series of suburban streets. The houses were spaced farther and farther apart until eventually long stretches of desert separated

them. In the rearview mirror Bolan watched the lights of
Preston change, first to isolated points, then to a dull haze,
an upside down bowl of faint illumination against the black
desert sky. The moon ahead of them bleached the night,
then passed behind the first cloud Bolan had seen since ar-
riving in Arizona.

A gigantic cumulus, the cloud glowed at its filamentary
edges as if it pulsed with an inner fire. Its passage across the
moon was more like that of something alive, the density
changing from moment to moment and the light behind it
throbbing, almost breaking free, then vanishing altogether.

"All right, slow down, now," Carlton said, whispering
as if he thought Allenson might overhear him. "It's just
ahead on the right."

Bolan eased the Renegade off the road. Nearly a mile
away a blocky shadow sat fifty yards or so back off the
road. There was virtually no vegetation, and distance was
their only cover. He turned off the engine and let the 4x4
coast away from the road until its momentum was exhausted. Then he reached over the back seat and hauled the
canvas sack into his lap.

With a small flashlight in one hand, he unzipped the bag
and spread the flaps on the bag with the other. A small
mound of black plastic boxes of varying sizes and shapes
sloped down and away from the center of the bag. Bolan
rummaged through the contents until he found what he was
looking for.

"That's one," he said. "Now for the receiver." He tossed
a few instruments aside, then grabbed a pair of look-alikes
and set the bag on the floor. "One of these ought to do it."

Finally he withdrew a small leather pouch and unsnapped the fastener. The pouch unfurled to reveal a set of

miniature tools, including several screwdrivers, needle-nosed pliers and an assortment of hex wrenches.

The warrior balanced the twin receivers on his knees and clicked both on. Then he switched on the smaller transmitter. Neither receiver responded to the beacon. Handing the light to Carlton, he said, "Here, hold this."

Turning the transmitter over, he thumbed open a sliding panel on the back, then brought the transmitter closer to the small pencil of light. The glittering green and copper of a printed circuit reflected the beam. In the lower left he found what he was looking for—a recessed setscrew, its tiny head tapped for a hex wrench. Slipping one of the wrenches from his tool kit, he tried it in the setscrew, but it was too large. He replaced the wrench and tried a smaller one. This time the wrench slipped easily into the screw head.

Turning the setscrew, he watched the receivers with one eye. Suddenly small red LEDs on both receivers started to wink. He continued to turn the screw until the lights winked off again, then backed up until the flashing red was brightest. With the frequency adjusted, he put the tool kit away and slipped the plastic lid back into place.

"That's it." Bolan turned off both receivers and slipped one into his shirt pocket, along with the tiny transmitter. He rezipped the canvas bag and returned it to the back seat. Yanking the door open, he stepped down to the desert floor. "Wait here, Randy."

He closed the door gently, and Carlton watched as he walked away in the moonlight, his clothing a pattern of neutral grays in the lusterless illumination. A moment later he was gone.

Bolan looked over his shoulder once or twice, trying to fix the location of the vehicle in his memory, then drifted slowly to the right, getting farther away from the highway. The big man settled into an easy lope over the dry earth, occasionally ducking low to pick up the blocky outline of Allenson's cottage. As he drew closer, he slowed his pace a little, conscious of the quiet around him, and of how easily sound traveled in the night air.

A faint crack of light slowly materialized out of the darkness, probably around a drawn curtain, and became a beacon for him. He was close enough now to distinguish contours among the shadows, and the details of the rear of the cottage began to take shape. Two dark bulks, probably vehicles, glinted in the shade against the house, and as he shifted direction, the front bumper of one fell into the moonlight, reflecting it from its chrome.

He slowed to a fast walk. Patting his pocket to make certain he hadn't lost the transmitter or the receiver, he dodged among a few scattered saguaros, which seemed more closely spaced as he drew closer to the small house.

When he was no more than a hundred yards away, he stopped. The house was isolated, and Allenson had no reason to expect an unwanted visitor at this time of night, but it didn't pay to be careless. Bolan got a fix on the rear of the cottage and dropped into a tight crouch. Easing forward cautiously, he angled for the left rear corner, where the car bumper was still visible. He was close enough to see the second vehicle, this one a chunky, squarish 4x4.

The light around the curtain seemed to flutter a bit, and Bolan realized the window was open. A soft purring sound, probably a fan, hummed in the darkness. The Executioner aimed for the window and slid in between the two vehicles. The car, a steel-blue Camaro with its spoiler painted the flat gray of primer, was up on blocks, and he was thankful he didn't have to decide which one should carry the transmitter.

Slipping between the Subaru four-wheeler and the house, he inched toward the front of the building and ducked down to find a suitable place to conceal the small radio beacon. A pair of powerful ceramic magnets would hold it fast to almost any part of the body or frame, but making sure it wouldn't be accidentally discovered wasn't as easy. He passed on the well behind the rear-mounted spare on the off chance of a flat tire.

Dropping to his stomach, he slid under the rear bumper, groping up in the darkness with one hand. Finally settling on a tight crevice where a flat strut with rolled edges supported the left rear panel, he rubbed mud and dirt off the metal until the surface under his fingers was smooth and free of grit. He slid the beacon up along the underside of the quarter panel while fighting the pull of the powerful magnets. When he had it where he wanted it, he let go and heard the sharp click as the magnets caught and slapped the hard plastic against the strut.

While he worked he heard the mumble of conversation drifting through the open window above him. It wasn't possible to understand what was being said, but Bolan was certain he'd heard no fewer than three voices. Hauling himself out from under the Subaru, he got to his feet and brushed the sand from his clothing. Unholstering the Beretta 93-R, he eased back between the 4x4 and the wall of the house.

He stopped at the window and leaned up against a screen. Through the narrow gap between the window frame and the curtain, he was just able to make out two men. He could see neither of their faces, but the size and coloring of the man on the right matched that of Buck Allenson. The other, visible only from the elbows down, was dark-skinned and slender. They were playing cards, but seemed more interested in their conversation than in the game. They were talking softly, as if they were afraid of being overheard.

Bolan strained to pick up their words, but the fan, sitting on a table just to the left of the window, was too loud. He worked his way around the back of the cottage. Another window, this one uncurtained and set high in the wall, was probably a bathroom. Bolan stood on tiptoe and could see over the high sill. The room inside was dark, but the door was open, and he could see all three men through the doorway. He'd been right about Allenson. The other two were both dark, either Chicanos or Mexican nationals. While he watched, Allenson stood and walked toward the doorway. Bolan ducked and pressed in against the wall.

Allenson continued to talk over his shoulder, raising his voice as he stepped into the room. A sharp block of light fell on the sand, and Allenson said, "Listen, let's get some shut-eye. I'm leaving at 6:00 a.m. sharp. If you boys don't want to walk, you'll be up and ready. I have to see Calderone at nine-thirty."

The rest of his words were drowned by a rush of water, but Bolan had already heard enough. Calderone wasn't a new name; he'd heard it before in Tyack's orange grove.

Now they were getting somewhere.

20

The light was very dim. A single pair of fluorescents, each with two of its four tubes dark, flickered from the ceiling. The whole room reeked of the acrid smell of burned ballast, the tarlike odor seeming to drip like fine mist throughout the room. Four hard wooden benches, arranged in a tight square end to end, sat at the center of the room, their backs surrounding a closed space full of old papers and crumpled paper cups.

The entire place had that stale, sweaty smell of a gymnasium locker room. Around the outside edge of the square formed by the benches, dark stains of old coffee seeped out in half-moons with tattered edges. Three of the outside walls were lined with wooden folding chairs, loosely chained together. Slats were missing from several backs, and more than one was missing a seat.

The desk was closed, its dark bulk occupying the fourth wall. A single bulb on a long chain dangled from the ceiling, shifting gently back and forth in the slight breeze churned up by a ceiling fan. The fan turned only slowly and wobbled from side to side, thrown off balance by its missing blade. The remaining three, coated with dust clinging to a sticky layer of oil, seemed uninterested in moving more than a token amount of the hot air filling the room.

Most of the chairs with seats were occupied by small men, little more than sinew and bone wrapped in rough cloth. They sagged and drooped, trying to get a little sleep in their discomfort, and looked like nothing so much as a band of destitute zombies suddenly stripped of life for a second time. The lucky ones, those who had come early and been willing to hold their ground, sprawled on the hard wooden benches, small bundles of spare clothing bunched into rough pillows under their heads and folded arms.

The San Carlos bus station was often closed but never empty. The northern edge of Sonora seemed to draw people like a magnet, from Guerrero and Yucatán in the distant south and Nuevo León in the east. There was no river between San Carlos and Arizona, just a line as imaginary as the comfort most of them would find if they managed to cross it. Generations had made the journey up and back, some men every year for as long as they could remember. They knew what it was like, and were stubborn enough to ignore that knowledge.

The disillusioned ones, those who had made the trip and come back with less than they had brought north, said nothing when they returned home. They remembered ignoring those who had been disillusioned before them. And they had themselves been ignored too often to bother trying to preach any longer to the unconvertible. But they no longer bothered to come to San Carlos. And no one missed them. In Mexico, as everywhere else, no one was so out of mind as he who was out of sight.

To those who did come, San Carlos was not merely a dusty, ragged town just large enough to escape being called a village. It was a staging area for dreams, a place where a rusty bus was as good as a golden chariot. If you wanted a ride, San Carlos was where you bought your ticket.

In the parking lot behind the bus station, a three-year-old Buick sat with its engine idling. Two men sat in the front seat. The passenger fiddled his hands in his lap, watching the man next to him in the driver's seat. The driver had angled the fur-covered rearview mirror down and to the left. With the dome light casting a yellow pall over the car's interior, he was busy rearranging the grooves in a thick, stiff pompadour. The car smelled of hair oil and imitation Aqua Velva.

"Shit, come on, man," the passenger said. "There's no ladies in there, Antonio, man. What you have to waste all this time for? Huh, man?"

"Fuck you, Angel. I got to look *right*. I don't look right, I can't work right, man."

"Next thing you tell me that sissy shirt you got on is extra especial."

"You don't like this shirt, man?"

"No, man, I don't like it."

"Why not, man? How come you don't like my shirt?"

"Because, man. That's why. Besides, man, it make you look like a fucking American candy-ass, man. That's another reason why I don't like your shirt, man."

"You know how much I paid for this shirt?"

"No, man. I don't care, neither."

"I bought this shirt in Neiman-Marcus, man. In Dallas. I paid two hundred dollars for this shirt, man. Feel that. Raw silk, man. Feel it."

"I don't want to feel your shirt."

"I tell you what, man. When we done tonight, I *give* you this shirt, man. You like that?"

"You give it to me?"

"Yeah."

"That shirt, you give it to me? For nothing?"

"Yeah. For nothing."

"All right, man. Thank you, man, really. I like it. I like that shirt. What color you call that?"

"Royal burgundy, man. That's what that color is."

"I like it. Thank you, man. That's a nice color."

"You welcome, man. Let's go to work now, okay."

"Yeah, sure. Okay."

"You really like the shirt?"

"Yeah, man. I do. It looks good on you. Real macho, like Omar Sharif or somebody, man. Really."

The driver slipped his comb into the pocket of the shirt and opened the car door. "I changed my mind, man. I think I'll keep the shirt."

The passenger shrugged. "Okay, man, whatever you say. You want to look like a faggot, go ahead." He opened his own door and got out of the car.

The two men continued to bicker as they walked around to the front of the bus terminal. Antonio grabbed his partner as soon as they reached the double doors leading into the waiting room. "Don't you fuck up now, Angel."

Angel looked hurt. "Aw, Tony, man, why you always putting me down? I know what to do."

"You say so. But you mess up, and you can forget about me, man. Calderone will be on your ass. Mine, too. I don't need that shit. I want to kill myself I can go home and stick my head in the stove. At least that won't hurt."

"You always worryin', man. Don't let Calderone get to you. He's a big talker, but he's interested in business. That's all he cares about. We deliver, we got no problem. And we always deliver, Tony, right?"

"If you say so. Let's go, then." Antonio pulled the doors open. "And, Angel, let me do the talking, all right?"

"Whatever you say, Omar."

Before Antonio could respond, Angel stepped through the open doors. Antonio followed him, then brushed past to get in front of his colleague. He stood with his hands on his hips, surveying the room for likely freight. This was only his second recruitment trip for Carlos Calderone, and he was anxious that it go smoothly. The first one had been only marginally successful, and Calderone was notorious for his short temper. The whole program was new, for Calderone as well, and Antonio knew he had some slack. What he didn't know was how much. And how he'd know when it had been played out.

He didn't want to find out, either.

Making his mind up was a complicated process. Choosing a likely candidate for transport was part instinct and part divination. The mystical element seemed to be the determining factor, and Antonio approached the problem with all the reverence of a newly ordained priest lifting the chalice for the first time. Reaching inside the royal burgundy shirt, he fingered a heavy gold crucifix and mumbled, "Here goes."

He crossed the room toward the benches, working on the assumption, inherently logical, that anyone on the bench was serious enough to have come early and persistent enough to have hung on. That seriousness and persistence translated into desperation in Antonio's mind. But that wasn't the hard part. The hard part was deciding, or rather divining, who had enough money to make it worth his while.

There was always bargaining, but that was no problem. For most Mexicans, regardless of station, bargaining was a way of life. It was in the air, or the soil, and came in mother's milk. Those who were desperate enough bargained because they couldn't afford not to. Those for whom money was no problem bargained just as hard, because the game was more important than winning or losing. As a result, there was no such thing as a fixed price.

But for the coyotes, the important thing was setting a price high enough. Nobody was willing to pay the full amount at the outset. Most of the chickens preferred to make three equal payments—one on reaching agreement, one on crossing the border and one on reaching their destination. The coyote shared the risk, but only when the third up front was satisfactory. He had to assume that his client might be lying to him. If a chicken beat you out of your money, you had three options: you could ignore it, but that was usually too risky. If word got out that you were too easy, you would be a sitting duck. You could take him back across the border and leave him where you found him. That, too, was risky, and it was twice as much work. Since most coyotes were about as interested in work as they were in reading Marcel Proust, that left option number three. Wasting the bastard. It was the easiest thing to do, and the one with least negative impact on future business. And if you got beat too often, all you had to do was raise your prices to make up the shortfall.

But now Antonio felt an added burden. He was negotiating for two. No one, especially Don Carlos Calderone, had said as much, but Antonio was operating on the assumption that if he got beat by a client, he would eat the loss himself. Don Carlos was a man of refined diet. Swallowing such a meal wouldn't appeal to him in the least.

Antonio dropped into a crouch alongside the head of a sleeping man. Reaching out with one manicured hand, he shook the man by his shoulder, gently at first and then, when the man started waking, more vigorously. "Hey, Chico, wake up, man."

The sleeper finally came to his senses and sat up, rubbing his eyes. "What's going on?" he asked. "Why do you wake me?"

Antonio held a finger to his lips. "Shh... Come on, Chico, don't wake everybody up, okay? We got to talk."

"About what?"

Antonio laughed with a conspiratorial wink. "You know, Chico. Where you headed?"

The man now stiffened a little, his sixth sense warning him to be careful. "Tijuana, to see my sister."

"Oh, sure. I get it. Ah, how you going, man? By bus, right?"

"Sure, by bus."

"You in a hurry?"

"Yes. Why?"

Antonio didn't answer right away. He knew the man was interested. And the man knew he knew. The deal was all but signed and sealed. The only thing at issue was price. "I think I can get you to *Tijuana* pretty quick." Antonio laughed, and nudged his client in the ribs with an elbow. Then he turned to the silent Angel. "Ain't that right, man? Can't we help Chico here to get to *Tijuana*?" The emphasis on the destination was now accompanied by an exaggerated wink.

"How much you want to pay, Chico?"

"That depends. How much is it?"

"Oh, I don't know. I think maybe that depends on how much you want to pay, eh?"

An extended period of haggling finally ended in agreement on the sum of 450 dollars.

"Okay, Chico, you get some sleep. We'll see you in the morning, okay?" The man nodded and he curled up again on his makeshift pillow.

Antonio moved around the square of benches, stopping on the far side in front of a tall, thin man who slept in articulated sections, folded like a carpenter's rule. He dropped to one knee and shook the sleeping man as he glanced at his watch.

"Hey, Chico, wake up, man," he whispered.

21

Mack Bolan watched the small red light on the dashboard wink on and off at regular intervals. Its rhythm was steady, even insistent, and the pulse began to stimulate a sonic echo in his head. An imaginary *beep...beep...beep...beep* kept chirping away. Bolan relaxed and let the rhythm take over.

They'd been on the road since just after sunrise. They had waited patiently all night long, taking turns napping in the close confines of the four-wheel-drive. Eventually the heightened expectations took their toll, and when the small green grid light first began to move, neither man noticed it.

The blip was almost off the tiny screen when Bolan happened to glance at the receiver, which lay on its side on the dash, tucked in up against the windshield glass. The sudden rumble of the engine coming to life woke Randy Carlton. For the first hour they were able to hang close enough on Allenson's tail to catch a glimpse of him now and then as he topped a rise and they topped another behind him.

The pursuit was steady and the pace rather relaxed. Long-range scrutiny through binoculars revealed the presence of three men. That one of them was Buck Allenson was an article of faith. Who the other two happened to be was a good question.

But now, as the green blip swerved off the screen and the Subaru struck out across the floor of the desert, it was no longer desirable to stick to Allenson's tail; they didn't want to get too close. The small blobs of light, red and green like a miniature Christmas motif, suddenly assumed a significance out of all proportion to their size. Neither man seemed willing to breathe normally, as if some careless gust of wind might extinguish one or both flames, leaving them in total darkness, despite the forbidding glare of a relentless sun in the cloudless sky overhead.

"I've been meaning to ask you something," Bolan said, taking one hand off the steering wheel to stretch an arm behind him.

"What's that?"

"The thing that puzzles me is that railroad car. How did it get to where it was? Ray Conlan told me it was supposed to be hundreds of miles away."

"Mistakes happen. Hell, if the railroads were perfect, there'd be more of 'em. I think it's that simple."

"Maybe, but I wonder..."

"Don't wonder too hard, Mike. We'll likely never know what happened."

"Look, I can accept a railroad car getting misplaced. I mean, it's a big system and there are hundreds of thousands of cars. I can also accept some poor souls getting locked in, either on purpose or by accident."

"Seems to me you don't really have a problem. You can accept those two things, and those two things are exactly what happened."

"Listen to yourself, Randy. Think about it for a minute. What do you think the odds are against either of those two things?"

"Pretty high, I guess."

"Damn right. And the odds on both of them happening to the same car?"

"Yeah, I suppose...math isn't my long suit. And probability theory isn't even in my vocabulary. I just take what's at face value, I guess. It works. So far, anyhow."

"But that isn't the half of it. Look, you admit it in small cases. Buck shows up at Sipe's when I'm supposed to meet you there. No way it's a coincidence, you say. And I agree."

"So? I still don't see what you're driving at."

"What I'm driving at is this..." Bolan pounded the wheel with the heel of one hand. "You know, if you ran the odds on each of these things through a computer, you'd be getting some pretty long numbers. You start asking the machine to figure all of them being unrelated, I think you'd probably need a new computer. The point is, there are too damn many fantastic coincidences. They're in little clusters, not superficially related in a single fabric. I'll grant you that. But that just makes it more unlikely that they're *not* connected. They have to be because it would be an even greater coincidence if they *weren't* related. Do you see what I mean?"

"No, but don't let that stop you." Randy laughed and reached into the back for a thermos. "You want some coffee while I have this thing open?"

"Not now, thanks."

"I wish we knew where that son of a bitch is going," Carlton said. "I've just about had it with riding around in the desert. I keep remembering the last time I was out here. With Will..."

Bolan glanced at him, but said nothing.

"You ever in a shoot-out like that?"

"Yup."

"Yeah, maybe so, but I mean, did you lose your best friend."

This time Bolan remained silent, but nodded.

"The war? Vietnam?"

"I don't want to talk about it, Randy. Okay?"

"Sorry."

Carlton turned his face to the side window. Watching the desert go by, he felt desolated, as if he carried too much of the desert inside himself. For a moment the world outside the Jeep seemed to be a metaphor for his entire life. It was as if someone had managed to project it on a gigantic screen, and it overwhelmed him.

He had always loved the desert. Whenever he thought about it, he would smile. It was a place he went to think, to explore his life for hours, sitting in his beat-up convertible, leaning back with the top down under the stars. He didn't even know how many long nights he'd spent revelling in the brutal aridity. It was pure, and that, he knew, was what had attracted him so strongly. But that was all ruined now. He could no longer look at the desert without thinking of Will Ralston.

He turned away from the searing glare and stared at the blinking red light on the receiver. He watched it closely, as if mesmerized by its predictable rhythm. The green locator was pale in the bright sunlight, and he paid little attention to it. Lulled, almost asleep, it took him several moments to realize the green light had drawn closer to the bottom edge of the grid. They were drawing closer to Allenson's 4x4.

"He must have stopped," Carlton said. "We're coming up on him pretty quick."

"I know. I've been watching it."

"Don't you think we ought to stop, too?"

"Not yet. If he stopped, it was for a reason. We won't know what it is by sitting here."

"What do you think's going on?"

"Unless your friend Buck came all the way out here for a picnic, I'd have to guess that he's meeting somebody."

Bolan swung the wheel to the left, and the vehicle started to drift off line.

"Where the hell are we going?"

"I want to get as close as I can, but if he turns around and comes back this way, he'll spot us. If we come in from the side, we might be able to see what he's up to."

Bolan eased the Renegade forward, watching the green blip on the locator grid. They were less than two miles behind Allenson. At one mile the Executioner stopped the vehicle and killed the engine. He grabbed a pair of binoculars and yanked the door open. He dropped to the ground and said, "Randy, you keep an eye on them. I'll use the other beacon to get as close as I can. If he starts moving back this way, head due west from here, and I'll get to you as soon as I can. If he keeps on toward Mexico, pick me up."

"You sure you don't want me to go, Mike?"

"Not in this heat, Randy. You need to get your strength back."

Bolan waved and started off at an easy lope. Carlton climbed down out of the Renegade and watched him, amazed at the big man's seemingly inexhaustible energy. He moved as comfortably under the desert sun as if he had been born and raised there.

When Bolan had dwindled to little more than a stick figure, Carlton took his own glasses and swept them across the landscape. Looking straight along the line intersecting Allenson's location, he saw something that chilled him to the bone.

Low on the horizon, like a glittering insect, a helicopter was headed straight toward him. It was several miles away, coming in from the south, but there was no mistaking what it was. For an instant he wanted to climb into the Jeep and race after Mike Belasko, but any movement on his part might call attention to him. If he stayed where he was, they might overlook him. And there was always the chance, he told himself, admittedly slim, that there was no connection between Allenson and the chopper.

Even as the patrolman considered it, he dismissed it. Belasko had been dead on when he talked about the frequency of apparent coincidences. There were no such things. And there was no more innocence.

The whole fetid mess smelled to high heaven. And coming out of the Mexican sky, at this precise moment, there was no way in hell that chopper was there by chance alone.

22

"Hey, Chico. Rosalita's Cantina, one hour, eh?" Antonio covered his mouth with his hand. Anyone more than three feet away would have thought he was just politely stifling a cough. The man he'd addressed looked at him with big eyes as if uncertain about what had been said.

"Hurry, Chico. Rosalita's, one hour. Let's go." Antonio swaggered away, his eyes darting nervously around the interior of the bus station. If possible, it was even darker during daylight than it had been the night before. The dim bulbs overhead were swallowed by the glare pouring in through the tall, narrow windows and the glass front doors.

Dropping casually onto one of the hard wooden benches, Antonio watched Angel in the doorway. He was acting more comfortable than he really felt. This was his first major run for Don Carlos, and he wanted to do well. Of the nine men he had lined up the previous night, he had so far found five. He started to stand again when the telltale flurry of activity that always signaled the arrival of the *federales* sent people on the sidewalk outside scurrying in every direction.

The usual procedure was to sit tight and see which of the policemen he knew. If both members of the two-man team were strangers, he'd simply walk away. A run with five chickens was better than no run at all. If he knew one or both, he would simply spread a little of the wealth around,

round up the remaining four and be off for a quickie at the local whorehouse before meeting his clients at Rosalita's.

But that was the old days. He wasn't working for himself now. He was taking orders, and although he wasn't sure he liked the idea, he knew better than to cross Carlos Calderone. No fewer than three of his friendly competitors had disappeared in the past few months. No one knew for certain what had happened, but there were rumors. And in a country fueled by idle gossip, rumors were more than sufficient.

As the people outside milled around, Angel drifted toward him, pretending to be absorbed in a newspaper. When he reached the bench, Angel turned to look at the vacant seat behind his knees, backed up a step, then fell onto the bench.

Spreading the paper out and raising it to cover his face, he whispered. *"Federales."*

"Who?"

"Nobody I know."

"Shit!"

"What are we going to do?"

"Wait."

"How long? We only have an hour. We wait too long, we miss the pickup. We miss the pickup, we get our balls in a pickle jar. I'm not ready for that."

"You make it sound like Don Carlos is some kind of savage. He's nothing of the kind."

"You think so?"

"Of course not! He's a businessman. Even now there's a meeting at his house—like the board of directors in a big company. This is gonna really be some operation. Besides—" Antonio leaned in to whisper through hands cupped over Angel's ear "—if he hears what you said, he might be angry, and we could lose a soft job, eh?"

"Uh-huh . . . I know what you mean. You seen Mendoza lately?"

"Who?"

"Mendoza, Felipe Mendoza. The one with all the Donna Summer tapes."

"Him. No, I haven't seen him. But what does that matter? He's a pig. Do you know what Luisa told me?"

"Who?"

"Luisa, from La Dicentra."

"The whorehouse?"

"Yeah."

"No. What did she tell you?"

"She said Mendoza wears silk underpants. Tiny things, like a woman wears."

"He has expensive taste, eh?"

"That's not the point. The point is, Mendoza is . . . he's a little, you know . . . funny."

"So?"

"So maybe he got himself into trouble. With that fancy underwear of his, no? It could happen."

"Maybe. So you're saying we shouldn't worry about no one seeing Mendoza. Not even if they found his car in the desert. And even if his shoes and wallet were in the sand alongside the car. Is that what you're saying?"

"His shoes?"

"Yeah, his shoes."

"Aha!" Antonio sat back, as if the interjection were the last word, and pretended to be dozing. He watched the *federales* through slitted eyes.

The policemen pushed their way into the waiting room, now very quiet. They turned to the left as soon as the door banged closed behind them. In a slow orbit of the room, they stopped every now and then, sometimes leaning forward to peer into averted eyes. As they drifted out of his view, Antonio whispered instructions to Angel, then got to his feet. He began to move toward the door, walking slowly, as if he weren't sure where he was going.

As his hand touched the tarnished push plate on the wooden door, he heard a sharp bark. "Just a minute. Stay where you are."

Antonio turned, wearing what he hoped was an expression of surprised innocence. "You talking to me, Officer?"

The two policemen took their time joining him at the doorway, their studied swagger overdone a little.

"You seem to be in a hurry," one of them said.

"Oh, yeah. Well, I just remembered something I forgot."

"Oh? And why were you here in the bus station to begin with?"

"I was waiting for my mother. She's coming to visit me."

"And you were going to leave her here alone, with no one to greet her?"

"No, I was coming back."

"I see. Maybe we should step outside, eh?"

"Whatever you say, Officer." Antonio turned and pushed the door open just as the blunt end of a riot baton was planted between his shoulder blades. He stumbled through the open door, nearly falling facedown on the littered sidewalk.

He scrambled to his feet with a clenched fist, coiling his body into a tight crouch. He came up ready to swing when the baton caught him on the left shoulder, knocking him back down. He lay on his back, holding the shoulder and moaning. His left arm was numb. He closed his eyes to block out the bright sun beating down on his face. The *federale* planted a foot on Antonio's stomach and leaned forward, then poked him under the nose with the end of the baton.

Antonio opened his eyes slowly, blinking in the glare. He looked past the cop's leg and saw Angel, one arm twisted behind his back in the grasp of the second *federale*. Angel put a finger to his lips, then winced as the cop jerked his arm a little higher.

"You ready to listen, my friend?" the *federale* asked, pressing his foot a little harder. "Huh?"

"Yeah, man, yeah. I'll listen. What's the problem? I wasn't doing anything."

"Maybe we should take a ride, eh, Ricardo?" The cop turned to look at his partner, who was grinning broadly.

Ricardo jerked Angel's arm for emphasis and said, "Yeah, let's take a ride. I'll get the car."

He shoved Angel forward, letting go of the man's arm at the last second, and Angel spun in a half circle, then grabbed his shoulder. "What you have to do that for, man? I didn't do anything to you. I didn't even say anything, man."

The cop ignored him and walked to the corner of the bus station. Antonio tried to get up, and the cop with the baton pushed him back down, then raised the baton and threatened to hit him again. A moment later a Jeep Cherokee backed out into the street with a blare of its horn. Pedestrians standing near the curb scattered out of the way, and the cop with the baton laughed.

"Okay, you, get up," he said. Hanging the baton from his belt, he unsnapped his holster, resting his hand on the butt of his pistol. He looked over his shoulder at Angel. "Get in first."

Angel did as he was told, backing toward the Cherokee and watching the man's gun hand. When Angel was seated in the back, Antonio felt the sharp prod of a boot in his ribs. "Get up, asshole." The cop backed off just a bit, and Antonio got to his knees. His shoulder still hurt and his ribs ached. He climbed into the rear of the Cherokee, looking over his shoulder at the grinning *federale*.

Getting into the front seat, then closing the door after him, the cop turned to rest his chin and arms on the back of the front seat. "So, where shall we go?" His voice was muffled by his arms.

"What?"

"I asked you where we should go, asshole. Can't you hear?"

"How do I know, man? I mean, this is your fucking idea."

"Watch your language, asshole. This is an official police vehicle." He laughed, but there was no humor in it. Antonio thought it sounded like the bark of a hungry coyote.

The driver, as if tired of waiting for the two men to decide on a destination, pulled into the traffic, narrowly missing a passing car. "I guess we'll just ride around for a while, huh?"

"What do you guys want?" Antonio asked. His voice sounded high and thin to his ears. The mixture of fear and frustration made his throat feel tight. He breathed in long, shallow gasps, and his mouth was dry. It felt as if it were coated with a thin paste.

"You think we want something?"

"Sure, doesn't everybody?"

"I don't know. What do *you* want?"

"I want to get out of the car, man. That's what I want."

"You think we can just let you go?"

"Why not? We haven't done anything."

"That's for us to decide. Not you."

"Okay, man, how much?"

"What?"

"How much?" Antonio reached for his wallet. The movement made his ribs throb, but he ignored the pain. All he could think of was getting out of the Jeep.

"You trying to bribe us?" The cop grabbed the wallet and opened the billfold.

"No, man, no. What do you think I am?"

"You mean you're not trying to bribe us? Then what do you need all this money for?"

"Nothing. I don't need it for anything, man."

"You know," the cop said, lowering his voice and frowning, "my mother is very sick." He nodded to his partner. "And his mother, too. Both our mothers are very sick."

"I'm sorry to hear that, man. I really am."

"Medicine is expensive, too. Very expensive."

Antonio turned to Angel with a grin. "You know what I think, Angel, man? I think we should help these guys out. They can't make too much money. And both their mothers are sick. Isn't that something?"

"Yeah, man, that's really something. Maybe we can buy the medicine for their sick mothers."

Antonio shook his head. "We could do that, man. But I got a better idea." He snatched the wallet and counted out two hundred thousand pesos. Folding the bills, he handed them to the cop. "Here, man, take it. For your mother."

The cop looked at the bills. "What about his mother?" he asked, indicating his partner.

Antonio slapped himself in the forehead. "What am I thinking of?" He counted out another two hundred thousand, then added several more bills. "For bus fare," he said.

"You don't have to do that," the cop said.

"No, I want to. *We* want to. Take it." He folded the cop's fingers tightly around the bills. "You keep it."

The driver pulled over to the curb. The cop in the passenger seat reached into the rear and opened the door. Antonio got out slowly, holding his ribs. When Angel joined him on the curb, the Jeep pulled away.

"Good thing their fathers are dead," Antonio said, gritting his teeth. "We couldn't afford medicine for four old people."

"You know what I'm thinking?" Angel asked.

"What?"

"You know how much medicine we could buy if we had the money Don Carlos has?"

23

On the outskirts of San Carlos Mack Bolan pulled the Renegade into a dusty parking lot in front of the Cantina La Paloma. He turned off the ignition and looked at Randy Carlton. They were both hungry and thirsty, and the place looked as good as any.

"This place looks like Germany after the war," Bolan said.

"That's Mexico for you." Carlton stared through the windshield as he spoke. "You know, I've been in a hundred places just like it. It's no damn wonder these people try to sneak up north."

Carlton opened his door and stepped down from the 4x4. He walked around to the driver's side and leaned on the open window. "When we get inside, watch your back, Mike. Gringos aren't too popular around here. This isn't exactly tourist heaven."

He stepped back from the door and waited while Bolan rolled the window up and climbed out. "Make sure it's locked."

Leading the way into the cantina, Carlton nodded at an old man in an armless rocker on the wooden porch. The old man ignored him, just a trace of a smile curling the corners of his thin lips. As Bolan walked past, the old man turned his head slightly, as if he were seeing something out of the ordinary. Bolan felt the porch floorboards throbbing under his feet in response to the blaring jukebox inside. When the two men pushed through the door, the old man turned back. There was no trace left of the sardonic smile. The music stopped suddenly, and the carnival glare of the jukebox went black.

Inside, the darkness was thick with conversation and the smell of overcooked rice. A sharp tang of chili cut through the background odors. The conversation came to a sudden, deafening halt as Randy Carlton led the way to a vacant table in front of the dusty, grease-smeared window. He scraped back a chair and sat on an angle, one shoulder canted toward the interior of the room, the other up against the dirty glass.

Bolan joined him at the table, conscious of a hundred eyes watching his every move. He turned his own chair a little and repositioned the table under Carlton's elbow. The noise of the moving furniture was the only sound, except for the continuous racket of pots, pans and dishes in the kitchen.

The Executioner checked the radio beacon by tilting his pocket forward enough to see the winking lights. "I can't figure why Allenson drove all this way," he muttered. "He sure as hell didn't come here for lunch."

"San Carlos is coyote country, Mike. My guess is he's here to pick up a month's pad."

"I'm not so sure about that, Randy. Seems like a lot of trouble. Unnecessary trouble."

"Maybe so, but the coyotes don't much like it north of the border. Too risky. They don't want to go roaming around up there, and the last thing they need is for some illegal to see them talking to somebody from the Border Patrol. It's bad for business. There are very few secrets on either side of the border."

Carlton turned to look over his shoulder at the Jeep. A crowd of small children milled around the vehicle. One, a little taller than the others, reached out with a bony arm and ran his fingers through the accumulated grit on the driver's door. There was something almost reverential in the gesture.

Bolan watched the kitchen expectantly. Through a glassless window in the center of the rear wall, he could see a cook working over a pair of blackened stoves. A dark-haired woman, her round face like a dark moon in the lightened rectangle, leaned forward to watch them for a long moment. Behind her, curls of steam rose in the air and hung like a pale cloud. She vanished almost as suddenly as she had appeared, then a block of light flashed in one corner as a door to the kitchen opened.

A moment later she was at their table, wiping her hands on a grimy apron. "*¿Señores?* What can I do for you? You are lost, no?"

"How's your chili?" he asked.

"*Caliente, muy caliente, señor.*"

"Two chilies, *señorita*, and two beers, please."

She took a pencil from her tightly wound hair and a pad from a pocket in the apron. After she had written up their order, she continued to stare at them.

"Anything else?" she asked.

"No, that'll do for now."

"You sure?"

"Yes, why? Is there something you want to recommend?"

She looked at Carlton, her face a flat, impassive mask. She tapped the pencil, eraser first, on the pad. "Two chilies and two beers. That to go?"

"No."

She shook her head slowly. Bolan watched the woman curiously. She obviously had something on her mind, and just as obviously didn't know whether to broach the subject. "That's what I'd recommend," she said. She turned abruptly and walked back to the corner of the room. A moment later the block of light opened in the wall, and she was gone.

Carlton turned to Bolan and whispered, "What the hell was that all about?"

Bolan shook his head. "I have no idea."

Continuing to whisper, Carlton leaned forward, keeping one eye on the Jeep. "There are probably a dozen chicken runners in here right now. I don't imagine too many white faces stop in asking for beer and chili."

The conversation around the room gradually resumed, starting as a sibilant undercurrent and slowly building in volume. By the time the woman returned with their order, the raucous thunder of the jukebox had been restored, but every other eye in the cantina was still directed at their table.

"I guess we don't canvass the room, asking if anyone here knows a Señor Calderone, do we?" Carlton asked.

"I think if we stick on Allenson's tail, we'll find him. I just wish to hell we knew more than a name. It's not exactly an uncommon one."

"If he's the one we want," Carlton replied, "they'll know who we mean."

He broke a piece of bread from a warm loaf and dipped it into the chili. As soon as he took a bite, he immediately reached for the beer. He fanned his open mouth with one hand. "Great chili." He was about to say something else when he stopped with his mouth still open. "We've got a problem."

Bolan turned to see what he was staring at. Buck Allenson stood on the sidewalk across the street, talking to three men. His back was to the cantina, but there was no mistaking the big man. One of the three kept glancing at the Renegade, and once reached out to point at the cantina, but Allenson stiffened, grabbed the extended arm and wrenched it down.

"Sit tight, Randy. If he doesn't know we saw him, we'll have the upper hand."

"The last time I had the upper hand, I got myself shot up. I'm not about to let that happen again. I have a score to settle with that son of a bitch." He started to rise out of his chair, but Bolan reached across the table and yanked him down.

The younger man watched the animated conversation through the window, trying hard not to stare. "There he goes, Mike."

"What about the other three?"

"They're still there."

"Okay, watch where they go."

"What about Buck?"

"Don't worry about him. He's only a little wheel in a big machine. We'll get him, but we want bigger game than he is. Don't forget that. You blow his brains out and you'll feel good for a couple of minutes. But as soon as you realize there's somebody a lot worse out there, how will you feel?"

"Why do you have to be so damned logical?"

"If I weren't, I wouldn't be sitting here now. And neither would you."

Carlton hung his head. Bolan watched the younger man clench and unclench his fist as it lay on the table between them. He knew the temptation the guy was struggling against. But more importantly, he knew, as Carlton didn't, the consequences of giving in to it.

Finally the patrolman looked up. "Okay, you win. What do we do now?"

"Finish our chili. It might be awhile before we get to eat again."

BOLAN CLIMBED behind the steering wheel and leaned over to unlock the door for Carlton. Randy slammed the door closed behind him and reached between the bucket seats into the back. He slipped a Browning automatic into his lap.

"You still see him?" Bolan asked.

"Yeah, he's in the alley across the street. I don't know what happened to the other two."

"It doesn't matter. As long as they're still interested in us, we can hook that fish any time we want to."

"What now?"

"I think we might as well find a place to stay. Any ideas?"

"What am I, a tour guide? I've been here once, Mike."

"Then let's go look for the local version of a Holiday Inn."

Carlton snorted. "The only thing they'll have in common is a nosy clerk. I can guarantee that."

Bolan backed into the street, swung in a half circle and headed into the heart of San Carlos. They steered through the town's traffic, narrowly avoiding a collision with a careering taxi, which roared off with its fenders flapping. In the uproar on the sidewalk that followed the near miss, Bolan noticed a rusty green Oldsmobile slide away from the curb and slip into the traffic three cars behind him.

The heart of the town was busy, but no less run-down than the outskirts, and as the traffic thinned, the Renegade was able to make decent time. At a crowded intersection, Carlton rolled his window down and asked directions

to a hotel. He realized it was unnecessary to follow the rapid
Spanish as he glanced in the direction pointed out by an old
man with a pushcart.

Bolan hung a right and nudged the Renegade through the
teeming side street. The green Oldsmobile also made the
turn, but pulled over just past the corner. A faded red ar-
row, inscribed with the word Estacionamiento, directed
them down an alley, and Bolan pulled in between two brick
walls. It was a tight squeeze, and he had to roll down his
window to tug the sideview mirror in toward the door.

The parking lot behind the hotel was empty. Bolan and
Carlton climbed down and hauled their light luggage out of
the rear, then locked the 4x4. They walked into the hotel
lobby through a side door just off the parking lot.

A tiny clerk, barely visible over the front desk, checked
them in, then stepped around the desk to lead the way to
their room. The creaky elevator seemed uncertain whether
it wanted to reach the third floor. The clerk unlocked the
door and extended an open palm in a less than subtle hint.
Carlton obligingly slipped a bill into the tiny hand. Before
closing the door, the clerk informed them that toilet facil-
ities were to be found at the end of the hall.

"God," Carlton said, "what a dump."

"All in the line of duty, Randy."

The patrolman laughed. "Now I know what combat pay
is all about. I'll bet the bugs in this place are bigger than I
am." He hefted his overnight bag and dropped it on one of
the two single beds. The sluggish springs continued to rock
for several seconds, and he shook his head. "Shit! I forgot
my medicine in the glove compartment. I'll be right back.
You want anything while I'm downstairs?"

"No, thanks."

Carlton stepped into the hall and started for the elevator. Then, realizing it was probably quicker to walk, he ducked into the stairwell.

Bolan sat on the edge of the bed and considered his options. A few moments later he heard a soft knock on the door. Drawing his Beretta, he walked to the door and pressed his back against the wall. "That you, Randy?"

When there was no answer, he reached for the knob, then hesitated. The door burst open almost immediately, and three men lunged into the room. Bolan fired at point-blank range, nailing the last man in the center of the back. The crack of vertebrae sounded like snapping twigs, and the man fell to the floor. His two companions whirled, one stitching the wall behind Bolan with a sustained burst from a silenced Uzi.

The warrior dived to the floor, the 9 mm stingers gouging plaster from the walls. Bolan squeezed off another round, catching the sluggish gunner on the left cheekbone. Incredibly the man continued his spin, the Uzi spitting the last rounds in its magazine before he fell backward onto the nearer bed.

The third man, obviously unprepared for this kind of resistance, backed up, raising one hand over his head. But the silenced .45 in his other hand was still wavering. Bolan watched the man for a heartbeat, then, as the pistol swung in his direction, the warrior fired a 3-round burst, catching the surprised hit man in the chest. The impact hurled him back against the window, where he seemed to hesitate for just a moment before the glass gave way with a shriek. Then he pitched backward, carrying broken glass and window frame with him to the ground three stories below.

Bolan got to his feet slowly, swinging the Beretta toward the gaping doorway. Catfooting to the opening, he peeked out into the hall and saw that it was empty. He holstered the

Beretta and was halfway across the room when four *federales* filled the doorway.

"That was fast."

"*Señor*, you are under arrest. Please come with us."

"Under arrest for what?"

The lieutenant in charge smiled. "You *narcotraficantes* are such kidders." He snapped his fingers and waved to an underling. "Take his weapons."

24

Carlos Calderone was in his glory. Standing under a huge skylight at one end of the hall, he paused with his hands on the podium. It was a calculated move, the kind of histrionics he admired from American movies. He could feel the heat from the sun as it poured through the crystal-clear glass and splashed over the podium and the stark white wall behind him.

He looked up at the sun, its outline blurred by the glass, and watched his own blood through closed lids. He could see the delicate network of veins and the throb of his pulse as the lids reacted to every beat of his racing heart.

He looked out over the audience members, relishing their presence precisely because they were there whether they wished to be or not. What made this gathering so sweet was the fact that these men, among them, had probably killed several hundred people and yet *they* were frightened of *him* and unwilling to spurn his invitation. He raised his hands to quiet the murmuring and tapped the microphone to make certain it was working. The echo of his tapping finger bounced throughout the hall.

"My friends, welcome to my home." He paused for effect, then waved his hand at the far wall where a dozen men in crisp black uniforms wheeled in a table stacked with glasses and a dozen ice-filled salvers. Quickly with the economy and precision of a well-coached drill team, the group split into pairs and moved to the end of each table.

Calderone gave another signal, and the teams went to work, one man swiftly and quietly placing a champagne glass in front of each guest, while the other filled the glass nearly to the brim.

"Don't worry about the champagne, gentlemen. I assure you the vintage is ideal. And the price is of no concern. Nothing is too good to celebrate the commencement of a grand adventure like ours."

The men murmured, raspy whispers cutting through the general undertone. When each guest had been served, a waiter mounted the stairs in front of the podium and presented a glass to Calderone himself.

"We will toast now before I explain to you what it is we are toasting. I am sure you will all indulge me in my taste for the mysterious. And I believe you know enough about me to believe that I would not have called you all here if it were not important."

Calderone hoisted the glass high over his head, where the sun flashed like fire, its light refracted by the shimmering wine, and spilled rainbows onto the white wall. Then, when every eye was on the elevated glass, he said, "To our future," and took a long sip.

The audience emulated him, hoisting their own glasses and echoing the sentiment.

"Very well," the flesh merchant continued, "let me explain to you what this is all about. As you know, we share a common business. As you also know, a great deal of effort and not a little money goes into the competition among us. For quite some time, as I am sure you are all aware, I have been expanding my business on the theory that what works for Pemex and General Motors would also work for me."

He paused again and took another sip of champagne. Watching their faces, he could see they were far from convinced. Many in attendance envied him; others resented him. Calderone didn't kid himself. More than half of the men below would kill him if they got the chance. But he didn't hold it against them, could understand why and even agreed with their reasoning. He had expanded to their detriment, and no man loves one who takes food out of his mouth.

But that was personal, and this was business. What he hoped to do was to make them see the wisdom of his plan. That wouldn't be easy. Small minds didn't handle large questions very well, and the ease with which he had built his empire was proof that most of the men gathered before him had small minds.

"You have all seen this place. Like you, I started with nothing. And this," he said, waving his hand in a broad circle, "is all the proof you need that I was right."

He waited for the men to look around them. That they were impressed was obvious. That they were envious was also transparent, but the crucial question was whether they were intimidated by what they saw. Anticipating them, he continued, "Now, I know some of you are saying 'Who is Calderone? What does he have that I don't have? If he started with nothing, then I am no worse off than he was at the beginning. If he can do it, why can't I?' And I don't blame you for asking such questions. They are the very questions I asked myself a few short years ago. But I not only can give you the questions, I can also give you the answers. You can't do what I have done for one very simple reason—*I won't let you!*"

An angry buzz filled the room. Before it could get out of hand, he leaned into the microphone and raised his voice to shout, "Would you permit it if you were in my place?" The edge to his voice and its increased volume hushed the crowd again.

Calderone smiled. "Of course you wouldn't. You know it and I know it. But that does not mean that I am a greedy man. Not overly greedy, anyway." He smiled at his own joke, and a few nervous titters joined in. "But I am reasonable, and I am fair. What I propose to you is that you all join me. I know you cherish your independence, just as I do. But if you are practical, you will see that I can offer you benefits more valuable than independence. I can bring to the table assets that none of you can match... organization, expertise and technology. To some of you, those are just words. You are proud men. I know that. But there is more to technology than a ten-year-old Chevy. And I don't mean just a good stereo system."

One of the men toward the rear of the room stood up. "Fuck you and your technology," he shouted angrily. A few approving murmurs echoed the sentiment, but others shouted him down.

Calderone held up a hand to quiet them. "Let him speak. He is only saying what a lot of you are thinking. If I can't convince him, I don't deserve your attention anyway. Raul, come on up here." He waved the angry man toward the podium.

Raul Ramirez looked around him uncertainly. Several men seated near him were leaning forward, urging him to accept the challenge. He took a tentative step forward, then staggered as a thrust from behind propelled him ahead faster than he was willing to go.

Calderone scrutinized Ramirez as he mounted the steps. The man was slovenly, his clothes rumpled and spotted with grease. A generous stomach protruded over a ragged belt from which the leather was cracked and peeling, and the tip of which was pitted with several makeshift holes made with a nail as Ramirez's girth had increased. A two-day growth of beard, long hair combed back behind the ears and shiny with oil, and the overly sweet fragrance of five-and-dime cologne completed the image. Ramirez was everything Calderone had come to hate. He resembled too much what the businessman had once been, and resembled too closely the men who had given him his start.

The Carlito who had started out in his early twenties had been buffed and polished until no one would recognize him now. No one, that is, but Don Carlos Calderone himself, who couldn't look in a mirror without seeing the young man he had been, buried, but not hidden, under the grand exterior.

Calderone swallowed his distaste and grasped Ramirez by the hand. He shook it firmly, conscious of the dirty cuff of Ramirez's cheap shirt. This man was the clay he hoped to mold, and he couldn't help but wonder whether he was equal to the task. He invited Ramirez to use the microphone, and waited while the man looked around the room.

Ramirez's eyes grew as big as balloons, yellowy whites swallowing dark irises. The perspective from the podium was vastly different, and Calderone was counting on intimidation to work in his favor. If Ramirez lost his nerve, he would play right into Calderone's hands. If he couldn't make an argument for his independence—and that of the others—then that independence was a thing of the past.

Ramirez bowed nervously and swallowed hard. Picked up by the sensitive microphone, the gulp echoed from every corner of the room. The crowd laughed, daring Ramirez to do it again. He looked apologetically at Calderone, then began to speak in a soft voice. "I mean no disrespect to Don Calderone, but there are many things he may have forgotten. Living in a place like this—" he gestured grandly while the crowd looked around "—living in a place like this, it is easy to forget."

"What is your point, Raul?" Calderone prodded him, trying to keep him off balance. The one thing he couldn't afford was for this man to beat him at his own game. Losing face in front of the others would be disastrous.

"Point? I don't know. I guess what I mean is that it's easy for you to scheme grand schemes. You're not out there in the sand like we are. You don't have to worry about the *federales* or the Border Patrol. We do."

Grateful for the opening, Calderone leaned forward. "What you say is true, Raul. I don't have to worry about them. That is precisely my point. If you join me, you won't have to worry about them, either. None of you will. I can buy the kind of protection you only dream of. And the more of us who band together, the more protection we can buy. We can have our own police, and why not? The politicians have theirs, so why should we be any different?"

The crowd applauded, and Calderone stepped back graciously, letting Ramirez have the mike again.

"This organization you talk about. What good is it to us?"

"Do you know where the Border Patrol is at all times? How many times have you been arrested, your money and vehicle confiscated? Which of you has not done a year in jail?"

"That comes with the territory, Don Carlos, and you should know that. If I am not mistaken, you are no stranger to the inside of a jail."

"That's right, I'm not. But of all the men in this room, I am the only one who can say I will never see it again. Why? Because I have bought into the Border Patrol. And because I have the very best electronic equipment that money can buy. I know where the patrols are, I know where the motion detectors are, and I'll bet a dozen cows that some of you don't even know what they are."

Ramirez shrugged. "So you have fancy toys."

Calderone slammed his fist onto the podium. The hollow thunder was picked up and reinforced by the microphone. "Toys? You think I am talking about toys? I'll tell you what I am talking about. I am talking about computers. I am talking about satellite communications. I am talking about the ability to monitor every Border Patrol radio transmission, right here from this house. Do those things sound like toys to you?" He appealed to the audience, and it was clearly his point.

"And I'll tell you something else. I can tell you where every single railroad car in the Southwest is, where it's been and where it's going. I can even do better than that. I can make it go wherever I want it to go. Why waste gasoline when the railroad will move your freight for you? Can you arrange such a thing, Raul?"

"No, Don Carlos, I cannot." Ramirez seemed cowed. It was time for the coup de grace.

"And can you deal directly with the American growers? Can you make deals with them and have them pay you, as well as the chickens? Can you do that?"

"No, Don Carlos. I cannot do that." Ramirez looked slyly at Calderone, as if he had sensed a hole in his defenses. Smiling slightly he asked, "Can you?"

Calderone raised his chin slightly so that he was looking down at Ramirez across the bridge of his nose. He hesitated for several seconds. "Yes, I can do that."

The uproar in the hall told him all he needed to know. He looked at the applauding men. Now all he had to do was decide who was sincere and who was trying to applaud himself out of a noose.

It wouldn't be hard. And, besides, he could always err on the side of caution.

25

The prison cell was crowded. Nine men, counting Bolan, shared a space barely large enough for four. The variety of insect life would keep an entomologist busy for a year.

On being taken to the police station, he had tried to explain what had happened, but it had been like talking to a stone wall. It hadn't taken him long to realize he had been set up. The police had arrived so quickly, they had to have been tipped off. Apparently they had been the second wave. If the hit men had managed to take him out, that would have been fine and dandy. But they hadn't fared very well, and the B team had been on hand to get him out of the picture.

He had expected to be asked questions, perhaps none too gently, but the *federales* couldn't have cared less what he had to say. Not only didn't they question him, they didn't even book him. It was as if he were a piece of paper that nobody wanted to read. It was simpler to file it and forget it.

Sitting on his bunk, he had watched the other prisoners carefully, fully expecting to be attacked as soon as the guards had left the cell block. It seemed like hours since he had been unceremoniously dumped into the cell, and no one had said so much as a word to him.

Something about the situation kept tugging at him. After wrestling with a vague uneasiness for a quarter of an hour, it hit him like a blow from a pile driver. He was a nonperson. And a nonperson not only didn't exist, no one existed who had ever seen or spoken to him.

The full significance of that fact dawned immediately. To these men, he wasn't there, and, a minute after he left the cell, he would vanish from their memories and, just as surely, from the face of the earth. To remember him was to place oneself in danger. The motley assortment of disreputable and objectionable and socially unacceptable men who shared his cell, and who peopled the one adjacent and the two across from his, had gone collective amnesia one better—they had developed it before the fact.

More troubling than the certainty that he was right was the realization that this phenomenon wasn't a new one to these men. They had seen it all before, knew what was expected of them, how they should behave. How many times must it have happened for them to be that perfect in their parts?

With a solid clang, its echo lingering in the air like a death knell, a master switch was thrown, and the cell block was plunged into near darkness. Only a quintet of low-wattage red bulbs, one in each of the cells, and one high on the wall over the entrance to the cell block, remained lit. The bulbs were recessed in the ceiling, encased in thick Plexiglas, itself securely defended by a thick wire mesh. The reddish light oozed down the walls and onto the floor like a pool of anemic blood. The eight men huddled in the far corner moved uneasily, their eyes either closed or reduced to virtual slits.

The cell stank, and its walls began to shimmer as the bugs came out of their crevices. The shimmering chitin of the cockroaches gleamed, even in the dim light, as hundreds of the vermin descended the walls. Bolan brushed them away by the dozen, not even bothering to try to kill them.

The sound of their wings made his skin crawl. The men bunched across from him seemed to be unaware of the insects swarming around them. A dull thud at the end of the cell block came as a welcome diversion. It got his mind off the poor conditions in the cells.

There was a second clang, and the four lights in the cells went dark, leaving only the single dim red bulb high on the wall.

The warrior heard footsteps, but refused to stand or make any move toward the bars. If whoever was there had come for him, he'd make the bastard walk every step of the way. His eyes not yet adjusted to the gloom, he blinked rapidly, trying to pick some features out of the center of the twin shadows that hovered just outside the bars.

The sound of a key grating in the lock caused him to bunch his muscles, gather his legs under him ready to spring, knowing as he did so that this was precisely what they hoped for. He was unarmed, and there was no way in hell he was going to get beyond the confines of the cell block. Unless they wanted him to, unless they either let him out or escorted him out.

Bolan decided to bide his time. The ball was in their court now, so he was willing to let them serve. If he couldn't volley, that was his problem, but there was no point in surrendering before he even had a chance to play. If he lost, it sure as hell wasn't going to be by default.

The barred door swung back, dull flashes of red reflecting from the bright metal scratches where the door met its seat. The rest of the door was as black as wrought iron in the near darkness, more like an insubstantial partition made of shadows than a physical impediment.

The shadows talked to each other, but the words were soft, almost as insubstantial as the shadowy door. He waited, his feet up on the cot, his back against the stone wall, feeling a hundred roaches crawling on his skin, slipping down his collar and inside his shirt. They crawled on his face and over the naked skin of his arms, but he ignored them all. The warrior was concentrating on the presence in the open doorway.

"Belasko, come on out."

The voice was a harsh whisper, as if the speaker were reluctant to wake the sleeping prisoners. Bolan ignored it.

"Belasko, man, come on out. You hear me?"

The nearer shadow took a step forward, and Bolan could tell the man was large and broad, but his face was featureless in the darkness. The figure took another step, and Bolan distinctly heard the rap of a hard heel on the stone floor. The sound of the pneumatic gun caught him by surprise. He felt the sting of the dart, then even the bit of light winked out.

THE RUMBLE of the engine through the floorboard made Bolan's cheek feel numb. Then he remembered...the dart, and the blackness that seemed to well up out of the floor and swallow him. He shook his head, but the pain that shot through his skull was excruciating. He could feel the sting of the dart high on his chest, under the left collarbone. He moved his arms slightly and realized his hands were shackled behind him.

He rolled onto one side, trying to relieve the stiffness in his arms and shoulders. He had no idea how long he had been out, but judging by the bit of sky he could see through a dirty window, it had to have been more than two or three hours—it was starting to get light. The car bounced and he landed on his shoulder hard. The pain that shot through his upper body made him wince, and he saw a bright flash as the pain overloaded and arced through his nervous system, transformed into light.

Gritting his teeth against the pain, he brought his legs around, tight into his body, and realized his feet were also shackled. The clank of the chains alerted the driver, who turned and looked over the bench seat.

The driver leaned forward a second, and the dome light went on. He turned to the rear, letting up on the gas as if he couldn't look and drive at the same time. He wore a puzzled frown. "Belasko? You awake?"

He didn't answer. The driver turned the dome light off and stepped on the gas, the vehicle lurching forward. Bolan opened his eyes, turned his body a little and found himself staring at the back of the driver's head.

The Executioner smiled grimly. If the man was no lawman, he was even less of a driver. It looked as if Buck Allenson wasn't good at anything. The man in the passenger seat was silent, but Bolan had seen him somewhere before.

A smear of light washed through the rear window. Allenson cursed and turned to look behind him.

"What fuck is that? Rodrigo, take a look."

The passenger crawled over the back of the seat and squirmed past Bolan. He held a machine pistol in his left hand, and it clanked against the wheel well as he maneuvered himself to a sitting position. Rodrigo cranked the rear window down.

"What is it?" Allenson shouted.

"I don't know, man. It looks like a Jeep or something, but I can't see. Not past the fucking headlights."

"Hang on. I'm gonna make a turn."

The Subaru swerved to the right, and Bolan was slammed into the side of the vehicle. His pinioned arms were twisted under him, and his shoulder felt as if it had caught fire.

"Can you see anything now?"

"It's black, man. That's all I can tell."

"Well, the hell with it. Cut loose at him. Take him out. Do whatever the fuck you have to. Just get him off my ass. I can't push this crate any faster in the goddamned desert. Too many freakin' saguaros."

Rodrigo poked the muzzle of his machine pistol over the rear door, and Bolan recognized it as a Skorpion, a 7.65 mm, Eastern Bloc specialty, the best Czechoslovakia had to offer. Rodrigo cut loose with a burst, and Bolan heard several slugs whining off metal. The headlines kept on coming.

"Stop, man. Maybe I can nail him if you stop. We're bouncing around too much."

"Oh, shit! You greaseballs are worthless fuckers. Hold on."

Allenson hit the brakes and swung the Subaru in a wide semicircle. Instead of following it, the pursuing vehicle cut across a tangent. Rodrigo pushed the tailgate down as Allenson threw the transmission into neutral and grabbed another Skorpion from the front seat.

The Mexican hit man slipped down onto the desert floor, but the deep, resonant boom of a heavy rifle covered the sound of his feet on the sand. He sprawled backward, slamming into the open tailgate with the base of his spine. Then he disappeared below the gate and out of sight.

Three more quick shots rang out, splintering the glass over Bolan's head and showering him with fragments. Allenson opened the driver's door as a fifth shot slammed through its window and out through the windshield. Bolan dragged himself back over the tailgate and dropped onto the sand. He landed beside the dead Rodrigo, and rolled onto his stomach.

Allenson had opened up with the Skorpion, and the short barrel rattled against the doorframe he used as a brace. Bolan spotted the smeared shadow of Rodrigo's Skorpion.

He swung his body around to face away from the gun, then groped in the sand until his fingers felt the warm muzzle.

Gripping the weapon tightly, he rolled back onto his stomach, balancing the gun in the middle of his back. With little leverage, it was a difficult maneuver, and he lost his grip twice.

The rifleman had stopped to reload, and Allenson fired several quick, short bursts. In the sudden silence Bolan heard him ram home a new magazine. The Executioner finally got the grip of the Skorpion in his fingers and heard the crunch of boots on the sand, realizing Allenson was about to charge.

Suddenly the big man shot past him, and Bolan squeezed off a burst. The 7.65 mm slugs chewed at the sand, and the warrior rolled onto his hip, trying to raise his line of fire. Allenson turned, frozen in midstride. He seemed to realize what had happened and brought the Skorpion around, muzzle up and tracking.

Then, like a rotten fruit, the renegade cop's head burst open, spraying blood and gray matter over the Subaru. A moment later Randy Carlton knelt beside Bolan.

"You all right?"

26

Calderone stood outside the room and listened to the grumbling. The men inside were confused. They were also angry. Calderone smiled to himself. "If they only knew," he whispered, "they would be terrified." He paced anxiously, stopping at either end of the corridor as if the wall were something he had never seen before. After a few moments he would turn jerkily, like a puppet in the hands of a novice, and march back the other way, only to stop and stare at the other wall.

He didn't hear the door open. It wasn't until Tomás Sanchez stuck his head in and called to him that he turned.

"Are you ready, Tomás? Are the men ready?"

"Yes, Don Carlos, we are all ready."

"You understand what you are to do?"

"Very well. I don't screw this one up. You will see."

Calderone nodded his head absently, like a man agreeing with someone he wasn't listening to. "Good, Tomás, good. Will you send Ramón out here a moment?"

Sanchez pulled his head back through the doorway, but left the door open. A moment later Ramón Santana stepped through and out into the hall. He waited patiently until Calderone turned away from the blank wall and started back in his direction. Calderone stopped for a second, a frown on his face. Then, remembering he had asked for the young man, he smiled.

"Ramón, you startled me."

"Sorry, Don Carlos. I thought you wanted to see me."

"I do." Calderone appraised his choice of a new body-guard thoughtfully. The kid—and he was that, barely into his twenties—was a big man. Santana's large head, with its flat, vaguely Indian features, sat on a stump of a neck that almost immediately broadened into massive shoulders. At six-two, he towered over his boss, and his 250 pounds were as hard as oak. His black hair, cropped close to his scalp, was so thick and dark that one had to look closely to realize he didn't need a haircut.

Calderone reached up to put an arm around Ramón's shoulders, pulling him down to listen. He whispered for several minutes, keeping one eye on the door through which Santana had come. Occasionally he backed away from the young man and scrutinized his features, as if trying to determine whether Santana truly understood what he was being told or was merely agreeing in order not to offend his employer.

Santana nodded his head every so often, usually in response to a pull on his neck from Calderone. When he was finished speaking, Calderone straightened up, still gripping the back of Santana's neck. "So, you're certain you understand me?"

"Yes," Santana said. "I understand."

"All right, then, Ramón. I am counting on you, okay? Don't disappoint me."

Santana shook his head. "I won't, Don Carlos."

"Okay, get me Tomás again, eh?"

Santana rushed away eagerly, as excited as a child. He seemed elated, as if he had just been given a piñata of his own, without the need to compete with other children for the prizes. He opened the door again, ducked through and left it open. Calderone could hear the young man over the grumbling coming through the opposite door. "Tomás, Don Calderone wants you. Tomás, you better hurry."

Calderone fitted a cigarette into his ornate cigarette holder, staring at the empty doorway while he twirled the cigarette firmly into place. He stuck the holder in his mouth and fished in his pocket for a lighter. He was still groping around for it when Sanchez reappeared.

"You wanted to see me?"

"Is everything ready?"

"Just about."

"How much longer?"

"Five minutes, maybe ten. No more."

"Very well." Calderone turned on his heel and resumed pacing, the unlit cigarette in its holder. He felt rather than heard someone coming up behind him and turned just as Sanchez reached out with a lighter in his hand. The round man thumbed the wheel and produced a flame, but it went out before the cigarette caught. His boss waved him away impatiently. "Never mind, Tomás. I'll do it myself."

Sanchez looked hurt, and Calderone turned his back rather than watch the man make a fool of himself. Sanchez was about to say something when Santana poked his head through the door. "All set, Tomás. Let's go."

Sanchez seemed torn, unwilling to leave such a foolish impression unaddressed, but was reluctant to delay implementation of Calderone's wishes any longer. Finally he walked off, looking over his shoulder at Don Carlos and yelling to Santana to wait for him. He yanked open the second door and hollered for quiet. The men milling around inside turned to look at him, but continued their individual conversations. Sanchez cleared his throat impatiently.

When he had their undivided attention, he asked them to follow him, then stepped through the center of the room, the men dividing like water ahead of a speedboat. As he passed through, the men behind him drifted back together, never quite closing ranks, leaving a narrow aisle to mark his transit. He threw open a pair of tall wooden doors on the far side of the room and stepped out into a graveled courtyard. Turning to face the doorway, he waited for the men to follow him.

"All right, all right," he shouted. "Quiet down. Those of you with the green name tags, get on the green bus. Those with blue name tags, get on the blue bus. Make it snappy. We're on a tight schedule."

"Where the hell are we going?" Raul Ramirez demanded.

"Never mind, never mind. You'll see."

"I don't want to see, asshole. I want to *know*."

Sanchez shook his head. "You want to be convinced, okay, be convinced. Don Carlos has arranged for a little demonstration to persuade you of the wisdom of his proposition. Okay, you satisfied, moron?"

"You watch your mouth, Sanchez. I'll eat you for breakfast."

Sanchez grinned. "You need a man, huh. Those little boys not enough for your big belly?"

Ramirez lunged toward him, but Sanchez stepped to one side and Santana moved in between them. He kept his eyes on Ramirez, but spoke out of the corner of his mouth to his comrade. "Tomás, I don't think Don Carlos would be happy to see you fighting with his guests."

Ramirez sneered over Santana's shoulder, but Sanchez ignored it. The younger man was right. He was already in the doghouse, and Santana was obviously angling for his job. He'd better be careful. There would be time soon enough to take care of a blowhard like Ramirez.

Sanchez moved away, urging the milling men to shut up and get on their designated buses. When they were all aboard, he climbed aboard the blue bus, Santana moving to the green. The blue bus led the way, Sanchez sitting right behind the driver, jabbering at him between instructions.

The rough terrain rocked the bus from side to side, and the driver kept cursing as he wrestled the steering wheel to a draw. Glancing in the driver's side mirror, Sanchez saw the headlights of the second bus as they rose and fell, and behind them a second pair of lights, lower to the ground and closer together, bounced wildly, the van's shorter wheelbase responding more acutely to the narrow gullies gouged in the soil by the infrequent rain.

So far, so good, Sanchez thought. He smiled at the driver's image in the mirror, then leaned forward to wave his hand. "About another mile, my friend. We're almost there."

The driver grunted, brushing away the waving arm. "Watch it," he said, "unless you want me to have an accident." He stepped on the gas, and Sanchez had to hang on to the sides of his seat with both hands. Constantly shifting gears, the driver had begun to work up a sweat. Sanchez stared in fascination at the small drops, which caught stabs of light from the following headlights and glittered like jewels on the driver's neck and arms.

Suddenly a huge mound of earth rose up off the desert floor like a pyramid. It was so tall, its peak rose high above the reach of the headlights, and seemed to hang in the air like a dark cloud.

"To the left," Sanchez shouted. "Left, for the love of Mary!"

He leaned forward to grab the wheel, and the driver swung a weak right at Sanchez's clutching hand. "Let go of the wheel, you idiot!"

"Stop here for a minute," Sanchez insisted.

The driver, grateful for a respite from the grueling drive, did as he was told.

"Open the door!"

When the pneumatic door hissed open, Sanchez climbed down and crossed in front of the bus. The driver watched him as he passed through first one headlight then the other, each time seeming to grow in size as the light expanded his figure like a balloon taking on additional air.

Off to the left, the driver could see a steep slope, its surface compressed by some heavy weight and wearing the twin corduroy strips of a pair of bulldozer treads. Sanchez waved, indicating that the man should drive the bus down the incline, but the driver shook his head. When twin beams lanced into the driver's eyes through the left window, he threw up his left arm to shield them, and squinted into the glare.

The second bus had swung around, and now steered perilously close to the edge alongside the excavation, stopping about midway. The driver heard the exhalation of air brakes, and the headlights of the second bus went dark. Its running lights glowed dark amber along one side, and the golden glow of its parking lights gave it the forbidding scowl of a huge cat.

Sanchez suddenly appeared just below the driver's window, rapping on the glass with a pistol. The driver started, backing away from the angry rapping until Sanchez twirled one hand over his head. The driver cranked his window open, and Sanchez stood on tiptoe to holler through the opening. "Move this damn thing. Now!"

"Down there?"

"You heard me, move it!"

The driver shrugged. He was reluctant to comply, fearful that the heavy bus would get mired in the soft earth on the floor of the pit. But one glance at the contorted face of Tomás Sanchez made him frightened not to obey.

He jerked the gearshift into first and raced the engine. Letting the clutch out slowly, he could feel the bus begin to strain forward. As it started to roll, he swung the wheel in a tight left turn. The nose pitched down at a sharp angle, and he hit the brakes, but the weight of the bus kept it moving downhill, its locked wheels skidding on the steep incline. Easing off on the brakes, the driver felt the wheels begin to turn, and the bus picked up speed.

Nearing the bottom of the ramp, he noticed another pair of headlights across the pit from the second bus. He leaned forward to look up over the lip of the excavation, but the sides of the pit towered high overhead, and he could see nothing but the shadow of the rim. The incline flattened suddenly, and the sheer wall of the pit loomed up ahead. He hit the brakes again, this time skidding to a halt.

Jerking the pneumatic handle to open the door, he slipped out of his seat and fell to the floor. Behind him his passengers began to shout questions, demanding to know what was happening. He nearly fell again descending the steps, and tumbled out on the freshly dug floor of the pit. Climbing to his feet, he looked up to see the stark outlines of several men peering over the edge and down into the hole. A sharp report echoed in the pit, and a bright white scimitar flashed overhead.

The passengers had begun to pour from the bus as a brilliant burst of white light exploded high above him, then started a long slow fall. The phosphorous flare showered sparks, swinging in a gentle arc as it dangled from its parachute.

Raul Ramirez grabbed the driver and spun him around. "You son of a bitch! What the hell is going on?"

The driver's answer was drowned by the first burst of gunfire from the lip of the pit. Wave after wave of automatic weapons fire poured into the bus, sparking rainbows from the metal as they ripped through the roof of the vehicle and ricocheted from the struts and bumpers. In a rising crescendo the windows shattered, cascading like a sheet of ice onto the damp earth.

The men in the pit began to scream, but it was already too late for them. An RPG ripped through the front window and detonated on impact, ripping the bus in two. The ruptured fuel line splattered gasoline over the wreckage, and the second RPG ignited the fumes. Thick tongues of greasy flame licked at the walls of the pit, charring thin tendrils to ash and blackening the earth.

Along the rim the passengers of the second bus absorbed their lesson in stunned silence. Tomás Sanchez leaned over the edge and shook his fist at the heart of the inferno. "Ramirez, you asshole, that'll teach you, you bastard."

Behind him Ramón Santana stepped forward, leaned down casually and reached out with his right hand. He tapped Sanchez at the base of the skull, then let the .357's muzzle rest on the protruding bone and pulled the trigger.

He turned before Sanchez disappeared into the holocaust, stepped back and sat down against the rear wheel of the bus. With a handkerchief he wiped the blood and tattered brain tissue from his arm and the Colt Python, shook the handkerchief once, then tucked it back into his pocket. Impassively he watched the flames crack like whips over the crumbling edge of the pit.

In the east the sun was just beginning to brighten the sky, bleaching the deep velvety black to a hard gray dawn. He hoped Don Carlos could see the thick black smoke from his balcony.

27

Everything was in place now, and Carlos Calderone was on a high. Nearly four years of sweating and planning were about to bear fruit. He had been awake all night, pacing the floor. Hours of trying to relax, hours in which he spun his web out to a hundred times its current size. Then, like Penelope, he took it apart strand by strand to start over, to weave some new, more intricate design. As each one was found wanting, he ripped it to pieces and began again.

Down in the kitchen he poured himself a half glass of vodka, splashed some tomato juice into the glass, dropped in a slice of lemon and downed the drink in two swallows. Unused to alcohol, he was hit by the vodka immediately. The air-conditioning was on, but he felt hot, almost feverish.

Calderone yanked open the freezer and grabbed a handful of ice cubes. He wrapped them in a towel and held the cold compress to his forehead. The melting water felt soothing, and he let it trickle down over his nose and eyes. Mixing another Bloody Mary, he climbed the stairs to the second floor and stood in front of the sliding glass doors. The desert was dark gray, and he glanced at a gaudy clock, shaped like an orange, hanging on the wall.

It was five o'clock, and sunrise was less than twenty minutes away. High in the sky, toward the south, a long slash of brilliant white light, so elusive he wasn't sure he had even seen it, crossed the sky just above the horizon. He made a note to ask Alfredo if it could have been one of the communications satellites they were tapping into.

The light was gone almost as soon as he noticed it, but he continued to stare at the place where it had been. He slid one of the doors to one side and stepped out onto the balcony, feeling his skin tingle as it shook off the artificial cool and began to respond to the predawn heat.

Walking to the edge, he set the drink on a table and leaned forward with his hands on the rail. He noticed a ropy smudge to the north and nodded. Below him, dimly lit by a few ground lights scattered among the shrubs, his garden took on an otherworldly appearance. Fronds waved in a slight breeze, and small frogs jumped in the fountain pools. Here and there a fish rose to the surface to catch a bug. He walked to a control box beside the doors, opened it and threw a pair of switches.

Back at the railing he could see the golden carp swishing back and forth, circling around the underwater lights he had just turned on. He had everything he had ever dreamed of, and felt cheated now that he realized it wasn't enough. Part of him wanted to turn his back and walk away from it all, as if he were being slowly crushed by the sheer weight of his material possessions. Another part of his being wanted him to accept what he had, find satisfaction and surrender himself to the fact that he was a wealthy man. But deep inside, so deep he couldn't even be sure he could find it if he wanted to, something kept challenging him, daring him to do more, to want more, to take more.

As the sun started to rise, he sat on a lounge chair, cradling the drink in his hands, swirling it idly in the glass. It was time to take the last steps to consolidate. It was all laid out, and he wondered why he should feel nervous. It seemed unnatural not to have some doubt, but then he was an unnatural man. He tilted his head back on the cushion and closed his eyes, enjoying the warmth. A moment later he was asleep.

CALDERONE JERKED AWAKE with a start. The hand on his shoulder continued to shake him, and he reached up to grab it before he realized where he was.

"Don Carlos," Alfredo said, "Don Carlos. It is seven o'clock. You'll be late."

Calderone rubbed his eyes with one hand. His head ached, and he was thirsty. It was the closest he had come to a hangover in years, and he looked distastefully at the half-empty glass on the table beside him. The tomato juice had clotted, leaving a thick skin of reddish-brown pulp on the sides of the glass. His stomach turned, and he got up hurriedly.

"Are you all right, Don Carlos?"

"Yes, Alfredo, I'm fine. Just a little queasy. I'll be down in a few minutes."

Alfredo excused himself, and Calderone walked to the rail again. The sun was well above the horizon now, its color a pale orange. It was going to be a scorcher, not the kind of day for a trip into Arizona. But he had an appointment with Big Jaime Tyack at eleven. Turning his back on the sun, he opened the door and stepped inside, the cool air luxurious as it washed over him. He walked quickly to his bedroom suite and stripped for a shower.

The hard spray lashed at his skin, washing away the stickiness, and he tilted his head back to fill his mouth with water. He swirled it around, then spit back at the shower head. The dry powdery taste in his mouth disappeared, and he shivered as he turned the water to full cold.

His doubts were all but gone. The momentary uncertainty was only natural, he told himself. But he had worked too hard, and come too far to turn back, even if he wanted to. He turned the water off and stood in the elaborately tiled shower, letting the draft of cool air from the vents dry him. His skin tingled and, wide awake now, he rubbed himself down with a thick towel.

Once he completed the deal with Tyack he would be on his way. A simple handshake would secure his future, and the border would be his, from Baja California to the Gulf of Mexico. Already news of the conference—and what had happened to those who would not accept his proposal—had begun to circulate among the coyote community. In a matter of weeks they would all be his. There was no room in his system for competition.

He dressed carefully, choosing one of his best suits. It was a good thing to impress the *yanqui* growers, and he wanted them to know they were dealing with a man of substance. The days of field hands straggling in on foot under the cover of darkness were over.

Calderone walked quickly down the stairs, brushing his hair back with one careless hand. Through the glass wall on the far side of the foyer, he could see the chopper, its blades turning slowly, the rotor wash fluttering the leaves in the garden beyond it. He stepped out into the sun and ducked as he had seen politicians do. Ramón and Diego, his new bodyguards, were already on board.

"Let's go," Calderone ordered. The pilot seemed to sense rather than hear the command, and he pulled back on the throttle. The blades, flashing overhead, whirled more rapidly, throwing off showers of sunlight, and the craft shuddered a little, then drifted slightly to the left as it started to climb.

Calderone looked out the side window as the chopper rose straight into the air and the house and grounds fell away beneath him. The higher he rose, the smaller and more insignificant it all looked. The gardens were little more than green smears on the desert. The thick walls surrounding the compound seemed as thin as paper, incapable of defending him against those who would try to bring him down. Even the buildings themselves were diminished by the perspective. They looked like a child's toy.

He tried to console himself with the knowledge that from this altitude everything was reduced. But it was still his, all of it.

And he knew it wasn't enough.

Not for a man of his substance.

As the compound fell away behind him, he turned and looked north. That was where the real money was, and he intended to have as much of it as he could gather.

Don Carlos was master of all he could see, and all he could see was desert—he was the king of the void. There would have to be more, there had to be something he could do. He stared as if hypnotized as the helicopter sped over the desert, the muted colors blurring.

The trip passed as if he were in a trance, and he was unaware of the chopper dipping low to fly under the radar at the border, was unaware of anything, until the rich green of the citrus groves began to appear scattered at first, then increasingly densely packed, until they stretched out ahead like a solid green carpet.

It was then that Calderone saw what he had to do. Supplying the labor was only a first step. It was a sap's job for chump change. Why should he settle for being a labor contractor when he could own the groves themselves? Once he cornered the market on the labor supply, he would be in a position to destroy any grower he chose.

When a grower tied into the system, he would be helpless. His crops would be at Calderone's mercy. Don Carlos could demand a piece of the profits, become a silent partner. It would be no harder than herding cattle. He could cut a grower out of the herd, brand him, then move on to the next.

The sky was the limit.

The thought revived him, and Calderone began to shake off the gloom that had enshrouded him since leaving the ground. He could even start today, with Tyack. The man had no pickers. He was at the Mexican's mercy. It wouldn't be a bad idea to make the proposal this very morning.

The huge white house at Waywayanda loomed up on the left as the chopper settled into the broad semicircle of grass surrounded by the driveway.

Calderone jumped lightly onto the grass, ducking his head to avoid the whirling blades. Ramón and Diego followed, racing to catch up. Calderone was on the steps when Tyack appeared in the doorway. Like the last time, he was dressed in coveralls and a checkered shirt. Unlike last time, however, he had a Winchester cradled in his arms, one thick finger inside the trigger guard.

"*Señor*, good to see you again," Calderone said, extending his hand as he mounted the steps.

"Get the hell off my land. You're leaving a grease stain on the lawn," Tyack barked.

Calderone stopped and looked back at his bodyguards. His face was twisted and confused, the brows knit together. "I don't understand. What is the problem, Señor Tyack?"

"The problem is you murdered two of my people and run the rest of 'em off. I'm way behind, and probably gonna lose a third of my crop."

"But that is no problem, Señor Tyack. I have already made arrangements for new workers."

"There wasn't nothing wrong with the ones I had. Now get out of here before I use this." The man nodded toward the shotgun in his arms, then swung it around to point at Calderone's chest.

"I thought we had a deal. We did, didn't we? Have a deal?"

"I told you I'd think about it. Nothin' more. You had no business intimidating my people."

"Your people? Is that what you said? Your people?"

"That's what I said."

"But they are not your people, Señor Tyack. They are *my* people." Calderone struck himself in the chest with a clenched fist. "I *own* them, all of them. And you will burn in hell before a single one of them picks so much as *one* orange for you."

"If you're trying to threaten me—" Tyack suddenly brought up the Winchester "—don't do it." Ramón had taken a step toward the porch, his hand inside his jacket. "Get your hand out where I can see it."

Calderone cursed, turned on his heel and walked down the steps. As he passed between his bodyguards, he whispered, "When I tell you, kill the bastard." He continued on across the lawn toward the waiting helicopter.

In the polished Lexan of the cockpit, he watched as Ramón and Diego gradually backed away, widening the gap between them at the same time until the big man could no longer cover them both. When he reached the chopper, Calderone turned. "Now!"

Ramón and Diego went for their guns at the same time. Tyack, sensing what was about to happen, stepped back. He fired once, catching Diego in the chest with a load of heavy shot. The bodyguard flew backward, his chest a mass of blood and shattered bone. One hand, its fingers wrapped around the butt of a pistol, was still half inside his jacket.

Ramón had drawn his own gun and fired three times. The first shot went wide, the .357-caliber slug blowing out one of the tall windows in the doors behind the grower. The second slug struck Tyack high on the left shoulder as he was raising the Winchester to get off another shot. The third round struck him in the left temple. The remaining window behind him turned red. Calderone watched for a moment as the blood streaked the glass, then he waved to Ramón, who was struggling toward the helicopter with Diego's body.

"Leave him. He's useless now. Burn the house and let's get out of here."

28

Carlton finally found the keys in Buck Allenson's pocket. Realizing his hands were covered with blood, he scooped up a handful of sand, rubbed it on his palms and fingers, then wiped them on his jeans. Bolan was sitting on the running board of the Renegade, and Carlton knelt to unlock the shackles and handcuffs.

"That was closer than I like to come."

"What do we do now?" Carlton asked.

"We're going back."

The younger man looked at his watch. "Ray Conlan should be here any minute."

"What?"

"Oh, unofficially. But Ray has had about enough of this crap. He told me Tyack was blown away. The old man's house was burned to the ground. They found his body, what was left of it, on the front porch."

"Who killed him?"

"I don't know all the details. Ray'll fill us in as soon as he gets here."

"How's he going to find us?"

Carlton tapped his temple with a long finger. "Used the old noggin. I've been watching you, Mike, and I've learned a lot. I gave him a rough idea where to look, then figured the frequency on one of the beacons."

"Nice work, Randy."

"You hungry? I got some food and water in the car."

Bolan stretched, trying to relieve the cramping in his stiff muscles, then sat on the running board beside the driver's seat while Carlton grabbed a canteen from the back of the Renegade.

A black smudge to the south caught his eye. The smoke began to thicken on the horizon as it caught the first rays of the rising sun. Bolan shifted his weight on the running board, guzzling the cool water the patrolman poured from a canteen. "I don't like the looks of that smoke."

"Neither do I," Carlton agreed, "but I can't figure what the hell it could be. There isn't anything over there. Nothing grows thick enough to support a blaze like that, so it's got to be man-made."

"Judging by the color of the smoke," Bolan said, "I'd guess there's a lot of gas or oil at the bottom of that column."

"Maybe we should take a look."

"No maybe about it. If Conlan can find us here, he can find us a few miles south." Bolan stood and stretched his arms again. The circulation had been cut off so long that he still felt pins and needles in one shoulder, and his wrists ached from the cuffs.

Carlton slipped the metal cup back into his canteen cover, slid the canteen back inside and folded the canvas flaps, snapping them shut with a pair of brittle cracks. He walked around the front of the Renegade, drumming his fingers nervously on the hood. Bolan leaned over to open the passenger door. The big kid winced slightly when he bumped his shoulder on the doorframe, but tried to hide the pain that sliced through his upper torso.

When he yanked the door closed, one hand automatically went to his collarbone, and he took a few moments to massage his shoulder.

"You all right?"

"No problem. Let's take a look. By the way, I got some thing for you." Carlton reached into the rear of the vehicl and retrieved Bolan's weapons. "Buck had them in hi truck. Guess he knew a good thing when he saw it."

Bolan smiled and turned the ignition, the Jeep roaring to life. Jerked into gear, the 4x4 bit into the desert, and it deeply treaded tires churned up clouds of gritty dust.

The thick black smoke was framed against the sun, the top of the column flattening to a cloud and beginning to spread in all directions. Bolan muscled the powerful truck through the desert growth with precise control, like a skier in a giant slalom. He skirted some of the taller saguaros so closely that Carlton thought he could hear the tips of the needles squeal on the Renegade's skin as they flashed by.

He turned to the rear of the truck again, this time grab bing a gun belt for himself. Bolan glanced out of the cor ner of his eye at the powerful .357 Magnum as the patrolman checked the action and chambered a round. The kid slipped the automatic into the holster, then swung i over his shoulder.

The sky ahead was so bright now that visibility was re duced to a few hundred yards. The smoke had begun to thin a little, turning from black to dark gray, and Bolan real ized the fire at its source was burning itself out. He hoped they found it before it vanished altogether.

A pyramid appeared just below the edge of the sky. It seemed to grow as they rushed toward it, like some bizarre plant rising into the air. Bolan couldn't quite make out what it was, but he drifted slightly to the left and lined it up over the center of the hood.

"What the hell is that thing?"

"We're about to find out, Randy." The structure was less than a mile away, and it continued to rise above the surrounding desert as they raced toward it. Bolan estimated its height to be fifty or sixty feet. Its near side was wrapped in shadows, and no detail other than its general outline was visible.

The smoke was everywhere, a pall, rather than a cloud. Another, paler haze began to mingle with the gray of the dispersed smoke. Bolan covered the diminishing ball of the sun with an extended thumb. At the base of the pyramid a huge bulldozer had begun to move along one edge, filling the air with dust.

Bolan eased up on the gas, not wanting to rush into something he didn't have a handle on. He spotted two more vehicles, a gigantic Mack tractor and flatbed trailer, its loading ramp down, obviously used to transport the bulldozer, and a jet-black van. The dozer continued to scrape away at the bottom of the huge mound, then tilted back sharply and began to climb its steep face, its blade high over the cab like the coiled tail of a scorpion.

Near the peak of the pyramid the driver dropped his blade and started back down the other side, shoving a thick wave of soil ahead of it. The driver backed and filled, scraping the peak of the mound to a narrow plateau. Bolan braked the Jeep and watched.

Carlton grabbed field glasses and scanned the mound. "Just look at that. What the hell is he doing?"

He let the glasses drop, and Bolan picked them up. He was more interested in the van. The blocky black vehicle seemed deserted. Sweeping the glasses to the right, he checked the bulldozer again; the plateau on top had nearly doubled in size. The pyramid was being disassembled.

It seemed odd, but no more odd than its having been built in the first place. Tracking down one edge, Bolan caught a glimpse of thick oil smoke rising in wispy tendrils, apparently from the ground. Refining the focus, he realized it was emanating from some sort of excavation.

"What do you make of that?" Bolan asked.

"Make of what?"

"The pit. You know anything about construction planned for this area."

"No way. This is stone desert, first of all, and nobody in his right mind, on either side of the border, would build anything out here. What the hell for?"

"Then I think we better take a closer look. The smoke was coming from the left of that mound." Bolan turned off the engine, reached into the back and pulled Allenson's machine pistol into the front seat. "You better get the other Skorpion, Randy. I've got a feeling we're going to need the firepower."

The two men left the vehicle quickly, anxious to get as close to the pyramid as possible before anyone spotted them.

Across the desert floor the snarling bulldozer sounded like an angry beast. It lumbered back and forth across the broadening plateau as it continued to chop away at the huge mound. Great waves of loose earth slid down the steep slope and tumbled out of sight into the pit.

When they had come within two hundred yards of the foot of the pyramid, Bolan hit the deck and dragged Carlton down with him. The kid landed hard on his shoulder, but before he could ask what was going on, Bolan pointed toward the van. One of the rear doors had swung open and jutted out past the van's near side.

A tall figure appeared and was joined almost immediately by two more men. While Bolan and his companion pressed themselves into the earth, the three men leaned over the edge of the pit and relieved themselves. The warrior put the glasses on them, and he could see they were joking and laughing, but the bulldozer's engine drowned out any trace of the sound.

When he had finished, the tall man zipped himself up and backed away from the pit to slouch against the side of the van. He and his companions wore similar clothing, a dark blue-green, like some sort of military uniform, although it belonged to no armed force Bolan was familiar with.

"Looks like some sort of private army," he whispered.

"I wonder how many of them there are?"

As if to satisfy his curiosity, three more men appeared around the van's open door. They joined their companions and sat heavily on the ground. One man jerked cans from a plastic web and tossed them to others.

"Six, plus one on the dozer, makes at least seven," Bolan said. He swung the glasses toward the tractor, but it was parked at an angle, and he could see virtually nothing of the cab. He scrambled to his knees and reached down to help the younger man to his feet. As he started forward, the bulldozer suddenly went silent.

"You want to take them head on, or try to take out a few of them from here?" Carlton asked.

"We don't even know who they are," Bolan reminded him.

"You're right. They could just be a bunch of guys who like to bury fires in the desert."

Bolan stood up and swung the Skorpion around where he could reach it easily. "Cover me, but don't show yourself unless you have to."

Carlton stayed flat on the sand. He worked the lever on his Winchester, chambered a round and sighted in on the tall, storklike man still standing at the rear of the van.

Bolan got to within thirty yards before they even noticed him, and he was close enough to see over the lip of the pit.

The ruined bus lay at the bottom, partly covered with soil. It was split open like a filleted fish, its wreckage stained black with smoke and charred by the roaring holocaust that had consumed it.

These guys were anything but innocent. Bolan had seen enough to know that. He slowed his pace as he glanced at the wreckage, and the tall man finally noticed him.

The stork shouted at Bolan, his words slurred. "Hey, gringo, you lost? You a long way from home...." As he spoke, he moved slightly, just enough for an Uzi on a leather strap over his left shoulder to swing clear of his rib cage. He grabbed the submachine gun with his right hand and let the strap slip from his shoulder.

Bolan stood his ground, and the other Mexicans got to their feet. The Executioner shifted to the left a bit, to make sure Carlton had a clear shot. In a quick inventory he realized that at least three of the other men were also armed with automatic weapons.

"I asked you a question, man," the stork said, taking several steps forward. "You lost, or what?" There was no mistaking the drunken slur. When it came to reflexes, Bolan had an edge.

The Uzi shifted in the guy's hand, and he came to an unsteady halt. Bolan started to back away when the Uzi jumped and the first burst of fire clawed at the sand to his left. He dived to the ground, his arms extended over his head, and rolled over several times before he was up and tracking with the Skorpion. Suddenly the stork's head snapped back sharply. For a moment Bolan wondered what had happened, until the unmistakable bark of Carlton's carbine rolled past. The remaining five seemed stunned for a moment, then scattered, tossing a porous 9 mm wall in his direction.

Bolan cut loose with the Skorpion, aiming waist-high to catch them as they dropped into a crouch. Two men crumpled to the ground immediately, and Carlton nailed another, splattering gore all over the gleaming black side of the van.

Bolan charged forward, zigzagging to throw the drunken gunmen off stride. He could see the shins of one man behind the open rear door of the van. The other was out of sight. The warrior sprinted straight toward the van, launching himself in a low arc as he neared its front. He landed on the roof and dug the toes of his boots in. They caught on the nearly vertical strip above the windshield and stopped him from sliding off the back end.

He clambered to his feet, and a burst of autofire ripped through the roof of the van from inside. The spot where he had lain just a moment before now looked like a ragged sieve. Bolan didn't want to move, in case he revealed his position, but he knew it was only a matter of time before the man inside sprayed another burst up through the roof.

He took the field glasses from around his neck and threw them at the rear edge of the van. Almost immediately, the roof exploded, blasting the binoculars into twisted junk. Gauging the angle, Bolan ripped a burst through from above, then leaped down. He hit the ground running and shoulder-rolled past the back end of the van. Swinging the Skorpion in one hand, he laid down a barrage of fire until the magazine was empty.

Bolan tossed the Skorpion aside and leveled his Desert Eagle as he climbed to his feet. There was no need. The man behind the van lay on his back, one arm severed just below the elbow and his lower rib cage smashed by the 7.65 mm slugs. He'd been hit from behind, and raw bone—the broken ends of several ribs—jutted through his uniform shirt.

The man inside the van was also dead. He lay on his back, his head lolling back over the rear bumper. The dead man's Uzi lay in the sand, the pistol grip stained red by a thin cascade of blood running down over the bumper and dripping onto the ground.

Another shot from the carbine spun Bolan around, and he dashed past the van in time to see Carlton sprinting toward the base of the pyramid. Bolan ran toward the figure squirming in the dust. The driver of the bulldozer lay on his back, hugging his knees to his chest. Blood from a shattered shin seeped through his fingers.

Carlton joined them a few moments later. He was breathing heavily and holding his shoulder. "I figured we might need a little information, so I didn't want to waste him."

Before Bolan could answer, he heard a whining engine and turned to see a cloud of dust spiraling up behind a Jeep racing toward them.

"We've got company."

29

Calderone sat in a high-backed chair, supporting his chin with one arm. Alfredo paced back and forth in front of his employer. The young man was nervous, but also proud of his achievement. Don Carlos tapped the tips of his fingers impatiently on the arm of the chair.

Ramón stood in the doorway, watching through hooded eyes. He didn't understand Alfredo's work, and he couldn't understand Calderone's fascination with it. With two dozen Alfredos working for him, Don Carlos would still be hustling chickens in a ten-year-old car. He should understand that computers were nice playthings, but the real work was done with a strong back and a loaded gun. Ramón understood that. Why didn't Don Carlos?

While Alfredo ran through his checklist one last time, adjusting switches and reseating patch cords, changing settings and flipping toggles, Calderone remained almost comatose. Only the quietly tapping fingers gave evidence that he was awake. Ramón shifted anxiously from one foot to the other. This kind of garbage bored him. He thought of asking Alfredo whether his toys could have taken care of Tomás Sanchez as easily as the pistol in his pocket.

But Calderone was too touchy these days. He seemed to resent any criticism of the electronic wilderness Alfredo was so busy putting together. But Ramón was no fool. He understood that as long as you worked for someone else, being indispensable was the key to success, or at least to keeping your job. And he suspected Alfredo understood it, too. If no one else could work with the computers and the satellite communications, Alfredo was guaranteed a job. It also meant he would stay alive.

Ramón kept seeing the look on Sanchez's face that morning as he realized what was about to happen. He was troubled by it, but not because of what he had done. What troubled him was the way, as he tried to focus on Sanchez's expression, the fat man's features shimmered, blurred and refocused, only now as it reappeared, the face was Ramón's own.

Ramón had come back all full of himself, as happy as a kid with a good report card, and his boss hadn't even asked how it had gone. He wanted to raise it himself, but that would just be an admission that he valued Calderone's approval. If he wanted to be as indispensable as Alfredo, he had to control himself.

He kept reminding himself that as long as Don Carlos didn't own him, he was a free man. And in the world they lived in, nothing was more indispensable than a free man, a man who could thumb his nose and walk away without looking over his shoulder, a man who could tell you to kiss his ass, and mean it. That's the kind of man Ramón Santana wanted to be.

But at the moment it would be a mistake to attack Alfredo, and he knew it.

Calderone suddenly sat upright and clapped his hands impatiently. "Alfredo, huh? Let's get on with it. I'm tired."

"Yes, Don Carlos. One minute, and I'll be ready."

"Now, Alfredo, now!"

Ramón stepped through the doorway and leaned against the wall. In the dim light his smile was almost lost. He just might not have to wait as long as he thought.

Alfredo dimmed the lights even more, then sat on a low chair in front of a control console. He clicked a switch, and the wall above him glowed softly. Pressing a button, he raised the phosphor level, increasing the diffuse glow. "First," he said, "the railroad system. What would you like to see?"

"Texas, show me Texas," Calderone demanded.

Alfredo pulled a keyboard toward him and punched in a set of numbers, which caused the screen to burst into a fiery lace. "There. Every main railroad line in Texas, and every spur, too, if I move in closer."

"Do it!"

He punched in a new set of numbers, and Galveston swam center screen. The spidery filaments looked almost like actual flames flickering on the giant screen.

"Now," Alfredo continued, "let me show you something special." His voice quavered, like a kid demonstrating his entry in a science fair. His fingers tapped at the keyboard again, and the map shrank and shifted to the left. The right of the screen was suddenly alive with crawling ants. On closer scrutiny it could be seen as a digit sequence. "Those numbers identify every single railroad car in the Galveston area shown on the map."

He clicked a toggle, and the numbers froze. Reaching for a bright red ball set in the console, he pressed it once and a bright red arrowhead appeared on the screen. Rolling the ball with his fingertips, he moved the arrowhead, selected a number at random and pressed the ball again. The columns vanished and were replaced by a single entry. "There," Alfredo said proudly, "is everything you could possibly want to know about that particular car. Who owns it, what it's carrying, departure and destination points, contents. Anything at all."

"What's the big deal?" Ramón demanded.

"Shut up!" Calderone snapped. "Let him continue."

"You want to send some chickens from Chihuahua to Phoenix, you find the nearest empty railroad car. I change its orders by tying into the computer lines. It sits on a spur. You move the cargo in, load it up and I change the entry again. Nobody knows but us. Beautiful."

Alfredo demonstrated that technique, then called up a different map. "This is a section of the border area in southeastern Arizona. The little green lights are the motion detectors. The red lights are Border Patrol vehicles."

"Bet you can't move them around," Ramón challenged.

"As long as we know where they are, we don't have to," Alfredo snapped. "Now I want to show you something else." Working quickly at the keyboard, he called up yet another map.

"That looks familiar," Calderone said. "What is it?"

"You're sitting in it." Alfredo laughed. "It's the compound. And—" He stopped suddenly. "What the . . . ?"

"What's wrong? Your little toy doesn't work? Maybe it needs batteries," Ramón taunted.

"See that blinking light?"

"What is it?" Calderone demanded. "What's wrong?"

"Someone is approaching in a large vehicle. About ten miles away."

"Probably just Miranda with the truck," Ramón suggested. "No big deal."

"No," Calderone said, getting to his feet. "Miranda was taking the truck back to Arizona. Alfredo, can you get a picture for me?"

"As a matter of fact . . ."

BOLAN SAT behind the wheel of the Mack tractor trailer, Carlton beside him, loading the weapons. Ray and Milt

Conlan rode in the black van ahead of them. Calderone's estate was fifteen minutes way.

The sun was already high in the sky, and it glinted unmercifully from the elaborate chrome trim on the tractor's hood. Bolan and Carlton both wore mirrored sunglasses and looked like a parody of good ol' boys highballing through a country-western song, with Dave Dudley on their tail.

They could try to bluff their way through Calderone's defenses, but Bolan wasn't convinced it would work. The fallback was something all too common—brute force. According to the wounded driver of the bulldozer, the gate through the wall was the worst place to attack. The tempered steel gates were anchored in steel-reinforced concrete pillars and could withstand high impact, even that of a tank. If they were going to go through the wall, they had better be prepared to make their own gate.

They were.

Bolan hadn't come this far to let something like a wall hold him back. He ran several contingency scenarios through his head as he drove, discarding one after the other. They would be facing approximately forty men, and the odds were about as high as they could get. Randy Carlton was a gamer, but he was still recovering from his wounds. Conlan was a gutsy old man, but it took more than guts. Milt Conlan was completely untested, an unknown quantity, and in the mathematical computations of the Executioner, all unknowns were equal to zero. It was no indictment of the young man, just one of the harsh realities Bolan had learned to live with.

The van threw up a constant trail of brown dust, and the warrior had to spritz the windshield periodically. He glanced at Carlton a couple of times, but the kid was keeping his own council. Bolan knew what was running through his mind, and respected the need for quiet. He'd lost more than one partner in his own life, and you had to slog your way through the desire for blind vengeance. There was no room for passion when a man was in combat mode.

Not if he wanted to walk away alive.

The desert rolled in soft hills, and the trucks slipped back and forth, sliding between the higher elevations. Bolan kept waiting for the first glimpse of Calderone's fortress, and when it came, he was impressed. High on a steep hill, it towered over the surrounding desert. The mountains in the distance were little more than smears of purple, like the rough brush strokes of a primitive landscape artist, suggestions more than details.

Bolan whistled softly. The walls around the compound looked like slabs of stone. Even at this range, he knew they were in for trouble.

At the very center, glittering in the bright sun, the steel gates looked like a sarcastic smile in an inscrutable face. Bolan rapped the horn, and Ray Conlan hit his brakes. The Executioner swung up alongside the van and hit his own pedal, the air brakes snorting, hissing.

Bolan jumped down from the high running board of the cab. The old sheriff opened the window, and the warrior leaned into a draft of conditioned air. "What do you think, Sheriff?"

"Looks like we got ourselves more than we bargained for, Mr. Belasko."

"You inclined to wait for backup?"

Conlan snorted. "Hell, man, why wait for something we know we ain't gonna git? You and I both know we got no jurisdiction here. But some things are more important than a few lines on a piece of paper."

"I take it that means you don't want to wait?"

"Hellfire, son, I didn't get to be this old by sittin' on my duff. You step on a rattler, you better move fast. The way I figure it, we already done the steppin', and I reckon it's time to move."

Bolan nodded. "I think we better forget about the gate."

"Me, too. How many of them RPGs we got?"

"Six."

"Reckon that's enough?"

"It'll have to be."

"Son, I like you. Ain't too often I can say that about a federal cop. Most of you guys are three-piece suiters, ought to be sittin' at a desk somewheres, one of them little bitty calculators in your hands. You're different. We come out of this okay, you want a job?"

Bolan laid a hand on the old man's shoulder. "Thanks, Sheriff, but I don't think so."

"Figures. Can't blame a feller for tryin', though, can you?"

"No, you can't. I think you and Milt should ride with us now. If they spot us, and they probably will, it's going to get a lot hotter than it already is."

Conlan nodded. "Lead the way, son."

Bolan climbed up to the driver's door and stuck his head into the cab. "You feel well enough to drive this rig, Randy?"

Carlton shrugged. "Sure, what the hell, why not? What you got in mind?"

"You'll see. Lower the ramp."

30

While Carlton fumbled with the hydraulic controls, Bolan sprinted back to the van. "Sheriff, you and Milt get all the weapons out of the van."

"You got it, son." Conlan hopped out of the driver's seat with more vitality than Bolan would have expected. Dressed in jeans and a denim shirt, the old man looked about twenty years younger than his age. He and his nephew opened the van's rear door and started to haul the weapons from it, carrying them a few at a time to the rear of the trailer.

"Make sure you get the RPGs," Bolan called out, then he scrambled up the ramp to the bulldozer and bent down to unlock the rear chain. The heavy steel sagged with a sharp clank as he pulled the steel retainer bar free. The dozer shifted slightly as the pressure of the chain was released.

"You ever drive one of these babies?" Ray Conlan asked as he joined Bolan.

"No, I haven't."

"It ain't easy, 'specially if you want to move the blade around. I done it a few times. I'm no expert, but a little experience is better'n none, I figure."

"You sure you want to?"

"Hell, yes. I didn't come all the way down here to sit on the sidelines."

"Okay, then. Hang on while I tell Randy what to do."

"Tell Milt to ride up there with Randy, will you? No point in taking the van. If we can't do it with what we got here, we ain't gonna do it at all."

Bolan stepped to the front of the trailer and leaned around the side of the cab to explain what he wanted. He waved Milt to the passenger side and waited until the deputy was in the cab. When he turned back, Conlan was already waiting for him in the dozer's cab.

The Executioner climbed in and grabbed the RPG-7, loaded the first grenade and rolled down the window. Randy looked back through his rear window. On the high sign from Ray Conlan, he started the Mack's engine. Ray cranked up the diesel on the bulldozer, and the noise in the cab was deafening. The whole thing shimmied, and Bolan had to clench his teeth to keep them from rattling together.

The truck's engine raced, and thick black smoke belched from its twin stacks. As the tractor strained forward under its heavy load, the dozer shifted uncertainly, rocking back and forth on the slack of its steel treads.

Conlan turned to Bolan and cupped his hands around his mouth. "Hold on to your hat, son," he shouted. "I want to try the controls."

He jerked one of the three joysticks, and the dozer started to shift toward the edge of the trailer. He jerked it back the other way, and it straightened. "Wrong one, I reckon." Conlan grinned. Bolan could barely hear him over the roar of the two big diesels. He tried another joystick, and the blade began to rise in the air. "There, that's the one I'm lookin' for." He brought the blade a little higher until it hovered right in front of the windshield of the dozer's cab. They could just see the top of the hill over the upper edge of the blade.

The old man leaned toward Bolan. "I think I'll leave her there until we get up close. A little extra cover never hurt nobody." The truck strained, and the dozer, unbalanced by the elevated blade, rocked unsteadily on the flatbed. Bolan brought his legs up and placed one foot on either corner of the windshield. He shoved, his thigh muscles bulging with the strain. The rubber seal around the glass began to move, and Bolan shoved harder. The glass started to come free and Bolan drew his feet back then kicked hard at both corners. The glass popped free and tilted outward at a forty-five-degree angle.

Kicking down with the heels of his boots, he knocked the glass loose and it fell onto the flatbed with a tormented screech as the rubber seal tried to hold it back.

In the tractor cab Randy Carlton wrestled with the wheel, swinging the truck into a tight arc at the foot of the hill. He hit the pedal hard, and the air brakes squealed like a stuck pig. On top of the estate wall, two men opened fire with automatic rifles. Carlton and Milt jumped from the tractor cab as the sheriff revved up the dozer. They dived under the trailer and scrambled away from the autofire chewing at their heels. The heavy rumble of the dozer made the trailer shudder, and sand sifted down from between the planks, covering their backs and shoulders with a fine grit.

When the dozer was on the ground, Conlan worked the hydraulics with jerky precision, and the huge machine swiveled on its tracks. It started up the slope, and Bolan took aim with the first RPG round. "Drop the blade a little," he shouted over the roaring diesel, and Conlan lowered their shield enough for the warrior to fire the grenade. It slammed into the base of the wall, sending slivers of rock in every direction and a geyser of sand high into the air. The impact site was obscured by a cloud of dust as Bolan took aim with the second grenade, sending the high explosive screaming home a little higher through the heart of the cloud.

The second blast blew the dust away for a moment, and before its own veil of smoky grit descended, the Executioner could see he'd been a little high. A ragged figure eight, tilted slightly to the right, had been blasted into the barrier. On top of the wall itself, Bolan saw several men running toward the dozer, firing their weapons wildly. The 7.62 mm hail rattled on the thick steel blade of the big Caterpillar and whined off the roof of the dozer's cab.

Two automatic weapons began chattering behind the dozer as Milt and Randy opened up with two of the captured Uzis. The men on the parapet scrambled for cover, bobbing up and down like ducks in a shooting gallery. Bolan slammed a third grenade into the heart of the figure eight, and a sliver of daylight appeared for an instant before swirling dust wrapped the wall in another cloud.

"Keep bangin' away at her, Mike. We'll get through. How many you got left?"

"Three."

Conlan didn't respond right away, gunning the dozer's engine instead and driving toward the wall with a voracious churning of its thick treads. "Bang it again, son...."

Bolan fired the fourth grenade, and the loud crump of its impact slammed into his chest where the concussion slipped past the huge blade. Quickly taking the fifth RPG round, he aimed to the right and launched. When the last grenade was ready, he waited for the dust to settle a bit. A hole, not wide enough for the dozer, but real enough, gaped in the wall. He aimed at the right edge and shot the last grenade. It blew a huge slab off the right edge of the hole, and the top of the shattered wall collapsed and tumbled into the gap.

"I don't know if it is wide enough, but we're gonna find out," Conlan yelled. "Hold on!"

The dozer reached the break in the wall, and the old man lowered the blades. Carlton and Milt banged away from beneath the trailer, keeping the guards on the wall off balance. An occasional burst of 7.62 mm slugs chewed at the dozer's cab roof, but the defenders were firing blind.

Conlan gunned the Caterpillar's big diesel, and the treads gouged the earth, throwing twin cascades of loose sand down the slope behind them. The wall creaked, but it wouldn't give. Working the controls with more confidence, the sheriff backed down the slope and swung the dozer in parallel to the base of the wall. He dug in and shoved a curling wave of earth ahead of them, stripping the soil away five feet on either side of the break. Backing up, he stripped away another layer.

While the sheriff worked, Bolan watched the top of the wall. One guard had crept to the very edge of the break, and the warrior nailed him as he was leaning out to swing his assault rifle into position. The Skorpion clawed at flesh and snapped bone as it ripped through the guard, and he fell into the breach.

Conlan backed up again and pivoted the bulldozer, slipping one end of the blade into the gap. He gunned the engine and reversed, hauling huge chunks of concrete and raw stone out of the ragged hole. The debris tumbled down the slope, raising a cloud of dust.

Hooking the blade on one side just above the foundation, Conlan opened the diesel all the way. The engine groaned and the dozer started to slip sideways. As the blade was about to pull free of the wall, he backed off the gas, pivoted again, sliding the blade deeper into the gash, then slammed backward. The impact shattered a long, vertical chunk of stone free, and the blade folded it back along the wall like a huge garden gate opening on invisible hinges.

With no support under it, the slab toppled over on its long edge.

"That got it," Conlan whooped. "Let's go get 'em, boys." He swiveled the Caterpillar on its treads and charged down the slope toward the trailer. He stopped alongside the flatbed, while Randy and Milt climbed onto the engine housing.

"Hold on to your hats," Conlan shouted, and swung the dozer around toward the break in the wall.

Raising the blade like a giant shield, Conlan charged the cumbersome vehicle up the slope. Bolan leaned out of the cab and sprayed random fire over the top edge of the blade, but the defenders knew the autofire was wild. They raced along the wall toward the gap, gathering in two bands on either side.

Bolan knew what they were up to, and he grasped the sheriff's shoulder. "Hold it a minute." He slipped a new clip into the Skorpion while Conlan slowed his charge. "Okay, when I tell you, drop the blade a couple of feet for about thirty seconds."

"Gotcha." He juiced the big diesel and suddenly jerked the hydraulic controls. The blade quivered an instant, then plunged. Bolan had a wide open field.

As he anticipated, the hardmen weren't expecting the sudden opening. He sprayed a pair of figure eights, one to the left and one to the right, emptying the clip just as the blade began to rise again.

"Got a few of the bastards, anyway, son," Conlan shouted. "Want me to do it again?"

"No, they'll be expecting it now. Just go through."

"These creeps'll be behind us, then."

"Not for long," Bolan said, ramming a fresh magazine into the Skorpion.

Turning to the rear of the cab, he rapped on the glass to get Carlton's attention. When Randy leaned down, Bolan mouthed the words "We're going in." The border patrolman nodded and shifted his grip to relay the message to Milt. As the slope under the wall flattened out, the dozer's angle flattened with it, and the two men at the rear of the cab began to fire short bursts toward the top of the wall. With the blade still elevated, Bolan didn't have a clear shot.

Three or four bodies lay in a heap at the base of the gap, but this was no time for courtesy. The Caterpillar forged straight ahead, its blade just clearing the ragged edges on either side. Milt and Randy sprayed fire in alternating bursts, scattering the gunners.

Clanking and rattling, the treads ripped over the broken stone, then roared through the opening. Once inside, Conlan switched controls and began to raise the blade high overhead, swinging it up until it hovered over the cab like a steel umbrella, then letting it fall toward the rear.

Bolan jumped down from the cab, Milt joining him on the ground.

Gesturing with one arm, the warrior explained what he wanted. On the count of three the two men charged into the open. The surprised guards on the wall were defenseless now—there was nothing for them to hide behind. Their mouths gaped in astonishment as they fell to the ground, their bodies stitched by a ragged red line.

Two more men leaped over the wall and down to the sandy slope on the far side. They would have to wait. Bolan didn't want a war with two fronts.

The four invaders scrambled in the dense green jungle of a garden. On the far side stood a cluster of buildings, their glass faces reflecting a hundred blankly staring suns. Bolan felt at home for the first time in days. He could understand jungle. He took the point. Carlton and both Conlans fanned out behind him.

31

"Ramón, I want you to take charge. They are already inside the walls. If they get into the buildings, I will hold you personally responsible."

"But, Don Carlos, I—"

"No argument. I got rid of Tomás, I can get rid of you. You think no one out there can do what you do, maybe even better?"

The man said nothing. He glared at Alfredo, who had turned away from the confrontation and made himself busy with the console.

Ramón shook his head. He was beaten for the moment. Right now he had more to worry about than becoming indispensable. Staying alive was going to be difficult enough. But Alfredo would pay, that was for sure.

One way or the other.

"Where are they?" Calderone demanded.

"In the compressor room, Don Carlos."

"How many?"

"I can't tell." Alfredo looked past Calderone, and for a moment Ramón thought he was going to apologize. The uncertainty passed, and Alfredo's features seemed to age. His face a mask of impassivity, he turned back to the console.

"All right, go ahead, Ramón. We'll wait here."

THE FIREFIGHT at the wall had cut the odds, but there was a long way to go, and Bolan wasn't kidding himself. Now that the initial surprise was behind them, the advantage was definitely Calderone's. As he reached the far side of the garden, he held up a hand and examined the buildings one by one. There was little but size to distinguish one from another. Most of the structures were arranged in a rectangular U, with a single large building occupying the center.

This was a cold read. They had no inside information, no idea of the interior layout, not only of the main building, but of the smaller ones, as well. They didn't know whether there were underground connections, but Bolan had a sneaking suspicion there might be. He noticed the dull gleam of polished aluminum at two or three places around the compound, like metal mushrooms jutting out of the sand. Two of the three were on a direct line from the open end of the U to a spot just to his left.

As near as he could tell, there could be as many as thirty-odd men inside the compound. Between the dark gray tint of the glass and the intense glare of the reflected sun, it was impossible to see anyone behind the facades. Chances were that they'd be seen long before they made it across the courtyard.

On a hunch, Bolan slipped back into the greenery and huddled with the other three. "Spread out and look for one of those aluminum vents. There's a chance we might be able to slip inside if we can get into the air-conditioning ducts."

The small group broke up without a sound, slipping in broad circles through the tangled foliage. Bolan concentrated on the area roughly extending the imaginary line he had drawn through two of the three ducts.

Beating the thick fleshy leaves of some dense ground cover, he swung one foot back and forth. Moving away from the buildings, back toward the wall, he searched carefully for a couple of minutes.

He was about to reconsider, when he found it. A three-foot disk, slightly conical in cross section, raised just a few inches above the ground and wrapped in dark green leaves. "Here it is," Bolan called in a harsh whisper. He examined the joint, trying to determine how the ventilator hood was held in place. Running his fingers over the joint, he felt for rivets or bolts, but the surface was perfectly smooth except for a vertical seam where the sleeve was welded into its cylindrical shape.

Bolan grabbed the disk at opposite sides and tugged. At first it wouldn't move. He rotated the lid and it turned freely. Getting to his feet, he leaned over the lid and pulled straight up. With a grinding protest, the sleeve slid free.

He leaned down into the opening but could see nothing in the section running toward the wall. The opposite direction, though, a softly glowing rectangle marked the end closest to the buildings. Bolan dropped through the opening and angled his body to slide into the duct. He was in a rectangular channel, nearly three feet by four feet.

He had barely enough room to get to his knees, and he stuck his head back out just as Ray Conlan stepped through some undergrowth. "Looks like you got us a way in, son." Carlton and Milt emerged from the shrubbery a moment later.

"Let's go." Bolan dropped onto his stomach and crawled into the duct to make room for the others. He could feel a draft on his face as the air flowed around him on its way toward the house. The duct was large enough for him to crawl unhampered, and he made good time, glancing around as he drew near the opening into the house.

He held up a hand to signal for silence, and left the others behind to crawl the last thirty feet or so on his own. A heavy wire screen blocked the opening, and behind it, a fine mesh that felt like plastic kept smaller animals and insects from slipping into the house.

Bolan pressed his face flush against the screen, but was unable to see anything other than an empty room. Two smaller ducts led off at right angles, but he couldn't see more than a few inches into either one. Directly opposite, the duct seemed to continue on. Sticking his fingers through the heavy mesh, Bolan pressed hard to dislodge the screen, but it wouldn't budge.

Groping along the edge, he found the flat head of four studs almost flush with the flanged edge of the ductwork. Leaning close to the screen, he spotted four wing nuts on the far side. He yanked a combat knife from a scabbard on his hip and cut a six-inch square out of the center, slashing the plastic screen and thrusting one hand in to feel for the nearest wing nut. It turned easily, and he backed it all the way off and brought it into the duct. When all four had been removed, he was able to push the screen free.

Something below caught his eye, and he called for a light. Instead of the concrete floor he expected, he was looking at a gigantic fan, its huge blades turning so fast they were little more than a blur. The turbo powering the fan was virtually silent.

Two metal bars, like the cross hairs on a sight, intersected at the center. The footing was less than ideal, but there was no other way in. Bolan swung around and lowered himself gingerly to one of the bars, boot soles smooth and slippery on the rounded metal. One foot slipped free, and he started to fall, catching himself at the last moment on the edge of the duct. Rough metal sawed at his fingers, but he hung on until he was able to regain his balance.

To the right, another screen, this one much larger, blocked the way. The sterile concrete of the room beyond looked inviting, but the last thing he could afford was haste. Bracing himself with one hand, he pressed on the screen, and it popped open almost immediately, with a snap of retaining clips. Bolan swung his way out over the floor and dropped to the concrete.

He checked the room, but it was deserted. One corner contained a folding table, which he lugged over to the fan and hoisted. It was large enough to cover half of the whirling blades, and he snugged it up against the wall.

One by one, the other men dropped through, landing on the table and hopping down to the floor.

The room was low-ceilinged, and empty, except for the air-conditioning unit against the far wall. As Bolan tiptoed to a metal door set in one wall, the compressor clicked on, filling the room with a deep hum. He could feel its vibration through the soles of his shoes.

Bolan went to the door and pressed his ear against its surface, listening for sound that might indicate what lay beyond. A distant sound, possibly metallic, echoed through the solid panel of the door. Sound traveled great distances through solid material, and Bolan remembered putting his ear to a railroad track when he was a kid, then waiting nearly fifteen minutes for the train to come. The principle was the same, but this time he didn't have fifteen minutes.

Gripping the knob, he twisted slowly, then pulled the door open just far enough to peer out into the hall. He was about to open the door all the way, when he heard footsteps racing toward him. He waved the others back behind the compressor and the turbine housing.

Leaving the door open a crack, he backed along the wall until he felt the corner, dropped to one knee and rammed the last clip into the Skorpion. Out of the corner of his eye he watched Carlton and Ray Conlan maneuver for a clear shot at the door. If he was right, the men rushing down the hall already knew someone had entered the basement. High on the wall, he saw the three-inch disk that confirmed it— a motion detector. They were probably all over the house.

The door banged open, and Bolan steeled himself for the charge. Instead of a headlong rush through the door, a single sphere arced through the doorway, bounced once and came to rest against the base of the turbine housing. It had already begun to release gas into the close quarters. The canister was within Randy's reach, but they'd cut him to ribbons before he straightened up.

The wispy gas coiled up in a thin stream, then vanished as it was sucked up by the whirling turbo fan. In a moment or two the bulk of the tear gas would be spewed, and the fan would be unable to handle the load. Bolan realized he had to do something, and do it fast. He brought the Skorpion around and zeroed in on the edge of the sphere, like a pool shark lining up a difficult shot. The slug just nicked the edge of the gas canister and sent it spinning in toward Carlton. It vanished behind the turbine housing, only to come arcing back a moment later to bounce out into the hall, belching a thick cloud.

The doorway disappeared in a blue-gray haze, and Bolan crawled along the floor on his stomach. At the doorway he waited a beat, swung around and slid toward the opening. Six or eight men, invisible from the knees up, milled around on the edges of the cloud. One of the men dropped onto his stomach to crawl in under the gas—and froze with his mouth open when he saw Bolan.

The big guy shoved the machine pistol into the guy's face and squeezed. Bringing the muzzle up and to the left, Bolan swept the Czech weapon in a flat ellipse, then whipped it to the right, his finger still on the trigger. Men in blue-green uniforms, the shirts as bloody as butchers' aprons, fell in a heap.

Crawling out into the midst of the carnage, he looked to the right at floor level. Several pairs of boots pounded toward him, thick soles slapping the floor. The Skorpion was empty, and Bolan tossed it aside, swinging up the Uzi. He felt a flat palm on his back and turned to see Ray Conlan sliding into the hallway beside him.

Bolan fired in an oblique upward angle. The charging platoon stopped dead in its tracks, two men falling to the floor dead, others diving out of the line of fire.

"You take the left, son," Conlan shouted, opening up with his own weapons. He waved the muzzle up and down like a retiree watering a pampered lawn.

"Let's go." Bolan stood, holding his breath and pausing long enough to help the sheriff up, then burst through the swirling cloud and into the clear air farther down the hall. He heard footsteps behind him and turned just as Carlton and Milt Conlan cleared the tear gas.

"Randy, you and Milt take that left door," Bolan instructed. "The sheriff and I will take the right."

"Gotcha."

Bolan hesitated for a second, then jerked the door open. Like a swarm of angry bees, slugs whined through the narrow gap, ricocheting off the wall and gouging long furrows in the concrete. Several slivers of metal ripped at his cheek and right arm before he let the door swing closed again.

Ray Conlan grabbed Bolan by the upper arm. "Get on the floor, son. They were aiming high. I'll get the door, and you shoot hell out of them soon's you see daylight."

Bolan nodded. "Be careful, Ray." He dropped to the floor and rammed a full magazine into the Uzi, stuffing the partial into his shirt pocket.

"You don't get to be an old man like me by not bein' careful, son. If the good Lord didn't want us to rassle a bull, he wouldn't have given 'em horns." He stepped across Bolan's prostrate form and flattened himself against the left wall. "Here goes nothin'."

Conlan grabbed the doorknob, grunted, "On three," and started counting. When he stopped, Bolan turned to see why, just as the old man fired a burst into the overhead fluorescents. It went dark, and Conlan fumbled for the doorknob again. "One...two...three."

And the door swung back. Down a long narrow corridor, six or seven men, gathered in a tight knot, some kneeling and some standing, opened fire. Bolan hosed the hallway with lead, emptying an entire magazine. The sound of the return fire was deafening, the bullets screaming off the metal door and whining over his head.

Conlan opened up with his Uzi, sticking his arm out from behind the door and waving it wildly while Bolan reloaded. The warrior realized the return fire had stopped, and when Conlan's magazine was empty, the hall was eerily silent. Wisps of smoke drifted lazily, occasionally ripped sideways as they drifted past an air duct.

Bolan got to his knees and waited. Still nothing. Then in the distance, far behind him and muffled by the other door, a brief firefight flared up and just as quickly died away. He climbed to his feet. The clatter took him by surprise, and he turned to see Conlan, one hand gripping his right shoulder, slide to the floor.

The old man looked up at Bolan with a tight smile. "You go on, son. I'll be here when you get back. Don't worry about it. Go on now, git!"

"I'll be right back," he whispered.

In the narrow hallway Bolan stepped carefully over the sprawled bodies, his slick soles slipping in the pools of blood on the tile. In a crouch, the Uzi held waist-high, he kept to the right-hand wall and inched along the corridor. An open door on his left stopped him, and he shifted across the hall and peeked in. The room was empty.

He crossed back to the right and resumed his careful progress. The next door was on his side, and it was closed. Bolan reached gingerly for the knob. It wouldn't turn. The door was a solid slab of polished walnut, and its hardware was bolted on from the inside. Stepping into the center of the corridor, he cut loose with a short burst, circling the knob and splintering the dense wood.

Bolan planted a sharp kick just to the left of the doorknob, and the door started to cave in. A second kick sent it crashing back against the inner wall. A single shot barked from somewhere inside the room, the bullet just missing him and splattering against the wall behind him. The room was dimly lit, and there was no way the warrior could tell how many men were inside.

He took a cue from Ray Conlan and blasted the hall lights overhead. He waited several seconds for his eyes to adjust. The greenish glow in the room outlined two figures for a second until both men ducked behind furniture. Pressed against the wall, Bolan shouted into the near darkness, "Calderone, it's over."

There was no answer. The echo of his question bounced off the hard stone across the corridor, then rushed back at him from both ends of the hall. "Give it up."

"Fuck you, gringo."

In the silence Bolan heard harsh whispers from deep in the room, then a gunshot. He ducked instinctively, and it took him several seconds to realize the shot hadn't been aimed into the hall.

"Come on out."

"Chinga tu madre." The insult was punctuated by a second gunshot. As the echo died away, Bolan held his breath.

And waited.

After several minutes, he called again, but this time there was no answer. The door behind him banged open suddenly, and Bolan turned, ready to hit the deck.

"Mike, you all right? Mike?" Carlton's voice boomed down the corridor.

"Yeah, I'm okay."

The younger man sprinted toward him in the gloomy hall, skidding to a stop just behind him.

"Calderone's in there, and at least one other guy."

"What are we waiting for? He's the bastard we came for. Let's nail his ass...."

Bolan agreed. He crouched and duckwalked into the room, ready to dive at the first sound. In the sickly green glow, he could see clearly now that his eyes had fully adjusted. Working his way past a row of desks, he slipped between two and peered into the wide aisle between them and an elaborate console.

On the screen above the console a chain of blinking lights flashed in unison, superimposed over a schematic that Bolan knew instinctively was the very building he was in. Just below the console a young man in a white shirt lay on his back on the floor, the perimeter of a dark ragged hole in the center of his forehead glowing silvery green.

Bolan crawled past the body, still alert for the slightest sound. All he heard was the rasp of his own clothing on his skin, and the sharp crunch of sand under his feet as he ground it into the concrete floor.

In a small opening between two desks, a dapper man in a white suit lay on his side, his legs curled up toward his chest. As Bolan crawled toward him, a soft green glint winked and sparkled. The glittering revolver was still clutched tightly in his fist, its warm barrel still in his mouth.

Carlos Calderone was dead.

From Europe to Africa, the Executioner stalks his elusive enemy—a cartel of ruthless men who might prove too powerful to defeat.

DON PENDLETON's

MACK BOLAN

Moving Target

One of America's most powerful corporations is reaping huge profits by dealing in arms with anyone who can pay the price. Dogged by assassins, Mack Bolan follows his only lead fast and hard—and becomes caught up in a power struggle that might be his last.

DON PENDLETON's
MACK BOLAN®

More SuperBolan bestseller action! Longer than the monthly series, SuperBolans feature Mack in more intricate, action-packed plots—more of a good thing

Take
4 explosive books
plus a
mystery bonus
FREE

TAKE 'EM NOW

FOLDING SUNGLASSES FROM GOLD EAGLE

Mean up your act with these tough, street-smart shades. Practical, too, because they fold 3 times into a handy, zip-up polyurethane pouch that fits neatly into your pocket. Rugged metal frame. Scratch-resistant acrylic lenses. Best of all, they can be yours for only $6.99.

MAIL YOUR ORDER TODAY.

Send your name, address, and zip code, along with a check or money order for just $6.99 + .75¢ for postage and handling (for a total of $7.74) payable to Gold Eagle Reader Service. (New York and Iowa residents please add applicable sales tax.)

Remove from pouch...

unfold once...

unfold twice...

and they're ready to wear.

Gold Eagle Reader Service
901 Fuhrmann Blvd.
P.O. Box 1396
Buffalo, N.Y. 14240-1396

GES-1A

Offer not available in Canada.